THE SECRET POET

What Reviewers Say About Georgia Beers's Work

Hopeless Romantic

"Thank you, Georgia Beers, for this unabashed paean to the pleasure of escaping into romantic comedies. ...If you want to have a big smile plastered on your face as you read a romance novel, do not hesitate to pick up this one!"—*The Rainbow Bookworm*

Flavor of the Month

"Can people truly change? Can you make up for your past mistakes? ...This book was very emotional. The characters of Emma and Charlie were relatable and believable. The reader was invested immediately." —Marcia Hull, Librarian (Ponca City Library, Oklahoma)

"The story plays out quietly and gently. It feels grounded in reality. Nothing felt either dragged out or too rushed. ...I appreciate that both women were given time to process their past feelings and become comfortable with their potential future. When they made their choice and declarations, I felt that they were thought out and this time they were ready."—*Dear Author*

One Walk in Winter

"*One Walk In Winter* by Georgia Beers is that perfect combination of idyllic setting, feel-good romance and a beautiful ending that had me sighing in contentment."—*Kitty Kat's Book Review Blog*

Fear of Falling

"Beers sets a nice pace...and just enough heat to keep you begging for more. It's the little moments of intimacy between Dana and Sophie that really hook you."—*Romantic Reader Blog*

"Georgia Beers always delivers and as usual this book doesn't disappoint. Dana and Sophia have great chemistry and despite this being a celebrity novel the story is entirely believable. The romance is well paced and sweet. A great holiday read."—Melina Bickard, Librarian, Waterloo Library (UK)

"Georgia Beers has never disappointed me with any of her contemporary romances. I can always count on a wonderfully written and touching story when I open any of her books."—*Rainbow Reflections*

The Do-Over

"You can count on Beers to give you a quality well-paced book each and every time."—*Romantic Reader Blog*

"*The Do-Over* is a shining example of the brilliance of Georgia Beers as a contemporary romance author."—*Rainbow Reflections*

"[T]he two leads are genuine and likable, their chemistry is palpable. …The romance builds up slowly and naturally, and the angst level is just right. The supporting characters are equally well developed. Don't miss this one!"—Melina Bickard, Librarian, Waterloo Library (UK)

Calendar Girl

"*Calendar Girl* is a perfect master class on how to write a breathtakingly beautiful romance novel. …Georgia Beers had me captivated from the start with this story. Two skillfully crafted characters, an enthralling plot and the best kissing scene ever!"—*Kitty Kat's Book Review Blog*

"*Calendar Girl* by Georgia Beers is a well written sweet workplace romance. It has all the elements of a good contemporary romance. …It even has an ice queen for a major character."—*Rainbow Reflections*

"A sweet, sweet romcom of a story. ...*Calendar Girl* is a nice read, which you may find yourself returning to when you want a hot-chocolate-and-warm-comfort-hug in your life."—*Best Lesfic Reviews*

The Shape of You

"I know I always say this about Georgia Beers's books, but there is no one that writes first kisses like her. They are hot, steamy and all too much!"—*Les Rêveur*

"[*The Shape of You*] catches you right in the feels and does not let go. It is a must for every person out there who has struggled with self-esteem, questioned their judgment and settled for a less than perfect but safe lover. If you've ever been convinced you have to trade passion for emotional safety this book is for you."—*Writing While Distracted*

Blend

"You know a book is good, first when you don't want to put it down. Second, you know it's damn good, when you're reading it and thinking, I'm totally going to read this one again. Great read and is absolutely a 5-star romance."—*Front Porch Romance Book Reviews*

"Georgia Beers hits all the right notes with this romance set in a wine bar. ...A low angst read it still delivers a story rich in heart-rending moments before the characters get their happy ever after. A well-crafted novel, *Blend* is a marvelous way to spend an evening curled up with a large glass of your favorite vintage."—*Writing While Distracted*

"*Blend* has that classic Georgia Beers feel to it, while giving us another unique setting to enjoy. The pacing is excellent and the chemistry between Piper and Lindsay is palpable."—*Lesbian Review*

Right Here, Right Now

"[A]n engaging odd-couple romance. Beers creates a romance of gentle humor that allows no-nonsense Lacey to relax and easygoing Alicia to find a trusting heart."—*RT Book Reviews*

"[*Right Here, Right Now*] is full of humor (yep, I laughed out loud), romance, and kick-ass characters!"—*Illustrious Illusions*

"The angst was written well, but not overpoweringly so, just enough for you to have the heart sinking moment of 'will they make it' and then you realize, they have to because they are made for each other."—*Les Rêveur*

Finding Home

"Georgia Beers has proven in her popular novels such as *Too Close to Touch* and *Fresh Tracks* that she has a special way of building romance with suspense that puts the reader on the edge of their seat. Finding home, though more character driven than suspense, will equally keep the reader engaged at each page turn with its sweet romance."
—*Lambda Literary Review*

Mine

"From the eye-catching cover, appropriately named title, to the last word, Georgia Beers's *Mine* is captivating, thought-provoking, and satisfying. Like a deep red, smooth-tasting, and expensive merlot, *Mine* goes down easy even though Beers explores tough topics."
—*Story Circle Book Reviews*

"Beers does a fine job of capturing the essence of grief in an authentic way. *Mine* is touching, life-affirming, and sweet."—*Lesbian News Book Review*

Visit us at www.boldstrokesbooks.com

By the Author

Turning the Page
Thy Neighbor's Wife
Too Close to Touch
Fresh Tracks
Mine
Finding Home
Starting from Scratch
96 Hours
Slices of Life
Snow Globe
Olive Oil & White Bread
Zero Visibility
A Little Bit of Spice
Rescued Heart
Run to You
Dare to Stay
What Matters Most
Right Here, Right Now
Blend
The Shape of You
Calendar Girl
The Do-Over
Fear of Falling
One Walk in Winter
Flavor of the Month
Hopeless Romantic
16 Steps to Forever
The Secret Poet

THE SECRET POET

by

Georgia Beers

2021

THE SECRET POET
© 2021 By Georgia Beers. All Rights Reserved.

ISBN 13: 978-1-63555-858-6

This Trade Paperback Original Is Published By
Bold Strokes Books, Inc.
P.O. Box 249
Valley Falls, NY 12185

First Edition: April 2021

Credits
Editor: Ruth Sternglantz
Production Design: Susan Ramundo
Cover Design By Ann McMan

Acknowledgments

I am not a poet. In fact, I have had a distinctly love-hate relationship with poetry over the past few years. Poetry takes a special kind of talent. It's so much more than simply vomiting emotions onto paper, and when it's done well, the poet is suddenly left open and vulnerable, his or her heart laid bare. I admire that so much, and while, as I said, I am not a poet, I *am* a lover of words, and I don't think you can be that without appreciating the talents of poets like Dr. Seuss, Emily Dickinson, Robert Frost, E. E. Cummings, or Walt Whitman. And if you really want to be spiritually moved and uplifted by poetry—especially during the crazy times in which we've been living—I highly recommend reading *The Desiderata* by Max Ehrmann. I know poetry is incredibly subjective, but those are poems that have made space in my heart and now live there permanently. To me, that is poetry.

Something that has always fascinated me is what's called the Cyrano De Bergerac trope—when one person cares so much and so deeply for another that they're willing to set their own desires and happiness aside—sacrifice them—in order to help their loved one achieve theirs. It's beautiful and selfless and only the best kind of person qualifies. I have always wanted to write her, and so I bring you Morgan Thompson. I hope you love her as much as I do.

As always, my heartfelt thanks to everybody at Bold Strokes Books for taking care of both me and my stories. My books are like my children and the entire gang at BSB makes me happy and confident that mine are being very well taken care of.

With each book, my editors—Ruth Sternglantz and Stacia Seaman—teach me new things and point me in the direction that makes me a better writer. My gratitude doesn't seem like enough payment for that, but I offer it anyway.

I have an incredible support system in my life, and I am well aware of how lucky I am. My writer friends, my "regular" friends, my family, everybody who understands (or tries their best to understand) this crazy, solitary career of mine gets a huge thank you from me. I'm not the easiest person, but my gratitude is genuine and overflowing. Thank you all for being (and staying) in my life. I love each and every one of you.

Special thanks to Jennifer Jordan for happily answering all my questions about life as a pharmaceutical rep. I owe you a drink!

And last, but never, ever least, my undying thanks to you, my readers. I am forever grateful to you for your support, your emails, and your social media posts. Your faith in me as you continue to go on these journeys with me means more than you could possibly know. As always, I give you this promise: I will keep writing if you will keep reading.

Dedication

To anyone who has loved from afar...

CHAPTER ONE

I think it's pancreatitis."
"Let's let the doctor figure it out."
"Or it could be gallstones."
"How about we—"
"What if it's a subtle form of appendicitis? Is there such a thing?"

I sighed, but quietly. Mr. Wilson was pushing ninety. A very sweet guy, but also a hypochondriac since his wife died a year and a half before. We saw him at least three times a month. Still, the worry in his watery blue eyes was real, and I reached across the counter, through the sliding glass window, and covered his hand with my own. His felt so bony, so fragile and delicate, and I had to hide my surprise, consciously lighten my touch.

"Mr. Wilson," I said gently, making sure to smile. But not in a condescending way. If there's one thing I'd learned from working with so many elderly people, it's that they're often treated like children. Know what else? They don't like that. "I'm sure it'll all be fine. Let's let Dr. Thompson worry about it, and not jump to conclusions until he sees you, okay?" I shook my hand a little on his, changed my tone so it was a little bit light and teasing, and said, "You have *got* to stop googling."

He chuckled, and I felt relief course through me. "My damn grandkids taught me."

I knew that. He'd told me multiple times, but I grinned and shook my head like it was the first time I'd heard that tidbit. My phone rang, thank goodness, and Mr. Wilson took that as his cue to have a seat in the waiting area. I watched him as I pushed the button on my phone to connect the call to my headset. He was a tall man, all gangly limbs, and age had bent him like a lamppost. I was reasonably sure he was lonely, and that's why we saw him so often. Something to do. People to talk to. An appointment on his calendar to look forward to.

Anyway.

My name is Morgan Thompson. I work at Northwood Medical for my brother, Perry. He's the doctor here, and I am his right hand. Or at least I tell him that all the time because I keep his appointments, his files, and his life organized, and I will never let him forget it. I consider that part of my job as the little sister.

The waiting room had four people in it, which was about average for a typical Wednesday at ten a.m.

"Here."

I was on the phone setting up an appointment when a cell phone clattered onto my desk. I looked up at my big brother and raised my eyebrows in question as the woman on the phone gave me way too much detail about why next Monday wouldn't work for her.

"Work your magic," Perry said quietly and gestured at the phone with his chin. He looked like a soap opera doctor standing there in his white coat, stethoscope around his neck.

Perry was a super good-looking guy. Even as his little sister, I could admit that. His sandy hair was cut short on the sides and longer on top in what I was pretty sure was called a fade, though what did I know about guys' haircuts? His light brows were thick and sat above eyes that were an unremarkable brown, but the way they crinkled at the corners when he smiled made up for it. He spent lots of time at the gym and on the tennis court and the golf course and, at forty-three years old, was in the best shape of his life. He was a definite catch, my big brother, but dating had been hard for him after his divorce.

He said nothing else, just left to see his next patient. I picked up his phone to take a look. His dating app was open on the face of a blond woman whose profile said she was thirty and the president and CEO of a home organizing company. I thought she was kind of pretty, but in that super made-up way that made you sure she'd probably look like a completely different person without her makeup on. Perry seemed to like that. Since he'd decided he should start dating again, every woman he'd shown interest in was much younger than him and very, very made-up. Listen, I have nothing against makeup, but I don't put mine on with a putty knife. Still, he was trying, so who was I to judge? It's not like I had women banging down my door.

Between calls, I did some quick research on this Kimberly Winter, checked social media and Google, and found that her organizing company consisted of a staff of exactly her, so of course she was president and CEO. I couldn't really fault her, though, as I probably would've done the same thing if I had a profile. How often do you get to be president of anything, you know?

"Another profile?" Joanne asked. She and I shared the same space behind the counter. My desk was right under the sliding window, and I dealt with patients, deliveries, phone calls, all that good stuff. Joanne was part-time and took care of the files and odds and ends that I didn't have time for. She was sixty-eight and had retired, then came back when she got bored, so she manned the desk farther behind me.

"Yeah. An organizer."

"Well, she's probably neat then. That's a plus." She rolled one wall of files to the left so she could get to the next batch. "What does he need this time?"

"Words, I think."

"It amazes me that you two came from the same parents." Her shoulders moved with soft laughter. "You wouldn't have the first clue how to diagnose the flu, and he couldn't write a speech to save his life."

"Hey, I could diagnose the flu. Maybe." I grinned at her. She wasn't wrong. Perry and I looked similar enough to be siblings, but it seemed like our brains were wired completely differently. He was a science and numbers guy. Always had been. Biology, physics, algorithms, chemistry. He loved it all, and he excelled at it all.

Me? I'm a words girl. I'm the creative type. I'd rather poke hot needles into my eyeballs than have to work on a math proof. But give me a book of sonnets or some classic Emily Brontë or the works of E. E. Cummings? I'd be in heaven.

It was another twenty minutes before I actually had a chance to look at the profile and the back-and-forth that Perry'd already had with Kimberly Winter. She'd asked him what he did for a living, and he blurted right out that he was a doctor with his own practice. I groaned.

"Did he lead with I have my own medical practice again?" Joanne asked, which made me snort because she knew him so well.

"How many times have I told him to be subtle about that?" I shook my head. While I didn't want him to lie or mislead any woman, I also thought jumping right in with *I'm a doctor* could attract for the wrong reasons. Call me cynical, but Perry had looked out for me my whole life, so I felt it was my turn to do the same.

Kimberly Winter had asked Perry what he liked to do for fun. His answer was there, though he hadn't sent it yet, and thank freaking God for that.

I love football. Action movies. Go to the gym. Play golf.

I shook my head some more as I recalled a meme I'd seen fly around Twitter a lot. It said simply *Why are men?* and it made me laugh every time. So true here. I deleted his response and stared up at the ceiling as I searched for the right way to say what he wanted to say.

*I guess you could say I'm a typical guy in some ways. I love Sundays at home on the couch watching the football game, and I consider myself a connoisseur of pizza...*I added a winking emoji. I loved emoji and had to be careful not to overdo them on Perry's behalf. *I'm also kind of typical in that I like a good action movie. Pretty much anything Mark Wahlberg is in right now, I'll take a look at.* I knew this about him and liked to tease him about his man crush on Marky Mark. *I try to get to the gym regularly and I've played golf since I was in high school, so that's kind of my go-to sport.* There. That sounded better. I then remembered to do what many guys forget, including my lovable lug of a big brother: ask about her. *What about you? What do you do when you're not organizing the world?*

I didn't hit Send. I always let Perry approve my messages before they got sent. He'd never really argued with me because he knew words were my jam. I set his phone to the side and went back to work.

It was after six by the time I locked up the office and headed to my parents' for dinner. I'm not a great cook. No, that's a lie. I'm not even a good cook. Because I don't like to cook. I wish I did. I don't cook. I don't bake. I do excel at ordering food to go, but I'm not sure that's something you get points for. So, if I wanted a decent meal every now and then, I'd go to my parents', and my mom would make sure I had one.

Though that night, it would be my dad because it was early spring, and if it wasn't snowing out, it was warm enough to grill as far as my dad was concerned. I could smell the burgers as soon as I opened my car door, the scent carried from the backyard to the front by the slightly chilly late-April breeze. I entered the open garage, went out its back door, and sure enough, my dad was standing at the grill, apron printed with the words Grill Sergeant tied around his waist, long-handled spatula in his hand.

"Hi, Pops," I said and kissed his cheek. His Old Spice was still detectable through the aroma of the burgers, and I loved it. He was the only man I knew who wore it, so the scent always instantly made me think of him.

"Busy day at the office?" It was his standard question anytime he saw me on a weekday for dinner. I wasn't even sure he knew it, but I counted on it. If he didn't ask me that exact question, I would've thought something was wrong.

"Yeah, a couple last-minute appointments that crammed up the day. How was your day?"

"Can't complain." Another stock response. My dad had retired from forty years in the advertising business, so one-liners were part of his existence.

"Mom inside?" He nodded, and I headed in through the sliding glass doors off the deck. "'Tis I, your favorite daughter and most revered child," I announced loudly.

My mother grinned from her spot at the stove, which was why I said it, of course. "Definitely my favorite daughter," she said.

Fun fact: I'm her only daughter, so…

I shed my jacket and toed off my shoes, then went to stand by her where she was manning the deep fryer. Yes, deep fried foods are bad for you, but my mom made *the best* French fries on Planet Earth using her deep fryer. So good that she'd ruined me for most other fries. She once offered to buy me my own deep fryer for Christmas, and I snort-laughed at her, telling her not to be silly because I certainly wasn't going to make them myself, was she high?

"How was your day?" she asked me, pulling a scoop of fries out with a big mesh spoon thing and then adding a fresh batch.

"Oh, you know—same old, same old. Answered the phone, chatted with patients, used hand sanitizer sixty-three times, helped Perry with his dating app."

Mom moved toward the sink and grabbed a bottle of cucumber melon scented lotion. It was brand new, and she handed it to me.

"Are you keeping Bath and Body Works in business again, Mom?" I teased. I knew if I went upstairs and opened the bathroom closet, I would see a hoarding situation like no other.

"Somebody's gotta do it. Was this a new date for Perry?"

"Yes and no." I rubbed the lotion into my hands.

"Translation—different actual woman, but same kind of woman."

I touched my cucumber-scented forefinger to my nose. "Bingo." I put the lotion back, grabbed a fry, and had to blow on it so it didn't burn through my hand. "I did my job, edited his *I love football and pizza* so he doesn't sound like a Neanderthal, but…" I sighed. "I think he's losing interest." The thought had hung out in the back of my mind the entire afternoon, especially after he'd left his phone with me for several hours, returned to my desk to get it, and barely read my words before shrugging and hitting the Send button.

"That woman did a number on him." My mother said that so many times, it was expected whenever we talked about Perry. She was, of course, referring to Christine, his ex-wife. She'd had more than one affair during the course of their marriage, but it was the fourth guy that actually talked her into running away with him. Perry had been devastated. Christine had asked for nothing. None of his money. Not the house. She even left the convertible BMW Perry'd given her for her birthday. She fought for nothing, which is, I think, what broke my brother almost completely. All she wanted was to run away with the new man, and that's exactly what she did, which wrecked Perry. His pain had been deep and crushing, and it was brutal for all of us to watch.

That had been more than two years ago.

"It's good that he's at least trying, though," I said, in an attempt to pull my mom back from that dark and stormy place she could slip off to when she thought about one of her kids in pain. "He's allowed to take a break if he needs to."

Mom scooped another batch of fries out and dumped them in the bowl lined with paper towel. "He is. You're right."

The sliding glass door opened and my dad came in. "Burgers are up," he announced. When I looked his way, he said, "Extra cheese on yours," before I could ask.

I had dinner with my parents, as I always do a couple times a week. We chatted about everything and nothing, I helped clean up, and I headed to my own house.

My cats, Ross and Rachel, made it known that they had not changed their minds about my dinners away by singing me the song of their very displeased people. I fed them before I did anything else, sat on the floor with them while they ate, apologized profusely for my complete ineptitude as a mother. As it always happened, as soon as their little kitty bellies were full, they loved me again, leaned into me, crawled into my lap, and rubbed their faces against mine. People say cats are aloof, that they're not nearly as loving as dogs. I will agree that cats and dogs are very different—and I love both—but my cats show me how much they love me all the time. *Sometimes too much*, I thought as Ross got particularly assertive in rubbing his cat-food-scented mouth against my chin. I laughed anyway and kissed his black-and-white head.

An hour later, I was all cozy in my favorite blue flannel pants with the penguins all over them as I carried a glass of sauvignon blanc to the spot in my living room I referred to as my reading nook. It was really just a corner near the fireplace, incidentally the thing I loved most in my entire house. I'd had a gas insert put in when I bought the place, and sitting in my rocking recliner near the fireplace with a good book, a glass of wine, and my cats was probably the closest thing to heaven I knew.

I sighed as I settled in, curled my legs up under me, soft and fleecy blanket over me. The cats found spots—Ross in the crook of my knees and Rachel on the back of the chair near my head—and we all seemed to sink into the chair in relaxation. I picked up my notebook, which I have several of all over the house. This latest had a longhorn on the front. With swoopy bangs. He made me happy, which is why I bought it. I opened to a blank page and clicked my pen.

He has cracks but he hides them
Perfect presentation, nothing less
He jokes. He laughs. He heals.
He is broken, but no one sees

"Well, Jesus, that's depressing," I said to the cats as I reread my words, the beginnings of the poem inspired by Perry. I set the notebook and pen aside, picked up my wine, and let go of a long, quiet breath.

I stared at the flickering blue flames, rocked the chair just a bit so as not to send Rachel flying. I sipped and set the glass back down, then reached behind me with one hand and behind my knees with the other and scratched my cats. This was when I was at my most content. I was warm. I was loved. I had a good book within reach next to a lovely glass of vino. My life was good, there was no denying it. I wasn't rich, but I was lucky or blessed or whatever description works for you. I had a nice existence. It was simple, but full. And most of all, it was uncomplicated.

Man, was that about to change.

CHAPTER TWO

It's never not busy at my job. There's always something to do. Filing, emails, invoicing, paying invoices. And if by some miracle of miracles all that stuff is done, there's the waiting room. Straighten the magazines, pick up the toys and put them in the toy box in the corner, make sure nobody left coats, gloves, hats, purses in the closet area. My point being, there is always something to do.

However.

When you've worked there for nine years, you have seniority, and the boss is your big brother, you kind of have the freedom to let some of that stuff slide if you need a break. Mentally or otherwise. And that Thursday, I just needed to lose myself for twenty minutes.

People have lots of ways to escape, and my favorite was with a good book. I read like crazy, I always had. I read just about every genre, but classics, romances, and poetry were my favorites. I never went anywhere without either a book, my Kindle, or both. In fact I'd purchased a bag the previous year that had a special pocket for my Kindle, so I never left the house without it. Yes, I'm that nerdy chick at the pharmacy or the dentist's office who sits alone and reads a book instead of making conversation with other people. My friend Adriana always rolls her eyes at me.

In addition to carrying my Kindle around, I kept a small notebook with me. I dabbled in poetry, for no other reason than I liked to play with words, and I found that writing them down often made me feel better if I was dealing with something stressful in life. Corny, but true.

I knew something was going to happen on that Thursday. I can't tell you why—I have no idea. I just remember that I woke up with an odd feeling. Not a bad feeling. And I don't want to say that things felt off, because that kind of implies that I was scared or worried, and I wasn't. But something was definitely different. By the time I decided I needed a moment to forget myself in the latest Kristan Higgins—an actual book today, rather than an electronic copy—the feeling had been forgotten, and I was my normal self again.

"Morgs, can you call and make sure the pharmacy on Dickins gets the revised prescription for Mrs. Curtis?"

I took a moment to finish the page I was on, something I always did when Perry came at me with no greeting and just demanded. Again, he's my brother. I can be insubordinate and get away with it. Sometimes. I carefully placed the bookmark and closed the book, then looked up at him. "I'm sorry. What did you need?" I smirked because I'd absolutely heard him, and he knew it. I could tell by the way he cocked his head and pursed his lips. I could also tell that he was in a bit of a mood today and maybe not so up for playing the annoying little sister game, so I set the book down and straightened up in my chair just as the front door opened and he looked in that direction.

It's funny when I look back on that memory now, because I didn't glance at the door. My gaze was on my brother, and he was almost comical. His eyes widened just slightly, and his lips parted, and I was kind of surprised to see some pink blossom on his cheeks. Perry was not a blusher. At all. My big brother was most often the epitome of calm, cool, and collected. When you sometimes had to deliver bad medical news to people, having a poker face was very important. But that day? Zero. He had zero poker face. Zero coolness. Zero chill. His expression was just this side of being dorkily cartoonish.

When I looked toward the door, I saw why.

Stunning.

I had read that word as a descriptor countless times, but I don't think I've ever actually *seen* a woman in person—until then or since—who elicited that word from me the first second I laid eyes on her. This one was brunette, and her hair was the first thing that caught my eye. Dark waves of it. *A lot* of dark waves of it. My fingers instantly itched to twirl it, dig into it. She was a little taller than average and carried herself with an air of authority, dressed in a smartly cut pantsuit that was a deep blue with a lighter blue top underneath the jacket. She shut the door behind her, turned to us, and smiled widely—and oh my God. The cheekbones. The gorgeous, do-a-double-take-at-that-color blue eyes. I swallowed some foreign lump in my throat as she crossed the few steps to my counter and stuck out her hand to me.

"Hi. I'm Zoe Blake."

And right then, on that day, in that moment, in that very second that I slipped my hand into hers, I somehow knew that life would never be the same. I didn't know how or why or when, but I knew something was going to change. Forever.

"And you must be Dr. Thompson," Zoe Blake said as she shifted those eyes from me to Perry, removed her hand from mine, and held it out to him. Only then did I notice that she held a plate in her other hand.

Perry did that rapid-blink thing that you do when you realize you've been staring for too long but quickly pulled himself back into Doctor Mode, and he reached over the counter and shook her hand through the window. "I am. It's nice to meet you, Zoe."

It turned out Zoe Blake was our new pharmaceutical rep with Calverson, a company we dealt with regularly. Zoe explained how she was new to Northwood, but not Calverson.

"I just wanted to pop in and say hi, show my face. And leave these." She handed me the plate, which was piled with about a dozen cookies. Oatmeal raisin, if I guessed correctly. "I know it's a little unconventional to bring something homemade, but like I said, I'm new to town, and I've been a little nervous, and when I'm nervous, I make cookies." She lifted one shoulder in what looked to be a slightly self-conscious half shrug and grinned, sort of sheepishly, then added quickly, "No nuts in them, FYI."

Her smile…God, what was it about her smile? I was able to study her as she spoke with Perry, and there was something there, something underlying—was it a sadness?—and I had a sudden, almost irresistible urge to start asking her questions, get to know her better. Like, right then. I bit down on my bottom lip.

My thoughts came to a screeching halt when I realized that both Zoe and Perry were looking at me, and it was like I'd been underwater, all sound muffled, and then broke the surface where sound became startlingly clear.

Perry's eyes widened at me, and he used them to gesture behind me.

The phone was ringing.

Whoops.

I hit the button and spoke into my headset, beyond disappointed that I couldn't stare at Zoe Blake anymore.

Probably a good thing.

By the time I finished the call, the whole time silently cursing Mrs. Jenkins for needing to set up an appointment at that very moment, the plate of cookies was on the counter to my left, and Zoe was heading out the front door. She looked back to pull it shut behind her, glanced up at me, and shot me that smile. It liquefied my insides. Instantly. Then she was gone.

Look, I need you to understand that I'm not a person who objectifies women, and I realize that's what it sounds like I was doing because all I've talked about is what Zoe looked like. But that's all I knew of her at that moment. Her physical appearance. And yeah, it was head-turning. It affected me. But know this: Zoe Blake was so far out of my league, we were playing different sports. A woman like her, should she happen to play on my team—which I was sure she didn't—would never look twice at somebody like me. I knew it, and I was okay with it. It was my life, and I was used to it. But I could look. There was no harm in that, was there?

And my God, she made the best cookies I'd ever had in my life.

Perry had finished with his last patient and came out to the front to grab one of the oatmeal raisin cookies, probably his fourth. As the day had progressed, I had developed a love-hate relationship with those damn cookies. They were the best oatmeal raisins I'd ever had in my life, and they lived way too close to my desk. I could literally reach the plate without having to get up. And I did. More than once. Willpower is not something I'm well acquainted with.

"God, take those home with you," I said to Perry, pushing the plate toward him.

"No way." His mouth was full, and it came out more like *nowo.* Joanne had packed up and gone home a couple hours before, the patients had all been seen, and the phones had clicked over to the answering service, which happened automatically at five thirty if I didn't do it manually first. It was just me and my brother left.

Perry dropped into Joanne's chair, still eating a cookie, and I never really understood the phrase *he chewed thoughtfully* until I saw my brother do exactly that.

I swiveled back toward my desk and waited him out, folding invoices and sliding them into envelopes to go out with the next day's mail.

Finally, he spoke. "Speaking of the cookies, I liked her."

That felt a little out of the blue. "Zoe Blake? Yeah, she seemed nice." I swiveled my chair so I was facing him again. His brow was furrowed and looked like he was thinking really hard about something. "What?"

He swallowed, pursed his lips as if trying to figure out how to tell me what he was thinking. "She was…" He shook his head, and I knew exactly what he was talking about.

"She really, really was. Wow."

"Right?"

I smiled. Nodded my agreement. Grabbed another godforsaken cookie. My mom made fabulous oatmeal raisin cookies, but they didn't come close to Zoe's.

"She has piqued my interest," Perry said, rocking back in Joanne's chair.

I gave him a squint. "What does that mean?"

"It means, I like her."

"You don't even know her. How can you like her?"

He turned his eyes to me, and they crinkled at the corners as he grinned, held his hands out, and said, "Excuse me, but did you not see her? Are your eyes broken?"

"Oh, I saw her," I said and mentally winced at the lasciviousness in my tone.

"Then you know what I mean."

"Well, thinking she's hot and liking her are two different things. You don't know her."

"No. But I like her."

I groaned and tossed a foam stress ball at him. He caught it, and I noticed the weird expression on his face. Perry's ten years older than me, but we've always been super tight. I know him as well as I know myself. But that evening, sitting there in his office, just the two of us, I'd never quite seen that look before. I shrugged and tried to keep it light as I said, "So get to know her."

And just like that, it was like he decided he was being silly. Which he kind of was, really. He pushed himself up from the chair like he suddenly remembered he had somewhere to be. "I'll just wait until she comes in again." And she would. We both knew it. Probably soon.

"Good call."

"Okay. I have to go check in at the hospital."

"See you tomorrow."

"When it'll be Friday," he tossed over his shoulder as he walked down the hall to his corner office. Then he did his weird fist-pump thing he always did that I told him was corny, and so I'm sure he did it for exactly that reason. I shook my head with a grin at my goofy big brother that I adored.

I took another half hour to finish up some last minute things, stamp the outgoing mail, and pop it into the tray for the mailman the next day. Then I got my things together. I took a last look around, part of my nightly routine, and made sure everything was in its place. I never left anything out on the desk. First of all, because we were a medical office, and there were very strict privacy laws around health care. I couldn't just be leaving important files and info out in the open. Second, because I couldn't stand for my work space to be cluttered or messy. I was good at my job for a reason—my organizational skills.

I loved to keep things orderly and easy to find, and Perry saw that in me right away. He'd hired me only a year or two out of college, and we'd been very tentative about entering into a working relationship, given our closeness as siblings. I dipped my toe, took careful measurements of how things were going, how they were working. For both of us. My first year working for Perry had been stressful, but only because we were both being *so* careful, while at the same time, he was cultivating a clientele.

I put on my coat, shouldered my bag, and hit the lights. I set the alarm—Perry was already gone out the back door—and locked the place up for the night. As I crossed the parking lot to my car, I noticed some of the spring flowers that were poking up, including a row of hyacinths along the building. One of them was an interesting, unusual blue.

I immediately flashed to the color of Zoe Blake's eyes. That arresting blue that I bet turned heads wherever she went. Once in my car, my brain tossed me an image of her from earlier, striding into the office—that air of authority, that gorgeously tailored suit, that smile.

And that element of sadness that floated just below the surface, clearly there, but also maybe something she didn't want others to see. I wondered about that as I drove. I was curious.

What was it about Zoe Blake? I had no idea. I shook my head and told myself to stop being silly. Who cared what her deal was?

It wasn't like we were going to be BFFs or anything.

CHAPTER THREE

R ainy Mondays suck.
     They just do. You have to go to work, and you have the
entire week left still. You've slept in and stayed up late for the past two
nights, and now you've got to answer to an alarm waking you up at
o-dark-thirty. And on top of that, it's gray and wet and gross outside.

I always parked at the far end of the parking lot, leaving the
closer spaces for our patients, many of whom were elderly or mobility
challenged in some way, and that day, I definitely needed my umbrella
for the walk from my car to the door of the office. I unlocked the
door and went inside, shook the umbrella off, popped it into a holder
near the closet, and shed my coat as a full-body shiver ran through
me. Spring in upstate New York could be all over the board as far as
temperature went, and that day was much closer to cold than warm.

My routine is the same each day, and I like that. I'm a very
routine person. I don't like my plans to change or my world to be
altered. I thrive on order. So every morning in the office of Northwood
Medical, I wake up the computer, turn on the Keurig so it warms up,
walk down the hall where the three exam rooms live to flick on the
lights, and check the supply of toilet paper in the restroom. There were
other supplies in the restroom that were for urine samples, but I left the
restocking of that sort of thing to Martha and Diane, Perry's nurses.

I really liked being the first one in. There was something about
the silence of the office then, the stillness in the air that anticipated
the day to come. It might sound silly, but I thought of the office as
my domain. I get that, in reality, it was Perry's, but I liked to look
at it like this: Perry was the star and I was the manager. So while

people actually came to see the star, the manager was the one who made sure those visits ran smoothly. I was the one who actually ran the show from behind the scenes, while Perry dazzled from the stage. And those early morning moments were like getting to walk around in the empty theater, before anybody was there, getting to walk out onto the stage and just…listen. Just soak it all in, the space, the scope, the anticipation of the show. Or in my case, the day's patients.

Yeah, it was corny. I know. But I loved my job. Everything about it.

At seven thirty sharp, I switched the phone over from the answering service to my desk. Both Perry and Martha would be in at eight, Diane at nine, Joanne at noon.

The first call rang through at 7:32.

Showtime.

By the time noon rolled around, I was ready to either pull my own hair out or grab my things and just flee. Yeah, yeah, I said I loved my job, and I did. I do. But just like any other job, there were *days*. And that Monday was a *day*.

Perry was really good about sticking to his schedule. He had to be if he wanted to avoid being at work until nine every night. Once in a while, though, he'd have a day where a handful of appointments took a handful of extra minutes. Or he'd get stuck on a phone call, which would bump everything by ten, fifteen, twenty minutes. Or, worst of all, the first appointment of the day would take up extra time, ask a ton of questions, not understand something and need more time for explanation, insist on more tests. Perry would never turn somebody like that away or hurry them out. He was good with his patients that way. He took the time and he listened. And because of that, the entire remainder of the day would run late. There were any number of reasons why his timing could get thrown off, and he'd become a pro at avoiding those things.

Most of the time.

That Monday was not one of those days. His very first appointment with a woman named Mercy Drummond knocked his entire day out of whack. Mercy wasn't a hypochondriac, but she was a self-diagnoser. We saw her at least once a month, and when she came in, she was certain she knew what was wrong with her. Gallstones. Irritable bowel syndrome. Hypoglycemia. Hashimoto's. She hadn't been right yet, and the majority of her appointments—and the general reason they always ran long—were spent with Perry convincing her that she was wrong. She'd show up with printouts from Google or WebMD or wherever she did her research. Luckily, she ultimately listened to Perry. If he promised she didn't have ankle cancer, then she accepted that she didn't have ankle cancer. But those conversations were rarely quick.

I was on hold with a lab, and I glanced up at the waiting room. Let me describe our office setup. So, as I sat at my desk, which was L-shaped, I could look over the counter through the Plexiglas into the small waiting area. It had about ten chairs, a couple small tables stacked with magazines, likely out of date, and a toy corner for occupying little ones. To the left of my desk was a door, and if you walked through that, that's where patients paid their bills, made their next appointments, or had me get referrals for them on their way out. To the left of the office's front door was a door that led to the exam rooms. So when it was somebody's turn, Martha or Diane would open that door and call the patient back, and when they'd been seen and were all done, they'd come to my counter, take care of business, and leave through my door that led back to the waiting room. As I sat on hold, the nurses' door opened, and Martha called for Mrs. Lopez just as Diane came up to my counter on the left and handed me a file.

"Mr. D'Agostino is going to need a referral for blood work."

I nodded my understanding, took the file, and added it to my inbox.

Diane leaned her elbow on the counter and blew out a heavy breath. She was in her forties, broad-shouldered and solidly built. Her chestnut brown hair was pulled back into a ponytail, as it always was, and she shifted her weight from one foot to the other, having recently recovered from a bout of bursitis in her heel. She focused her rich brown eyes on me. "I'm starving," she whispered, just as the woman on the other end of my phone call finally returned, and the front door to the office opened at the same time.

Like some unexpected angel of mercy or a genie from a magic bottle, in walked Zoe Blake. She was carrying a big tray, and as she got closer, both Diane and I could see it held an array of sandwiches.

"Well, hello there, new best friend of mine," I heard Diane say as she straightened up, and I grinned. She opened the door to let Zoe back to my desk and get her out of the waiting room.

I admit I had a hard time focusing on my phone call, as Diane has one of those voices that can boom if she gets excited, and apparently, those sandwiches excited the hell out of her. I squinted as I listened to the woman in my headset—Why do we do that, anyway? Squint while we listen harder. Does that help somehow?—then jotted down the info I needed and hung up with relief.

Diane turned to me with a huge grin. "I don't know if you've met my new best friend Zoe, but she brought lunch, and so she's the queen of all things as far as I'm concerned."

Zoe's startling eyes landed on me, and she gave me a shot of those high cheekbones when she smiled, adding a humble little half shrug.

"Your Highness," I said by way of greeting. "Good to see you again."

"Same. Thought maybe you could use some lunch around here. Mondays can be rough."

"You have no idea," Diane said, grabbing half of what looked to be a turkey sandwich off the tray. "Thank you so much for this." She held up the sandwich, then took a bite, turned on her heel, and headed back to her desk, I assumed.

Zoe watched her go, then shifted her gaze back to me. "So. Hi."

"Hi," I said as I felt little butterflies fluttering around in my belly and wondered what that was about. "How are you settling in?"

"Pretty well. I'm finally unpacked. Which is a sentence I didn't think I'd ever get to say." She laughed softly then, a sweet, slightly musical sound that made me smile in return.

"Moving is rough even when you're moving in the same town. I can't imagine how much harder it must be coming from somewhere else." It was true. I'd never lived outside of Northwood, so I had no idea.

"It was…an adventure. Let's put it that way." Zoe was wearing black pants and a black-and-white striped button-down top that day. She looked a little more casual than her last visit when she wore a suit, but there was still something classy and elegant about her.

"I bet." I looked up as Diane opened the nurses' door and called Sarah Park back. "Listen," I said, turning back to Zoe, and I felt a weird catch in my lungs, something that would become a regular occurrence later. "I know you want to sit down with Dr. Thompson, but I'm afraid he's running behind today." I rarely felt bad turning any kind of rep away. It was nothing personal—it was the nature of the business, and they all knew that. Their chances of actually getting five minutes with Perry were often slim, and they were aware of that the second they stepped in the door.

"Life of a pharma rep," Zoe said, her tone good-natured. She lifted the lid on the tray. "How about you? Have you had lunch yet?"

❖

Zoe Blake was excellent at shifting into Sales Mode. It was subtle and seamless, and I didn't even realize we'd gone from talking about her new house to talking about her company's new migraine drug until I'd asked my third question about it. She was that good.

"I forgot to get your card," she said at one point, and I handed one over, then took a bite of the chicken salad sandwich I'd snagged off the tray. I noticed her hands. Pretty. Clear polish on the neatly filed nails. Probably a manicure.

She glanced at my card, then did a double take. "Morgan Thompson? Is Dr. Thompson your husband? I had no idea."

"Gah, no," I said, shaking my head like a cartoon character and making a face like I'd eaten something sour. Then I laughed. "No. He's my brother."

"Really." Zoe cocked her head. "I don't think I've ever met siblings who work together. How did that come about, if you don't mind me asking?" And just like that, she'd slid back into Regular Person Mode.

"I mean, the short version is that Perry was just starting his own practice after working in another for a bit, and I was having trouble finding a teaching job, so the stars kind of aligned. Of course, this was supposed to be temporary for me." I made an *oh, well* face.

"How long ago was that?"

I scrunched up my face, did the math in my head. "Nine years?"

"That's a long temp job." Zoe's tone held no accusation, no judgment. She put that last bite of her turkey sandwich into her mouth.

"I liked it way more than I ever expected to."

"Yeah? Not many people can say that about their job."

"Can you?" I asked, honestly curious now. I liked that time with her, just the two of us in the break room. It was my lunch, so Joanne had taken over the phones. Everybody else was busy. Only Zoe and I sat at the round table, the big sandwich tray between us, Diet Cokes from our fridge popped open and covered in condensation in front of us.

She didn't hesitate. In fact, she nodded before I'd finished my question. "Absolutely. I love the freedom this job gives me. I believe in our drugs. I love that I'm part of the chain that helps those who are sick. I love meeting cool, new people." Those cheekbones sharpened as she smiled, focused those eyes on me. She began to clean up. "Well, let me get out of your hair. Thank you so much for taking the time, Morgan. I know how busy you are, and I really appreciate it." We both stood, and she held out her hand. "I'll come by next week, and we'll talk samples."

I took her hand. Warm. Soft. "Hopefully, you'll get to see Dr. Thompson next time."

"Maybe."

I tried to picture her with Perry as we left the break room, tried to decide how that would work. They'd make a striking couple, that was for sure. I let my gaze roam over her as she walked in front of me. Stopped on her very shapely ass. Stayed there until I had to force myself to look somewhere else.

I slid behind my desk and gave Joanne a nod that I'd take over the phones. Zoe smiled that smile at me, rapped her knuckles once on the counter, then gave a wave as she pulled the door next to my desk open.

"Thanks for lunch, Zoe," I said as the phone rang. I put my headset on, hit the proper button. "Northwood Medical, this is Morgan, how can I help you?" My gaze never left Zoe's form until the front door closed behind her.

CHAPTER FOUR

"Are you trying to hurt me? I thought you invited me for drinks because you missed me, not so you could rip my heart out and stomp on it." Stefan gave a dismissive hand-wave flourish, picked up his appletini, and sipped.

"You are a walking, talking stereotype, you know that, right?" I grinned with affection. He might have been annoyed with me, but Stefan had been my best friend since we were sophomores in high school, and we'd known each other for a good ten years before that. I could honestly count Stefan as my longest relationship outside of family members.

"You know how much I love your brother, that I want him to make an honest man out of me one day. How long have I crushed on him?"

"Ever since you got hair on your manly parts, I think."

"Exactly."

"He's straight."

"Everybody's straight until they're not."

We'd had that conversation about seven hundred times. It always went the same way, in the same rhythm, always with a lot of flourishes and tsks and *mm-hmms*. And it always ended with me laughing and Stefan rolling his eyes and sighing like he was the most misunderstood homosexual on the planet.

"Pretty sure you're out of luck with Perry, but hey. I mean, you can give it a shot." I shrugged, took a sip of my pinot noir.

"Make the first move? Me?" Stefan pressed a hand to his chest and scoffed. "Please." Another sip of his appletini. A shake of his head. Mock disgust. "I am the pursued. Never the pursuer. Do you not know me at all?"

Pizzeria Cannavale was our place. It was about halfway between my work and Stefan's work. It had a bar, a fantastic wine list, and amazing wood-fired pizza, and Stefan's boyfriend Justin was the bartender.

Yes, Stefan had a boyfriend. And the two of them crushed on my brother together. It was kind of hilarious, and they always made me laugh about it. Even Perry found it amusing when I'd told him a few years earlier.

We sat at the bar on Friday, sipping our drinks and waiting on our pizza. Justin popped by when he wasn't busy with other customers, which wasn't often because there was a good crowd that night. Marissa Cannavale, the owner and chef, was busy bustling around in the open kitchen, and we watched as she slid our pizza into the huge brick oven.

"So. Serious now." Stefan turned his body on his stool so he faced me, and his bony knees poked at mine. "He says he likes this new girl?"

I nodded as I swallowed my wine. "I mean, he doesn't know her. He's only laid eyes on her once, so it's purely physical. But I've never seen him that smitten that fast." I told Stefan how Zoe had shown up earlier in the week, but Perry had been too busy to see her. "When he finally got to take a break, I told him she'd stopped by, and I swear to God, he got mad at me for not telling him. I was all, was I supposed to yank you out of the exam room in the middle of an appointment so you could have a moment of eye candy? I think he got my point."

"Is she eye candy?" Stefan asked.

"Oh my God, yes." I finished my wine and waved to Justin for a refill when he got a second. "I got to visit with her a bit, and I tried to get some info on her without making it weird."

"To see if she and Perry have things in common."

"Exactly. For example, does she love football and NASCAR and the *Fast and Furious* movies?"

Stefan snorted a laugh. "And you call me a stereotype."

Marissa slid our pizza in front of us with a smile and asked how we were. I was always surprised that she recognized us given how busy her place constantly was, but at the same time, I wasn't. It was the sign of a good business owner, knowing your clientele. Stefan and I were in there several times a month. We always ate and drank at the bar, in full view of Marissa as she cooked, so I guessed it made sense that our faces became familiar.

She told us to *mangia,* and we thanked her as we both leaned over our veggie everything pizza and inhaled deeply. "Seriously," I said to Stefan. "Is there any better smell in the world than tomato sauce, basil, and garlic?"

Stefan's eyes were closed in obvious bliss. "If there is, I haven't experienced it."

We dug in.

Isn't it funny how you can be chatting away with somebody at dinner, but once it arrives—assuming it's as awesome as Marissa Cannavale's pizza—you shut right the hell up? Stefan and I made some various humming sounds and a few soft grunts, all of which added up to the wordless version of, *Oh my God, this pizza is to die for,* and silence reigned for a few minutes.

Back in verbal communication mode, Stefan said, "So, what did you find out about this girl? Does she have anything in common with your beautiful hunk of a brother?"

I thought back on my conversation with Zoe earlier in the week and then chuckled and shook my head. "You know, she did that thing that salespeople are so good at—she got me talking about myself. I didn't even realize it."

"It's a skill."

"She thought I was his wife."

Stefan snort-laughed. "No way."

"Way. She saw that our last names are the same." I shrugged as I finished my first slice and reached for the triangular server thingy to scoop myself another. "It was a logical assumption."

"I mean, really, you should be so lucky."

"Ew, no," I shot back. "Gross."

Stefan laughed at his own humor—one of the things about him I loved. He thought his own jokes were the funniest and couldn't do deadpan to save his life.

"Maybe she plays for your team," he said then, and it was my turn to laugh.

"Doubtful."

"How come?"

I opened my mouth to answer and realized I didn't have a good response. My shoulders dropped as I looked at my best friend, blinked a couple times, and said honestly, "I don't really know. She doesn't ping my gaydar?"

"Honey, I love you, but God skipped right over you when he was handing out the gaydar."

It was my turn to snort-laugh because Stefan was one hundred and fifty percent correct. A woman could walk right up to me and kiss me full on the mouth—with tongue—and I'd squint and tilt my head and wonder if maybe she was possibly a little bit gay, but conclude that she probably wasn't. I was truly pathetic in that department.

"Wouldn't matter anyway," I told him, then took a sip of my pinot. "I doubt she'd look twice at me."

"Oh, are we going down this path again? I forgot to look at the agenda for tonight." Stefan always got mad when I said something like that. He said I was looking down on myself, and he hated when I did it.

"Look, I'm just being realistic." My response was almost always some variation of this, and it was true. "I mean, she's her and I'm…" I lifted one shoulder. "Just me."

Stefan made a sound that was close to ugh and waved his hand, dismissing the entire conversation. He was clearly not up for stroking my ego, and that's not ever what I wanted anyway. What I said to him was the absolute truth—I was simply being realistic. Stefan didn't get it because he constantly had men hitting on him. I was sure a big part of that was his level of confidence. He could be flamboyant. He could be snarky, but he was never cruel. He held his head high and was unapologetically himself, and I loved that about him. I envied it.

Not that I wasn't comfortable with myself. I was fine. I was out. I didn't pretend to be something I wasn't. But I was rarely hit on by women. Men? All the time. But gay women or bi women? They barely looked at me. And somebody in Zoe Blake's league? If she happened to like girls? God, no, I would never expect her to show any type of interest outside of selling me her company's drugs.

Stefan finished his appletini and signaled Justin for a refill. When he turned his gaze to me, his face was all serious, his light brows dipping into a V at the top of his nose.

"Uh-oh," I said and clenched my teeth. "That's your I mean business face."

"Damn right. I'm only going to say this once tonight, and you're going to hear me. Understood?"

"Yes, ma'am." I winked, trying to keep some levity in a situation that had somehow slid into super serious without my noticing.

Stefan turned so his knees were pointing at me. The he grabbed my knees and turned my entire stool so I was facing him. Keeping his hands there, he leaned in, bracing himself on my legs, until he was looking me square in the eye, the tips of our noses only an inch or two apart. His green eyes had gone dark and stormy, and I couldn't tell if he was angry at me or for me, but when he spoke, his voice was both gentle and firm, both pleading and matter-of-fact.

"You are amazing," he said. "You're smart and funny and fucking gorgeous, and I don't care if you can't see it. I can, and that's why I'm here—to remind you. Having you would be like hitting the jackpot for any woman. *Any* woman. You deserve the best, and one day, you'll have it. You are my best friend in the world, and I love you with every cell in my body, but I really, *really* need you to get the fuck out of your own way. Okay?"

Whenever this speech happened—and it was a fairly regular occurrence, I'm ashamed to say—I would smile or laugh softly or bump Stefan with a shoulder. This time? My eyes filled with tears. I had no idea what that was about, and I was mortified, scrambling to grab my napkin from my lap to hide the emotion.

Stefan, to his eternal credit, did not make fun of me for crying. He just smiled softly, squeezed my knees, and turned back to his pizza.

We took a moment…well, I took a moment, and Stefan graciously let me do so. When I had pulled myself together and shoved the emotions back into the dark corner from whence they came, I cleared my throat and spoke. "So, how's business for the most in-demand salon in the city? Prom season is upon us, and wedding season isn't far behind."

Stefan's face lit up, and he began telling me a story of a super-spoiled rich girl and her friends he'd dealt with that week.

And just like that, we were back to normal.

❖

My little house is just inside the city limits of Northwood, which made my lower taxes the envy of all my suburban friends, and I loved that location. I lived in a cute little neighborhood but had the ability to walk to several fun spots, including Jefferson Square, which was a large up-and-coming area made up of eclectic shops, restaurants, bars, and salons. Each year, the Pride Parade traveled down Jefferson, and since my street was just off there, I could carry my chair and a cooler to the corner, sit down with a drink, and watch the whole thing without ever having to drive through the gridlock or search endlessly for affordable parking.

One of my favorite things to do was just to wander Jefferson Square. I loved it when the weather was nice, but I'd also do it in the winter because all the businesses would be decorated for the holidays, and it made me happy. Sometimes, I'd shop. Sometimes, I'd stop for a drink or some lunch or dinner. Sometimes, I wouldn't go in anyplace, I'd just walk. The personality of the area was enough to hold my interest. A huge percentage of businesses had some kind of gay pride symbol either in the window or hanging outside in flag form. Some of the little shops were unique all on their own—tattoo parlors and a cobbler and a store that only sold candy in bulk like an old-timey candy store. There were psychics who wanted to read your palm or your tarot, and a tiny detached building, which looked like a shed in somebody's backyard, that only sold hot dogs. Halfway down the block was a park that boasted some gorgeous sculptures, along with several benches. I'd spent more than one sunny afternoon just sitting and reading there.

It was still a bit chilly to sit outside and read. The sun was bright, and spring was in the air, but there was a breeze, and its purpose seemed to be reminding me that we were on the tail end of a dwindling winter that just didn't want to let us go, rather than heading into a happy, warming-up-fast spring. I pulled the zipper of my jacket up to my chin when that wind tried to cut through it, and I pushed open the door to one of my very favorite places on earth, Happily Ever After.

It was kind of hard to describe Happily Ever After. Owned by Sylvia and Michael Abbott—but it was mostly Sylvia's baby—it was a combination tiny bookstore and café. But because it was so small, it wasn't a full one of either. Sylvia had started it after she retired from her paralegal job. She'd gotten bored quickly, wanted a hobby, and loved reading anything about love. As you can imagine, keeping a small independent bookstore open these days is nearly impossible, especially one that only carried specific books and not necessarily bestsellers, so Sylvia decided she needed more of an enticement and added the café part. And when I say café, I really mean just coffee and tea and some comfy places to sit. Michael was in real estate and owned the building, and I was pretty sure the Abbotts kept the place open with their own money because I couldn't see how she made much of a profit. If she'd had to pay rent for a shop in Jefferson Square, she'd have closed before she opened.

I headed straight back to the counter where Sylvia stood in a puffy white peasant blouse, her salt-and-pepper hair pulled back into some kind of twist I couldn't see the detail of, open smile on her face. That smile was one of the things I loved most about Sylvia. It was always so clear that she was happy to see me, and who doesn't want to feel like that, you know?

"Good morning, my friend," she said as she reached under the counter and pulled out a book. "I have something for you." She gently set a gorgeous hardback copy of Jane Austen's *Pride and Prejudice* in front of me.

A very soft *oh* slipped from my lips because I'd forgotten I'd ordered it many weeks ago. I ran a hand over what I then realized was a leather-bound cover. My gaze snapped up and met Sylvia's.

"I thought this would look classier on your shelf than a boring old hardcover or paperback." She gave a sort of offhand shrug like it was no big deal that she got me a far nicer version of what I'd been asking for. "Same price, though," she tacked on quickly, and I gave her a look. See? Not much profit.

"No. I will pay for this because you're right. It will look far classier, which will make me look far classier, and who doesn't want people to think they're classy, right?"

"I want people to think I'm classy," came a familiar voice from behind me. "Should I get a copy, too?"

Zoe Blake. I knew it before I turned to meet those eyes.

Her out-of-context presence must've made me look as confused as I felt because she laughed softly and said by way of answering my unasked question, "I live nearby and was looking for a place to hang for a bit—*that's* what I'm doing here." She shifted her attention to Sylvia. "Plus, this woman makes a mean cup of Earl Grey." Sylvia blushed a pretty pink as Zoe looked back at me. "I thought that was you walking in. Hi."

"Hi," I said, wondering how I'd missed her. She looked super cute. Washed jeans, a plaid shirt in pinks and blues over a navy tank, all that dark hair in a messy bun at the back of her head. Around her neck dangled a silver chain with a small—no, two small stones of deep ruby red, sitting comfortably between her collarbones. I swallowed.

"So," she said as she stepped closer to look over my shoulder. "What is it that's making you instantly classy?" She smelled like strawberries and vanilla, and the mix was both fresh and warm. "Jane Austen? Huh."

I turned to her. "I'm sorry. Did you just say *huh?*" I made air quotes with my fingers.

Zoe looked up at me quickly, her eyes slightly wider than usual. "Well, yeah, I guess I just didn't peg you for somebody who reads romance."

I tilted my head, and she immediately held up her hands and backpedaled.

"No, no. That came out wrong. There's nothing wrong with reading romance."

"I know there isn't." Seeing her all flustered was amusing me for some reason, and I rolled my lips in and bit down on them to keep from smiling.

"I just…" She dropped her hands to her sides in defeat, but then one corner of her mouth lifted. "You surprised me is all."

I wasn't sure how to take that, so I gave a little laugh through my nose. "Well, it's an excellent book. A classic."

"So I've heard."

I felt my own eyes widen. "You've heard? You mean you haven't read *Pride and Prejudice*? Like, ever?"

"I'm ashamed to say I haven't."

"Now I'm the one who's surprised."

"Yeah? Why?"

I blinked at her. Again. Then I burst out laughing. "I don't know," I said honestly, and she joined me, her laughter light and musical.

"Oh, good, I feel better now." Zoe's smile showcased those gorgeous high cheekbones. "I was worried I'd missed out on something really important. Missed the memo or something."

"I mean, it may not be important, but you are missing out."

"Am I?"

"Absolutely."

Our gazes held. I'm not fantastic at eye contact. I manage it, but it's not my favorite thing and always makes me feel a little twitchy. Eye contact with Zoe was different somehow. I didn't feel the insistent urge to pull away.

Finally, she did and turned her attention to Sylvia, who had been standing behind the counter and observing the entire exchange with what I now noticed seemed a lot like great interest. She hit some keys on her computer.

"I can order you a copy. Just add it to your current order."

"That would be great." Zoe grinned at her.

I suddenly felt a little guilty. "Listen, I don't want to bully you into reading something that doesn't interest you." I lightened it, though, by adding, "Of course, I also don't want to get in the way of Sylvia making a sale."

Zoe blinked at me, turned to Sylvia then back, and was completely deadpan as she said, "You mean this isn't all an elaborate charade to sell books?"

I looked at Sylvia and muttered, "I think she's on to our schtick."

"No worries," Sylvia said softly, playing along. "I'll write us up a new script tonight."

"Ladies and gentleman, the comedy stylings of The Book Pushers. They're here all week." Zoe's eyes were bright and those cheekbones almost waved to me. "Don't forget to tip your waitress."

"You're funny," I said as Zoe set a book I hadn't noticed her holding on the counter and fished her wallet out of her purse.

"Hey, looks aren't everything." I squinted to see that the second book was one of poetry by E. E. Cummings. "Wait a minute. Hang on here. You mock my romance reading while you're buying a book of *poetry*?" I raised my eyebrows high and didn't tell her that her stock had just risen in my eyes because poetry was something I had discovered an affinity for.

"Touché. I've never been much into poetry—I thought I didn't get it most of the time—but my mom was, and Cummings was her favorite. I started reading it, and his words, his moods, just drew me. I'm by no means a poetry connoisseur. In fact, I don't know much beyond some of his work." She tapped the book with a finger. "I saw this, and it made me think of my mom, so I decided to buy it." There was something different in her smile then, that thing I thought might be sadness the first time I'd met her. "His stuff is…" She shook her head.

"His words are brilliant," I said. "The longing, the depth." I pressed a hand to my heart. "His work always makes me feel… human." She seemed to study me, and I felt my face heat up.

But her eyes widened in what seemed to be recognition at my words. She pointed at me and said, "Yes. That's exactly it."

She paid. Sylvia offered a bag, but Zoe opted to just slide the book into her purse, then glanced at me, and those eyes made my breath catch. "I'm looking forward to reading Austen, you know," she said, her gaze on me serious.

"I mean, you did just order it. It would be kind of silly if it came in, and you bought it, then decided not to read it."

She bumped me with a shoulder, gave me a smile that seemed less sad, and said, "See you around, Book Pusher."

"Not sure how I feel about the drug dealer nickname, but okay," I called to her as she made her way toward the front door. She waved once and was gone.

"How do you know her?" Sylvia asked as she poured me a cup of coffee and slid it to me across the counter.

"She's a new pharmaceutical rep. Comes into the office every so often."

"She's gorgeous."

"Tell me about it." I think it came out more like a dreamy sigh than words, and Sylvia caught it.

"Any possibilities there?"

I gave her a *pfft*, my eyes still on the door even though Zoe was long gone. "Perry likes her, though. Asked me to help him make an impression."

"You'd better tell him to brush up on his poetry then."

I snorted a laugh. "Perry? Never gonna happen."

Chapter Five

It was the middle of the following week when I saw Zoe next. The waiting room was about half full. Not a super busy day, but steady, lots of people showing up with spring colds. It was twelve thirty, and I was on the phone when she came through the door, looking fresh and professional in a black suit with a skirt. It was the first time I'd seen her bare legs, and listen, it took *a lot* of effort for me to keep from staring at them. My God. They were long and creamy and shapely, and legs like that should be illegal. Super distracting.

Zoe mouthed a hi to me and gave me a wave with the hand that was not carrying the tray of food she'd brought with her. I was talking to the receptionist for an orthopedic surgeon, and I waved Zoe in through the door next to my desk and back toward the break room. She smiled, winked at me, and disappeared down the hall.

The receptionist put me on hold, so I took the opportunity to shoot Perry a quick text letting him know Zoe was in the break room. Earlier in the week, I'd filled him in on my unexpected encounter with her and what I'd learned, which didn't amount to much more than she drank Earl Grey tea and enjoyed E. E. Cummings's poetry. But he couldn't really use any of that info right off the bat, or she'd know that I reported it all to him, and he didn't want her to know I was helping. So you can probably imagine the blank expression my brother gave me when I told him those things. After he stared at me for a moment, he sighed with irritation and said, "You're supposed to be *helping* me, Morgan." 'Cause I guess knowing those couple of things about a woman you're interested in asking out won't assist you at all? What exactly is wrong with men and their brains?

He texted back within ten seconds: ty. Which was his version of thank you. Perry never texted in complete sentences. Everything was a fragment or an abbreviation. I got that he was a super busy and very important doctor and all that, but to somebody who loves words as much as I do, those texts were like little pinpricks to my skin every single time.

The stupid orthopedic surgeon's office left me on hold for nearly twelve minutes, but the receptionist finally came back and gave me the info I needed. The whole time I was jotting notes, I was also thinking about poor Zoe sitting in the break room all by herself. Pharmaceutical reps know it's par for the course, that doctors' offices are crazy busy much of the time, and that getting a face-to-face with a doctor, even a two-minute one, is not always a possibility, but I still felt bad for making her sit there. I finished with my notes, pushed my chair back, and hurried down the hall after her.

I stopped just before the door when I heard voices. Specifically, laughter. Zoe's. I thought about peeking around the doorjamb but then heard my brother's voice and realized he was making her laugh. I leaned closer, wanting to know what he was saying that she found so entertaining.

"Hey." Diane's voice came from behind me, and I jumped like she'd poked me with a cattle prod.

"Jesus," I said, hand pressed to my chest. I kept my voice low. The last thing I wanted was Zoe to think I was spying on her and Perry, but they kept on talking in the break room, so I didn't need to worry.

"Sorry." Diane's smile was amused. "I just sent Mrs. Calhoun and her son your way. Also, I smell food. Is there food in there?" She gestured to the break room

"No idea. You should check it out." I hurried back to my desk where Mrs. Calhoun and Jaeden, her thirteen-year-old son, were waiting for me. I checked them out, made a follow-up appointment for six months down the line, and said good-bye as they left, and Martha popped her head out to call in the next patient.

I hadn't had lunch yet. I was curious what Zoe had brought, but I didn't want to go look. Didn't want to interrupt. So I took a slug of my Diet Coke, which had been sitting on my desk for over an hour and was disgustingly warm and also flat, and stayed at my desk.

Perry had taken the time to sit with Zoe. That was good. I wondered what they'd talked about, if he'd used any of the—admittedly limited—info I'd provided, and I hoped he hadn't spent the entire time talking about the Patriots. Or the Red Sox. Or the Bruins. We lived in upstate New York, but like so many people there, Perry was a fan of a lot of Boston teams. I had no idea why. I think it was the popular thing to do when he was a teenager—and let's face it, our closest football team was the Buffalo Bills and they *sucked*—and it just held on into his adulthood. Perry loved his sports, and it occurred to me in that moment that I had no idea if Zoe was at all interested in them.

"Penny for your thoughts."

I flinched, slightly startled, and blinked rapidly. The way you do when you've been daydreaming, and you're suddenly yanked back to reality. It's a shock. Zoe stood at my desk, warm smile on her face, the scent of strawberries and vanilla floating in the air around her.

"Oh, hey," I said and wondered if that was too loud as I sat up straighter. A glance at the clock on my desk said another ten minutes had gone by. "You got a good twenty minutes with him. That's great."

"It really was," Zoe said, still smiling. "Super rare, as I'm sure you know."

"I do." Twenty minutes out of Perry's day was unheard of. I was impressed by his effort.

"He said I could take a look at your sample supply. To ask you to show me."

"Oh, of course." I hopped up and came around the counter. "Follow me."

We passed Diane in the hall just as she popped the last bite of what looked like a sub into her mouth. My stomach chose that moment to remind me with a loud rumble that I had yet to eat.

Zoe said from behind me, "I brought lunch, you know. You could feed that beast."

I couldn't help but smile. "Look, if I always give the beast what it wants, it'll take over completely. I need to remind it who's boss." I led her to the closet in the nurses' office where we keep all the drug samples, used my key, and unlocked it. Zoe slipped an iPad out of her bag, did some scrolling and tapping, then began to look through the samples we had.

I didn't really need to stay and watch her. There was no need for me to hover. She was our drug rep—she wasn't going to steal drugs from us. But Joanne was manning the phones, and we weren't crushingly busy that day, and my God, Zoe smelled so good.

"Was my brother nice to you?" It was a weird thing to say, and I realized that as soon as the words left my lips.

Zoe didn't miss a beat, though. "He was great," she said, keeping her eyes on the closet shelves, using her finger to count. She made a notation on her iPad, then looked back up at the closet. "He's a big sports fan, it seems."

I mentally rolled my eyes. "Yeah, he is. I hope he didn't bore you too much."

"Not at all," she said. "I'm not a big fan of hockey, but I watch football in the fall and winter, and I don't mind catching a baseball game here and there." She turned to me, and her face went comically serious as she lowered her voice. "*Not* on TV, though. Oh my God, that's like watching grass grow."

My laugh barked out of me before I could catch it. "I agree with you seven hundred percent. If they could cut out the stepping in and out of the batter's box and all the crotch-grabbing, they could shave a good hour off televised games."

"Such a snoozefest, right?" Zoe turned her gaze to me as she spoke, and the blue of her eyes…I felt like she'd lasered me in place. I couldn't have left the room then if I'd wanted to. Apparently oblivious to her powers, Zoe finished counting, then shut the closet door. "I'll take a closer look at all of this, then pop in for Dr. Thompson to sign it. Okay?"

I nodded as she slipped her iPad back into her bag. "Fine."

"By the way," she said as she stepped aside so I could lock the closet back up. "My book came in, and I'm going to start it tonight. It's my first night all week that I don't have to be anywhere or catch up on anything. So, Ms. Austen and I have a date."

Lucky Ms. Austen was the first response that popped into my head, but I still had enough control not to say it out loud. "Well, I hope she doesn't let you down."

"I have a feeling she won't."

"You'll have to let me know."

We walked back to my desk, and she opened the door that would lead her to the waiting room. Turning back to me, she said, "Eat some lunch, okay?"

"Yes, ma'am," I said and waited until she'd left the office completely before I jumped up. I hurried to the break room before I could faint from hunger and grabbed half a tuna sub. As I bit into it, I wondered if I should tell Perry he should read *Pride and Prejudice*. I knew my brother, though, and that would never happen. Perry was crazy smart, and he liked to read. But his fiction preferences ran toward books from Michael Crichton or Lee Child. He'd never read a romance. And certainly not a classic. He hated English lit class, if I remembered correctly.

"SparkNotes," I said to the empty break room. "I'll get him the SparkNotes."

❖

I've mentioned that I'm not a good cook. You know what I did excel at, though? Ordering in. I was pretty sure I single-handedly kept my local Grubhub offices in business by ordering dinner at least twice a week. Sometimes more. Yes, it could be costly, but I was also a pro at finding specials and coupons and secret deals, so I actually did okay when it came to the money I spent. It should be noted that my mother would roll her eyes over this.

That night, I kept it simple and ordered a pizza from Vinnie G.'s. I consider myself a bit of a pizza connoisseur, and I'd tried pretty much every pizzeria in Northwood at one time or another. While I loved Pizzeria Cannavale more than most, Vinnie's was much closer to my house. The sauce was amazing with a blend of oregano and spices that screamed Italy at me, and Vinnie's crust was the best I'd ever had. Crunchy on the outside, soft and chewy inside, never overcooked, never doughy. It was perfect every single time I ordered, so they had a loyal customer in me. The fact that I could order online and have it arrive at my door in half an hour without having to deal with talking to anybody, other than saying thank-you to the delivery person, was a bonus. Sometimes, after talking to people all day long at work, I just wanted to be quiet at home.

I stretched my legs out on my couch, some soft jazz playing on my Bluetooth speaker. I like jazz because you don't have to think about it. You can, of course, but you don't have to. It meanders, and most of the musicians riff and improvise, which will never not astound me, and I can simply lose myself in it. Ross and Rachel were both big fans of Vinnie's pizza, too, so they immediately found themselves spots—Ross along the back of the couch by my head, Rachel between my legs, so I'd get a good shot of her big, sad, starving eyes every time I looked down at my plate. She was no dummy.

Many of my nights were spent that way. Quiet. Peaceful. Stress free. Cats. Jazz. It was an atmosphere that I realized some might find lonely or sad, but it was neither for me. Being on my own was something I'd grown used to and eventually began to love. Would I have liked to have somebody to share some of those evenings with? Of course. I wasn't a hermit. I wasn't a recluse. I'd have very much enjoyed having a girlfriend. It just wasn't at the top of my list.

I pulled tiny bits of cheese from my pizza and gave a piece to each cat, watched them sniff, examine, sniff some more, taste gingerly, then finally pick it up and eat. If that was my process every time I ate something, I'd have been a lot skinnier than I was.

I had the fireplace going, but it was a nice, mild May evening and I didn't really need it. Emphasized by the fact that I was sweating and could feel that my face had grown hot to the touch. I groaned when I realized the remote for the fireplace was on the mantel instead of within reach.

"Okay," I announced to my cats, "up." I waited for Rachel to move, then set my empty plate on the coffee table and walked the four exhausting steps to the fireplace to click it off. I have built-ins on either side, and they're filled with books, framed photos, and a few little knickknacks that hold meaning for me, and they were my favorite part of the living room. I scanned my books and ran my fingers over the spines lovingly. My collection was eclectic…and not.

I had Jane Austen and both Brontë sisters and Shakespeare. I also had loads of more contemporary romances, both hetero and LGBTQ+. It was a really nice mix, and I was proud of it. Some of them had gotten me through rough patches in life just by providing me with an escape for an hour or five.

My gaze was drawn back to my leather-bound copy of *Pride and Prejudice* which—Sylvia hadn't been kidding—looked regal and absolutely classy on the shelf, all burgundy leather and gold stamped letters. I suddenly found myself thinking about Zoe, wondering if she'd actually started reading it or if it would sit on her shelf, remaining pristine and unopened, unlike mine which would be worn soft and pliable within the year.

I sat back down on the couch, Rachel taking that as her cue to hop right back up and curl against my knee. Ross was purring loudly near my ear, his head up but his eyes closed, and I gave him a gentle scratch. "Love you, buddy," I whispered as I grabbed my laptop from the table and opened it in my lap.

On Amazon, I searched for the SparkNotes for *Pride and Prejudice*, just in case. If nothing else, Perry would get a kick out of it.

I briefly considered ordering him a book of poetry as well, which really would be a joke because my brother was a great guy, but he wasn't terribly romantic, and poetry would just make him blink at me. Then he'd burst out laughing and tell me how funny I was.

I did a quick Google search anyway.

Can we talk about poetry for a minute?

I haven't always loved it, but much of it has drawn me to it, had a pull of sorts. I don't really understand the rules, and maybe that's why I have very specific poetry likes and dislikes, because there really are no rules. As a kid, I liked when poetry rhymed. Give me some Dr. Seuss, and I was a happy camper. Still am. The man was a genius. And I think as I grew up, the poetry that was not rhyming or in any way close to the cleverness of Dr. Seuss just annoyed me. And don't get me started on social media. That's where I want to tear my hair out. Apparently, things like, *You broke my heart, I am now heartbroken,* are considered poetry. And I guess, if I can take a moment and not be a complete snob about it, it kind of *is* poetry. Which means just about everybody with a Tumblr is a poet.

I have written my share of it. As I've said, I'm a words girl. Words are my jam. I love to listen to them. I love the sound of them. I love that they are endless in their expression and emotion.

To be clear, I don't post any of my stuff on social media. In fact, I have never shown it to anyone. It's private. It's for me. Just me. It makes me happy.

The poet Zoe's mom loved—E. E. Cummings—was one of the first poets I fell in love with. There was something about his words, and I knew what it was immediately.

He wrote love poems.

He was basically a romance writer in poetry form, so it made sense that he'd be a favorite of mine. Not everything he wrote was about love, but a lot of it was.

I had a weird moment of wishing I'd known Zoe's mother because I'd never met anybody who shared my love of Cummings. I was reading "I Carry Your Heart With Me" for the millionth time and being pulled in by the sheer volume of emotion in the words, letting it wash over me, drown me, when my phone pinged, announcing a text and yanking me rudely out of the lovely place I'd been so snugly tucked into.

Hello, swingers! Guess what. Our first round is tomorrow, and the forecast is gorgeous. Yes!!

I grimaced at my phone. I might have muttered, "Son of a bitch."

The text was from Robin McKinney, the point person for the golf league I was only in because my cousin Bridget had bullied me into joining three summers ago. *It'll be good exercise*, she'd said. *It'll get you out of the house*, she'd said. *You'll meet new people*, she'd said. That last one proved to be true. Actually, the last two turned out to be true. I liked most of the women I played with—Robin could be a little much—and it did give me a reason not to sit home alone. But Bridget hadn't counted on one very important thing: I sucked at golf. I was terrible at it, and I hated it. It made me want to throw things. But every year, she talked me into it. Don't judge me with, *If you don't like it, then don't play*. It's not at all that easy. If you knew my cousin Bridget and if you saw her sweet face and knew her kind heart, you'd do anything she wanted you to, too. I was helpless to fight back.

I always went, and to be honest, once we were a couple weeks in, my self-consciousness turned to I-don't-give-a-crapness, and I was more able to enjoy myself. The first round or two at the beginning of the season always beat me into the ground, though, and I dreaded it every time.

Robin had made it a group text, of course, so for the next half hour, my phone pinged nonstop until I stopped reading the responses once they went off on seventeen different tangents. I finally turned off the notifications and set the phone aside. My interest in the poetry now squelched, I quickly ordered the SparkNotes for Perry and decided it was time to turn in.

After all, I was going to have to golf tomorrow, and I hadn't even looked at my clubs—which were somewhere in my garage, I was pretty sure—since last fall.

I fell asleep that night and dreamed of swinging at floating hearts with my seven iron.

CHAPTER SIX

I liked Thursdays. Thursday might be my favorite day of the week that wasn't a weekend. It holds promise, you know? I feel like Thursday says, Hang in there, baby, tomorrow's Friday and then you are *free*! Plus, we closed up a little early on Thursdays, which helped me get to golf on time.

It had been a steady day, and I was glad when Perry's last patient paid her bill and left. I waited until she was safely in her car and backing out of the parking spot before I crossed the waiting room and locked the front door.

Diane waved to me, her bag slung over her shoulder and her sunglasses already on as she headed home for the night. "Have fun whiffing the golf ball," she called over her shoulder.

"I hate you," I called back in a singsong voice. But I laughed out my nose anyway because Diane wasn't wrong. Whiffing the golf ball was exactly what I'd be doing within the hour.

I was shutting things down at my desk when Perry came up to the counter. Out of the corner of my eye, I saw him lean on his forearms and sway a little bit back and forth, like he was waiting for something. I let a good ten or fifteen seconds go by, and he finally spoke.

"So…" He stood up then and looked back toward Joanne's empty desk and the movable walls of files. "That book you like has more in it than just mush."

I squinted at him. "What book?"

"I mean, Elizabeth is way ahead of her time, really."

Blink. Stare. Blink. "I'm sorry," I said with a disbelief that made me speak super slow. "Are you *reading Pride and Prejudice*? Like, actually *reading* it?"

Something flew across his face, and I was pretty sure it was insult. "I'm not a Neanderthal, you know."

The way he said it, the slight tint of hurt in his voice, took me by surprise, and I felt bad. "No, of course you're not. I'm sorry. I didn't mean to imply that." It was the truth. My big brother could be a lug of a guy and he ticked a lot of guy stereotypes, but he was smart and kind and generous, and I felt bad for insulting him. I felt worse when he spoke next.

"Zoe mentioned it when she was here last week, said she was reading it for the first time and how interesting she found it. You're always telling me I need to pay attention to a woman's interests"— that was true, I told him that constantly—"so I thought I'd give the book a shot."

I had no idea what to say. I wondered if I could still cancel my SparkNotes order, since it seemed now I didn't really need them.

A corner of his mouth quirked up. "I wasn't going to mention it to her at all if I hated it." Then his sandy brows dipped down into a V above his nose. "I didn't expect to actually kinda like it."

"Who are you, and what have you done with my brother? And *oh my God, are you blushing?*" Perry's face went an even deeper red. It was adorable and I felt a swell of affection for him right then.

"I'm gonna ask her to dinner, I think." Now, look, my big brother has never lacked confidence. He faces everything in life head-on, shoulders squared and chin up. He will come out on top and he knows it. But right then? In that moment when he told me about asking a girl out? I have never seen him look more unsure of himself, and it squeezed my heart a little bit.

"Yeah? Well, she'd be silly to turn you down."

Instead of scoffing at my ridiculous notion that being turned down was even a possibility, he grimaced and said, "God, I hope she doesn't."

This was the part where I probably should've talked to him about the whole working-together thing, was it a good idea to date somebody you had any kind of authority over, etc., etc. True, Zoe wasn't his employee, and there was nothing in the regs forbidding a doc from dating a pharma rep. Not that he would ever let his personal life interfere with his work—he wouldn't, he wasn't like that—but it was important stuff to touch on, and as his sister and employee and confidant, I should've said something.

Yeah, I didn't.

Because he just looked so vulnerable. It was super rare for me to see him looking anything other than strong and confident. He really liked Zoe. I didn't quite understand it, as he hadn't spent much time with her at all, but that's why you date somebody, right? So you can get to know them?

"It's a great book," I said instead. "A classic. I'm super impressed that you're reading it. My big brother, lover of romance novels."

"Yeah, don't go spreading that around. It's not like I'm gonna start reading..." He raised his gaze to the ceiling and scrunched up his nose. "Who did Mom read all the time? Nora Steel? Something?"

I snort-laughed. "You're right. Don't give up your day job."

"Not planning to."

"Zoe also likes poetry, you know." The face he made then—scrunched nose, furrowed brow, grimace as if he'd eaten a lemon—reminded me of some of the old photos I'd seen of him as a kid, long before I came along. I laughed as I said, "Is that a no to the poetry then?"

"Let's not push it."

We laughed a bit more and then I asked, "When are you asking her out?"

Perry straightened up slightly—probably didn't think I noticed—and lifted his chin. Then he shrugged. Actually shrugged like this was no big deal after I'd just seen him basically slit his wrist and bleed his feelings all over my counter. "Gonna give her a call this weekend sometime, probably."

"Probably?" I arched a brow at him, making my *oh, this is the game we're playing now* face at him, but it didn't seem to register.

"I mean, yeah, if I get a chance. I've got basketball Saturday morning, going over to Mom and Dad's at some point, rounds at the hospital. Busy weekend."

"Mm-hmm," was all I could say because I didn't want to call him on his bullshit, but also? I *so* wanted to call him on his bullshit.

"All right." He smacked his palm against the counter, his way of wrapping up the conversation. "I've got to hit the hospital quick before I head home. What about you?"

"Golf night."

"Cool. First round of the season?"

"Yep." No enthusiasm. At all. I couldn't find any.

"Remember what I keep telling you."

I joined him and we said together, "It's not a softball."

He grinned at me. "You'll be great. Just have fun." He could say that because he was a fantastic golfer. Like he was fantastic at just about everything he tried. "See ya." And he was gone.

I sighed. Loudly. There was nobody left to hear it but me, so I did it again just because.

"All right," I said to the emptiness around me. "Just have fun." I repeated Perry's advice a few more times in my head. Just have fun. That's all I was supposed to do. And I'd get there. And I'd have a little bit of fun.

Once I got a few whiffs out of the way.

Northwood Hills was not nearly as fancy as it sounds and certainly not to be mistaken with Northwood Country Club. NCC was where the wealthy folks played, where national tournaments were hosted. Perry was a member of NCC.

I, you'll be unsurprised to hear, was not.

Northwood Hills was the public course where people who were not networking or schmoozing clients or proposing expensive business deals went to play golf. The rules were a little more relaxed, though normal golf etiquette was still expected, but it was a nice place with an impressive clubhouse, and The Drive—its bar and grill—had a decent reputation for good food and craft cocktails.

The parking lot was pretty full, but I found a spot between two SUVs and slid my small Honda Civic in. It seemed like eighty percent of the population of Northwood had SUVs, which were very practical for northern winters but made life a little harder for people like me with normal-sized cars who looked out their driver's side window and often saw nothing but *door*.

I hauled my clubs out of the trunk and used the golf towel I had to dust them a bit. I hadn't had time that morning, and after sitting in my garage for the better part of seven months, they'd collected a bit of a covering and some cobwebs as well. I prayed the creators of those cobwebs weren't camped out deep in the bag, waiting to scare the bejesus out of me when I pulled out a club.

"You know, if you kept those in the house instead of in the garage, you wouldn't have to work so hard at cleaning them off every spring." I glanced up to see Mary Beth Stevens, one of the players in my league. Dressed in jeans—how she played in them, I'd never understand—a white long-sleeve T-shirt, and a windbreaker, she had her bag of clubs slung over her shoulder and a smile on her face as she waited for me.

"I don't really have a spot inside." Lies. I had plenty of spots. I just didn't want them in my house, taking up space and reminding me of the sport I sucked so bad at. I was pretty sure they could take away my lesbian card for being that terrible. But I liked Mary Beth and didn't want to be all whiny and complaining on the very first night. As it was, the weather was decent—it would get chilly in an hour or two, but I had layers—and it was good to be out of the house and doing something, so I just smiled back at her, slung my clubs over my shoulder, and walked with her toward the clubhouse. I felt this way every year in the beginning. Dreading it. Not excited or enthusiastic. But I knew that once I got into the swing of things—pun intended—I'd loosen up and have fun.

I started to relax once I'd met up with the rest of my group. Every year, the league boasted anywhere from twenty-five to thirty-five people. I didn't know all of them well, and there was always at least one new person, but I knew pretty much everybody's name, and by the end of the season, I'd have played with each of them.

Carts were gathered and parked as we all met around the first tee. We'd play the front nine that night and the back nine the following week.

"Okay, listen up." Robin McKinney stood in front of the group and waited for our chatter to die down. I had a love-hate relationship with Robin. I liked regular Robin a lot. She was funny and smart and nice. But too often, regular Robin was shoved aside by in charge Robin. She owned her own business and she ran our golf league. Both things that took a lot of work and a lot of energy, I didn't deny that.

But sometimes, by the middle of the season, some of us wanted to punch in charge Robin in the face. Luckily, we weren't there yet, and we quieted down and gave her our attention.

"Welcome back, you guys. I'm so happy to see you all. We're just waiting on a few more people—the first day is always hard to get to on time—and we'll get started." She rattled off the first couple of foursomes so they could get their clubs onto their carts and buy their alcohol if they wanted. Most people came right from work and were so ready for a drink by then. I normally stuck to red wine, but the craft cocktails at The Drive were so fun, I often let the bartender talk me into whatever was featured that day, and he'd send me off with my plastic cup to play a round. That night, though, I opted for just a Diet Coke. Wasn't really in the mood to drink.

Until…

"There they are," somebody said, while at the same time, I heard my cousin Bridget's voice call, "We're here. I brought a sacrifi—err—newbie. The party can start now." She walked quickly. Bridget always walked quickly because she was short and said she'd been trained early that if she wanted to keep up with her taller brothers, she'd have to pick up the pace. Her clubs clacked together as she moved, and then her next words and the newbie registered at the same time.

"Guys, this is my friend Zoe. I convinced her to sub for Connie tonight."

"You mean you browbeat her until the only way to get you to leave her alone was to agree to sub." That was Amanda, another player, and she winked and grinned to make sure Bridget knew she was teasing.

"That's probably pretty accurate," Bridget agreed while at the same time, Zoe said, "Nooooo," and the group laughed.

Introductions went around, Zoe shaking hands with everybody. She wore a pink hat with a Nike Swoosh on it, all that wavy dark hair in a ponytail and pulled through the opening at the back, and her smile was big. Genuine. She nodded at each person and stopped when she got to me. Her beautiful eyes widened in surprise as she said my name in disbelief.

"You two know each other?" Bridget asked, then got it before either of us could answer. "Oh, I bet she sells to Perry, right?"

I nodded, having a hard time with the context of Zoe in the midst of my golf league. "She does. I'm wondering why she's not offering me doughnuts or a sandwich right now." That made Zoe laugh, and I took a moment to revel in that. I loved making other people laugh, and Zoe had an especially contagious one. Then I turned to Bridget, curious. "How do *you* know her?"

"She lives on my street," Bridget said. "We ran into each other a few times, started chatting, and then she came into Vineyard over the weekend."

Vineyard was an adorable little wine bar where Bridget worked. I had no trouble picturing Zoe there. Somehow, it seemed like her kind of place. "Did you like it?"

"Oh my God," Zoe said, and her face went all dreamy. "It's amazing. If I could live there and just exist on wine, bread, and cheese, I totally would."

I made a mental note to tell Perry how much Zoe liked Vineyard. Then I lifted my arms and dropped them to my sides, and I could feel my own smile form. "It's so weird that you're here. What a small world."

"I know, right?" Zoe said. Bridget had moved a few steps away and was chatting with Amanda, and I noticed Zoe shift a little closer to me. "It's so nice to see a friendly face. I was nervous to be the new girl."

"You're in sales," I said and bumped her with my shoulder. "You meet new people all the time."

"Yeah, but that's work. This is play. It's different."

Was it? I guessed maybe. I did know that I was happy to be the friendly face. "Well, I'm glad you decided to come. This is a nice group."

"Do you know everybody?"

I lifted one shoulder in a half shrug. "I don't know everybody *well*. I mean, some of them, I only see during this league. And then we go for almost seven months without any contact. But I know everybody's name and enough about them all to ask about jobs and kids. I'd say I'd consider myself to be personal friends with about ten of them." I began to point out different women, give Zoe a quick rundown of occupation, number of kids, how long they'd been golfing, that kind of thing.

"What about you? How long have you golfed?" I could feel Zoe's eyes on me, and it was the strangest sensation. Both comforting and nerve-racking.

"When was 2018?" I asked.

"Three years ago."

"Then three years."

Dark brows climbed upward. "So you're pretty new at this."

I nodded. "True."

Before we could say anything more, in charge Robin raised her voice and began rattling off foursomes. I was surprised when I was grouped with Mia, Kate, and Zoe. Apparently, the Universe was giving me more opportunities to get to know Zoe. I would do my best to remember any important tidbits to pass on to Perry. I changed my mind about the Diet Coke and grabbed myself a drink from the bar. We decided to share a cart and put our clubs on the back as the first foursome teed off.

We were set to tee off fourth, so we sat in our cart and waited.

"What are you drinking?" I asked Zoe as she took a sip from her cup. Sitting next to her, I could smell peaches and…something with a bit of a zing. Her hair? Lotion? Perfume? I couldn't place it, but I liked it. A lot.

"Gin and tonic," she said. "I'm not a huge fan of beer. I wish I was. I've tried over and over again. I just don't like the taste. I feel the same way about coffee." She turned to me, and I noticed the gentle lines that appeared near her eyes when she smiled. "I fail at drinking popular things."

I laughed through my nose. "I like both of those things. However…" I held up my cup. "The bartender said this is a Tropical Storm. I think it's coconut rum, Amaretto, pineapple juice? Or something."

"Good?"

"Very." I held the cup out to her, then watched her glossy lips touch the rim of my cup and leave a light, shiny print.

"Oh, yum."

"Right?"

"As I suspected, you are way cooler and hipper than I am. Don't judge me."

There was no planet on which that would ever be the case, and I almost said it out loud but managed to keep it to myself. Instead, I commented, "No judgment here, I promise. As for the coffee and beer, maybe you just don't like things that are bitter."

This time when she looked at me, she cocked her head a little. "I'd never thought of that. Huh."

We sat in silence and watched as the foursome before us teed off.

"I'm really glad you're here," Zoe said softly, and the words surprised me. But then I understood.

"Like you said, it's hard to be the new girl. I'm glad I can help with that."

She looked at me for a beat, then another, before giving a quick nod and turning her attention back to the others.

A few moments later, we were up. The first hole was a par four, and Mia drove first, followed by Kate. As Kate picked up her tee and hopped into the cart next to Mia, Zoe pulled on her glove.

"How long have you been playing golf?" I asked her.

She slipped her driver out of her bag. "Since I was ten." She pushed her tee into the ground, lined up her shot, and swung.

You can tell when you hit a perfect drive by the sound. The thwack of metal hitting ball. My drives rarely sounded like that. Zoe's sounded exactly like that.

A hush fell over those of us who were still there waiting, and we watched Zoe's drive sail perfectly through the air, drop right in the middle of the fairway, and settle, waiting for her to come take her next shot. It couldn't have been more perfect.

A chorus of *nicely done* and *beautiful drive* buzzed through our group. I closed my eyes, let out a long slow breath as I forced myself to walk to the tee. I felt like I was walking to the stocks in the center of town where they'd lock in my hands and head and throw food at me while they taunted me about what a terrible golfer I was. I made a mental note then and there, and I didn't care if it was against everything my mother had taught me about manners and politeness. No, this was a new rule, solid. Set in stone.

Never, ever let Zoe Blake tee off first.

CHAPTER SEVEN

So, where did you learn to play?" Mia walked very close to Zoe, as she'd been doing the entire nine holes whenever Zoe wasn't in the cart with me. Mia also touched her a lot. A squeeze of an arm here, a shoulder bump there, a claim that Zoe had a leaf or something in her hair.

I saw no leaf.

Zoe was polite the entire time, though I caught a couple of expressions as the evening went on that might have been tediousness. I didn't really know her well enough to be sure.

I knew Mia, though. There were only three of us on the league who were gay—me, Mia, and Char, who I didn't even remember seeing that evening—and Mia had zeroed in on Zoe instantly. Not that I could blame her.

"My mom loved to golf," Zoe said, as we trooped into the clubhouse. I didn't know her well, no, but I felt like I'd been around her enough to be able to recognize a few of her expressions, and the smile she was giving Mia, while perfectly acceptable, was not the real, genuine smile I'd seen in the coffee shop. Or in my office, for that matter. The one that lit up her whole face and made her eyes dance and her cheekbones pop.

I tried to tune out the conversation. I mean, it wasn't my job to rescue Zoe, right? She was a big girl. But as I headed toward the bar, I could feel that she was right behind me, and when I glanced over my shoulder, Mia was right behind her.

Girl needed rescuing. Yup.

"Hey, what are you drinking?" I asked Zoe as we made it to the bar. Before she could respond, I made eye contact with Mia. "Oh, hey, I think Robin was looking for you." I pointed in the general vicinity of far-away-from-us and waved my hand around a little.

"Oh." Mia blinked and completely failed to hide her disappointment. "Okay." She looked at Zoe. "I'll catch up with you later."

"Can't wait," Zoe said. That same smile of hers made me hide my own. Once Mia was out of earshot, Zoe turned to me, a little wide-eyed, and said, "Good Lord. Remind me to thank Robin for taking her attention."

"Robin will have no idea what you're talking about. You should be thanking me." I quirked an eyebrow. "What would you like to drink?"

Those arresting blue eyes blinked once. Twice. Then Zoe elbowed me gently out of the way as she said, "I wasn't going to stay, but I will for one now because I owe *you* a drink."

Zoe ordered us each the featured drink, which was a chocolate martini that night and looked as delicious as it tasted. When they arrived, we touched glasses, took tandem sips, then both hummed our approval at the same time, which made us both laugh.

"I am a total weirdo for anything chocolate," Zoe said. "I don't care if it's bacon or potato chips or peas. If it's covered in chocolate, gimme."

"Can't say I've ever had chocolate-covered peas." I made a face.

"Me neither, but they're covered in chocolate, so they must be good, right?" Zoe set her glass down and leaned one elbow on the bar. "Seriously, though. Thank you. I mean, Mia is nice enough but"—she shook her head, scrunched up her nose—"not exactly my type, you know?" A shrug.

I was impressed by the diplomatic way she put it. Not mocking Mia for her sexuality or acting revolted or shocked. Just telling me simply that Mia wasn't her type.

I wondered if Perry might be, though.

Before I could steer her to that subject, Bridget joined us with a chocolate martini of her own. "So?" she asked Zoe. "Did you have fun? How'd it go?"

I answered instead, pretending to be annoyed as I said, "How did it go? How did it go? Did you know that Zoe should be on the LPGA circuit?"

Bridget's eyes widened in surprise. "She's good?"

"Oh, she's better than good. She made me look pathetic."

Bridget tipped her head to the side, wrinkled her nose. "Did she, though?"

I hung my head in mock-shame. "No. I did that all by myself, as usual."

Bridget laughed her high-pitched laugh as Zoe jumped to my defense and said adamantly, "No! You did great."

It was my turn to tip my head, scrunch up my nose, and say, "Did I, though?"

Silence held for a beat, then two, and then Zoe shrugged and said, "Okay, yeah, you were kind of pathetic."

I gasped in feigned horror as Bridget laughed even louder, and then the three of us were cracking up.

"Seriously, though," Zoe said once we'd gotten ahold of ourselves. "This was great. Thank you so much for inviting me. It's good to get out, and moving to a new place and meeting new people isn't always easy if you're not twenty-five and prone to going to bars and clubs."

"Where did you move from?" I asked, curious to learn more about her for Perry.

"Philadelphia," she said as she took a sip of her martini, a bit of chocolate clinging to her upper lip. "I grew up there, lived there my whole life until now."

There was something a little wistful in her tone then, and I suddenly had so many questions, wanted to know so much more about her. "What made you move to Northwood?" I asked. Best to start general, right?

Zoe inhaled a big breath and let it out quietly. Not really a sigh. Back to the wistful. Then she seemed to buck up a bit and said, "My mom passed away." Matter-of-factly. Soberly but seriously. Unemotionally.

"Oh my God," I said, my voice low. "I'm so sorry."

Bridget echoed my sentiments.

Two blossoms of red appeared on Zoe's cheeks, and I knew she was talking more seriously and personally than she was okay with, and I couldn't bear to see her uncomfortable. I scrambled for a new subject.

"So, Eagles fan?" I ventured.

"You know it." As if a switch had flipped, her entire demeanor changed. She was back to light and smiling and enjoying herself.

"I wouldn't say that too loudly." Bridget made a show of looking around. "You're in Bills country now."

Zoe snorted. "Is that supposed to worry me?" But she raised and lowered her eyebrows once to show she was just kidding. Oh, Perry was going to love that she was a football fan.

Noticing somebody across the room, Bridget waved, then said to us, "I gotta go talk to Mary Beth." Shifting her glance to Zoe, she said, "Twenty minutes?"

"I'll be right here." Bridget scooted off and my expression must've been questioning because Zoe explained, "We drove together."

"Aha." We sipped, and I was surprised to realize that I was completely comfortable standing there with her. I wanted to talk more to her, but I also didn't feel a need to fill the silence with chatter the way I often did with a new person. Companionable silence can be hard to come by, but it was right there sitting between Zoe and me. It wasn't until I saw Mia looking in our direction that I turned to Zoe and said, "Seriously, though. How did you become such a good golfer?"

Those cheekbones. God, those cheekbones. I wanted to make Zoe smile every second of every day just so I could see them.

"Well, like I said, my mom golfed a lot. She wasn't necessarily a great player—she did just fine—but she loved it. *Loved* it. And as soon as I showed any interest at all in learning to play, she'd take me with her. I think I was ten when we started. Something like that. Weekends. Evenings. Anytime she had off from work, if the weather allowed it, we'd go golfing. It was our thing."

I loved the way her entire face softened as she talked about her mother. She got this dreamy quality in her eyes, and a small smile stayed on her lips the whole time she spoke.

"My drives were always pretty accurate. She said I was a natural. I played on the golf team in high school. Then in college. I was ranked pretty high when I was at Penn State." There was a nice mix of pride and humility as she spoke. She wasn't bragging at all, and I liked that.

"That's impressive," I said, and it was true.

"This is the first time I've played since my mom died." She said it so softly, I wasn't sure I'd heard her right. And then I didn't want to ask her to clarify, because ouch.

"I'm sorry." It was all I could think of to say.

Zoe smiled, her eyes on mine. "Thank you. She'd be glad, though. She hated when I didn't make time to play because she knew I loved it as much as she did."

"Well, then, I'm glad you joined us, and I hope you're going to keep coming as needed. You could join permanently next year."

"I think I might." She sipped her drink. "What about you? I take it golf isn't your thing." Her grin softened the comment, and I knew she was teasing. "Did you play any sports in school?"

"I did, and that's why I'm terrible at golf and whiff the ball at least once every couple of holes. I played softball from the time I was about twelve. I still play now and then with a rec team."

"My turn to be impressed. That's a long time to stick with a sport. You can't be older than—what?—thirty?"

"Dangerous choice, guessing a woman's age." My tone was a little flirty, and it just came out like that, and I was horrified. I felt my own eyes widen in surprise, and I turned to my drink so Zoe wouldn't see. "I'm thirty-three. So you were very close."

"I've got you by five years," she said, and if she'd been bothered by—or even noticed—my overstepping, she hid it well. "And by the way, your playing softball has little to do with your not being good at golf." The expression on her face was soft, almost tender. She reached up and tapped her forefinger against my temple. "I think you might be stuck in here over that."

"My brother is always reminding me that the golf ball is not a softball. He thinks I swing too hard."

"I disagree. It's not that you swing too hard—it's that you *expect* to miss. So you do."

Before I could respond, Bridget returned. "Ready?"

"Yes, ma'am." Zoe downed the remaining bit of her drink, then signaled for the bartender, closed out her tab, and gathered her things. "I imagine I'll see you again in the office soon," she said to me, and there was something amazing and warm about having all her focus on me. It was like nobody else in the room existed. A weirdly comforting feeling that I didn't quite understand.

"You know how to find me," I said, then internally rolled my eyes at myself for my corniness. Thank God Perry had way more chill than me.

"I do." The cheekbones. The sparkling eyes. My brother sure did have good taste. I had to give him that.

"God, she's fucking hot, huh?" Mia had sidled up next to me, a glass of what looked like whiskey or scotch in her hand. She stared at Zoe's retreating form. No, she *leered* at Zoe's retreating form, and I felt a little dirty just standing next to her.

"Hot and straight," I said, stressing the second word for some reason.

"Hey," Mia said with a shrug. "You never know." She slugged back the rest of her drink, set the glass on the bar more loudly than necessary, and gave me a wink. "See ya next week."

A full-body shudder ran through me, and suddenly I wanted nothing more than to go home and take a shower.

❖

It was the following Friday, and the entire week had gone by without a visit from Zoe. Which wasn't unusual for a pharma rep. I knew from my nearly ten years working in a medical office that Zoe had many other clients, most of whom were probably bigger than our little office in the suburbs. I didn't want to admit that I was bummed not to see her, especially given how obviously bummed Perry was.

Every time he needed to come to my desk for some reason, he'd crane his neck to see out the window in front of my desk.

"Subtle you are not, big bro." I didn't have to look to know what he was doing. "She's not here. I haven't heard from her. She'll be back at some point. All things you know."

Perry cleared his throat, pretended to scrutinize the paper in his hand.

"Also, if you had called her last weekend like you said you were going to, you'd have seen her already."

He sighed and looked at me then. "I know. I chickened out like a loser." I tried to read his expression. He seemed a little bit crestfallen and a little bit disappointed in himself, and those were things I rarely saw on my big brother's face. Ever.

"So call her."

"You think? Maybe we should text a bit more first."

"Sure, what have you got to lose? She's an Eagles fan. Give her some crap about that."

"She is? How do you know?"

I tipped my head to the side. "Dude, do you ever listen to me when I talk?"

"Oh, right, you saw her last week. Right." His focus went back to the paper he'd brought to me.

"Seriously, do men listen to women at all? Like, ever?"

A beat passed, and then, in a move that couldn't have been timed more perfectly if it had been scripted by Nora Ephron, he looked up at me, raised his sandy brows, and asked, "Hm?"

I threw my pen at him. "Unbelievable."

He grinned and tossed me his phone. "Would you send her a text for me? Something witty and charming, but not too pushy." He narrowed his eyes as he thought. "Not needy. You know? Just…" He started to bob his head in this weird sort of…groove was the only word I could think of. "Casual. Yeah. Casual. No big deal." He continued to groove as he left.

I opened his texts. Zoe was three messages down in his inbox, and he hadn't texted her since last week. Did he know she was from Philly? I was pretty sure he did. I chewed on my lip for a moment, searching for the right way to break the ice of the day.

Hey there. Happy Friday. Good day? Busy here.

Typing two-word sentences went against every word-loving fiber of my being, but I was supposed to be Perry, so it fit.

Zoe's response came quickly. *Hi! It's been a chaotic week, yes!*

Hmm. Professional. Of course. Perry was a client, and I was sure Zoe wouldn't ignore or blow off a client.

Totally get it. Fridays can be nuts! I read it over several times, trying to decide if it sounded like Perry. I made a second attempt. *Word. Fridays are crazy!*

Right? A smiley. *Have a great weekend!*

Lotta exclamation points in her texts, I noticed. That always spoke of forced cheerfulness to me, but I was not giving up for my brother. He turned the corner then, and I held up his phone wordlessly.

"Good?" he asked, taking it back.

"Eh. She sounds super busy, so probably didn't have a lot of time to chat." I fudged my observations a bit.

"S'okay. Fridays are crazy." I grinned at my accuracy as he shrugged and turned away. I called him back. "Hey." When I had his attention, the words tumbled out before I could stop them. "I could write up a little something. A little ditty, as Dad would say. And you can send it to her when you ask her out."

"A little ditty?" he asked and made air quotes.

I gave him a look. "Do you want to impress her or not?"

He looked properly scolded for a second before he blew out a breath. "I do. Yes."

"All right. Give me a little time."

His smile grew and softened. "You're the best. Thanks, Morgs." And he headed to the exam rooms to see his next patient.

The phone rang and I answered, then shifted in my seat as I listened and tried to remember why I wore those particular pants. We were business casual in the office, so I mostly wore jeans and nice tops to work. The jeans I'd chosen felt fine when I'd put them on in the morning, but it was almost two in the afternoon now, and I felt like they had decided to strangle my entire body. I unbuttoned them in my chair and tried not to sigh in relief.

Something to know about me—I have zero fashion sense. I never know what to wear or when. I have no idea what goes with what and have been known to buy entire outfits right off the mannequin because I figure if somebody who works in the clothing store put that outfit together, it *must* work, right? I can't accessorize to save my life. My closet and drawers mostly consist of my Levi's, a few dress pants, a handful of dresses that I like but never know when to wear, shoes I have no ability to pair with clothing, and some shirts I thought were cute at the time I ordered them.

I shook my head in frustration because the one article of clothing I felt I could handle—jeans—were now out to get me. It was hopeless. "Why can't I just wear yoga pants to everything?" I muttered.

"I don't see why you can't," Joanne said from her seat behind me. "It's not like Perry would notice."

I laughed and glanced at her over my shoulder. "You make a fine point, my friend. Though I kinda think if you start wearing yoga pants to *everything*, you've pretty much given up. Like a guy who wears sweatpants twenty-four seven."

The door opened and Mr. Jones walked in for his two thirty. Every time I saw him, I broke into song, singing the Counting Crows' *"Mr. Jones"* to him. He was in his eighties, and I don't think he knew the song, but he grinned big every time, so I kept doing it. It was our thing now.

My cell pinged a text notification as I sent a message to Diane telling her Mr. Jones was here. I glanced at the screen, saw it was my niece Brittany.

Toes tom noon you in?

I grinned because I always teased her about how she tried to use as few words as possible to get her message across. And aside from question marks, she rarely used any punctuation. Her run-on sentences could be epic. I knew, of course, that this was the way normal people texted. My full, properly constructed sentences, complete with punctuation, made me the weirdo in this scenario, but I loved to pretend otherwise. I deciphered her text to mean she wanted me to go with her tomorrow at noon to get a pedicure.

Of course, to combat her brevity, I went for verbose.

Why, yes, dear niece of mine, Brittany Michelle Thompson. I believe I would very much enjoy accompanying you to an establishment where they have people who will spend much time and energy making our feet beautiful. I shall await your arrival at the hour of noon at the entrance of my humble abode.

I double-checked all my spelling and grammar and, when satisfied, sent it on its way. And waited.

Ur soooooooooo weird, came back a few moments later.

You wouldn't have me any other way, I typed back.

Now's probably a good time to tell you that there's another one of us, in addition to me and Perry. The oldest sibling, our brother Carter. He's forty-six and because of the thirteen year age difference, he and I were never really that close. But I adore his daughter with every drop of blood in my body. I was only eleven when Brittany was born, and obviously still living at home, so whenever baby Brittany came to visit Grandma and Grandpa, I got to be there, too. She was more like a little sister to me than a niece, and we stayed close the whole time she was growing up. At twenty-two, she was smart, funny, and one of my favorite people on the planet. I'd do anything for her.

The other thing about Brittany was that she had the confidence of Oprah, and I envied that. She didn't let anything tip her off balance. As I glanced down at my unbuttoned jeans, an idea came to me, and I picked up my phone and sent her another quick text.

A little shopping after toes? I sent it and waited. I didn't have to wait long.

OMG yes

That was it and that was all I needed. The front door opened, revealing another patient to see Perry. I exhaled as much air as I could, fastened my jeans back up, and smiled at her as she walked toward my desk.

That night, I sat in my living room covered in cats, my longhorn notebook open on my lap. Pen in hand. Brain whirring.

Zoe would like a poem, right? She seemed to appreciate words, and poetry made her think of her mom, which I didn't think could be a bad thing. But we were also talking about Perry. Not that I was a master of words and poetry, but I was way better than Perry, so this would have to be Perry-ish. That meant not too deep. Witty. A little silly, just enough to make her laugh.

"Hmm." I tapped my pen against my lips. Ross, in his usual spot on the back of the couch, lifted his head to blink at me. "What would Uncle Perry write a poem about?" I asked him. He blinked again. "Football, yes, that's a good suggestion, but that might be too on the nose for a guy. What else?" This time, Ross yawned. His little kitty mouth cranked open, and his pink tongue unrolled as he gave me an impressive shot of his needlelike fangs. "Lunch! Yes! That's a fabulous idea." I ruffled his fur, gave him an ear scratch. "You brilliant kitty."

I found a blank page and began scratching out words. Lunch. Food. Sandwich. Doughnuts. All things Perry might say. And remember when I talked about poetry and rhyming and Dr. Seuss? I knew that would definitely be Perry's version.

More tapping of the pen against my lips. More scratching of notes.

Bread, chewy and soft
Chicken, turkey, ham
I hold my sub aloft
Cuz sandwiches are my jam

I read it. Read it again aloud. Laughed at my own ridiculousness. But it sounded just like Perry, and that's what I loved about it.

"We're gonna call this '*Ode to the Sub*,'" I told the cats. Then I laughed some more while they looked at me with a boredom only cats can portray.

I typed the the poem up on my phone, then texted it to Perry. *Tell Zoe you appreciate that she brings lunch and send her this. Should make her laugh.*

It was short and dorky enough that it shouldn't seem like I told him she liked poetry. I hoped she'd laugh and find Perry charming. That was the goal. To win her over. For him.

Zoe's face appeared in my head, various images of her. Those cheekbones. Those eyes. God, those eyes. I turned the page in my notebook and wrote some more, just because I was in the mood.

To lose myself in azure
To be pulled under, but gently
Softly. Invited. Enveloped.
To feel seen, to feel safe
To be home

A long, slow breath left my lungs, and I felt my body deflate like a balloon as I lay there. The words were pretty, but I wasn't going there. It was ridiculous to let my thoughts run way far into a future that might never be, but I did. Glancing at Rachel as she lifted her head to gaze at me, I said, "What if she ends up being my sister-in-law? I can't be writing poetry about my sister-in-law's eyes, right? That'd just be pathetic. And sad. And a little bit creepy."

Rachel stared at me. Blinked her yellow eyes. I took that as agreement.

"Damn right."

We headed up to bed.

Chapter Eight

My niece turned heads.

Everywhere we went, people took notice of her. And she was attractive, yes, with her blond hair, long legs, and kind eyes, but I think it was more the way she carried herself. Self-assurance came off her like heat from a radiator, and you could see it. Sense it. She was a woman people wanted to be around. Sometimes it was sexual, I'm sure, but often it was just because of that confidence. You felt safe with Brittany, like she could take care of whatever might come your way. I know I did.

That Saturday was no different as we walked through the mall to Nailed It! where she'd made us appointments. I watched as people's gazes stayed on us even after we'd passed them. Brittany seemed oblivious. Or completely aware and owning it. Probably the latter.

Once in the chairs, we settled in and talked about anything and everything. Nothing was off-limits between us.

"How's your last summer off going so far?" I asked her as our feet soaked.

She sighed and let her head fall back against the black massage chair. "It's fine, but I'm anxious to get started at work." She'd gotten herself a job in the sales department of a very large marketing firm downtown with the very first interview she'd gone on. The company had been her first choice, she'd landed an interview, and she was hired before she even graduated.

"You start when? A month?"

"Yeah. July fifth. I'd start tomorrow if I could." She had her phone in her hand and began typing.

"Listen, savor this time off because it won't be long before you'll wish you had more and start wondering why you wasted that summer off you had that one time."

She grinned. "Probably true." Kept typing.

I learned a few years earlier that it was fruitless fighting with Brittany about how being on her phone when she was spending time with me was rude. There was just enough of an age difference that she had never known not having a cell phone. I had one fairly early on, but Brittany had had one always. It was part of her life, an extension of her, and asking her to set it aside completely was like asking her to hold her breath. She and her friends really could multitask, and while I still didn't love having her looking at an electronic device while talking to me, I knew she was paying attention, that she heard everything I said, and she responded. So I'm fine with it now.

Couldn't say the same for her parents. Or mine...

"Do you have to cold-call? Or will they give you existing clients to call on?" I asked as my pedicurist wrapped my legs in warm towels.

"A little of both, I think. Nobody likes cold-calling, but it's the first step in taking me to account executive and then senior account executive. That's when you get to travel and service the biggest clients." Her brown eyes sparkled with excitement, and I had a quick flash of when she was small and her adrenaline kicked in about something. She was always a girl who let any kind of excitement wash right over her. Completely. She embraced it, surrendered to it, wasn't overly cautious and analytical like her aunt. "I've been watching YouTube videos and online tutorials from salespeople to get a better sense of what the first few weeks will be like." Phone in her lap, she turned to me. "I mean, I'll be fine, but I really want to be more than that. I want to *impress*."

I grinned at her. "You have always been like that," I said, hoping my fondness for her was obvious. "You have never, ever done anything halfway."

"I mean, they're gonna give me a sort of mentor to help me my first week, but he's another salesperson there and kinda my competition, so..."

A thought struck me then. "You know, I have a…sort of a friend who's a salesperson. I bet she'd have some advice if you wanted to talk to somebody not in your company."

"Yeah? Who?" Back to the phone. Typing, typing.

"She's a pharmaceutical rep that comes to the office. She's super nice, very successful, has been in sales for a while, I think. I'm sure she'd talk to you if I asked."

Now, I have no idea what my face was doing or what tone of voice I was apparently using, but Brittany gave me a look. That look where the other person tips their head forward and kind of looks at you from under their lowered eyebrows like they're on to you for whatever you've done.

"What?" I asked.

"You like her."

"Me? What? No. As a matter of fact, your Uncle Perry likes her and I'm…helping him."

"O-M-G." The phone was put down again, and I had all Brittany's attention. "Tell me everything."

For the remainder of our pedicures, I talked about Zoe and Perry. But Brittany kept asking about Zoe, so I kept talking about Zoe, so by the time we were in flip-flops and paying at the front desk, she knew as much about Zoe as I did.

"Do you think Uncle Perry will ask her out?"

"I hope so," I said, sliding my credit card back into my wallet. "He's been talking about it enough, but hasn't pulled the trigger."

"What's he waiting for?" Brittany's eyes were wide. "He's Uncle Perry. Has she *seen* him?"

A laugh shot out of me as we walked back into the mall. "Listen to you, pimping out your uncle."

"I mean, she could do way worse. Come on."

"True."

We walked, and she typed on her phone, and I absently wondered if she'd ever walked right into something while walking and looking down at her phone. Another person? A pole? A wall?

"There," she said. "I gave him a little nudge."

"Oh. Well, good." I felt…weird. I didn't know why, but it was there, this uncomfortable buzzing in my gut.

"Hey," Brittany said, grabbing my arm and hauling me out of my head. "Come with me. Let's look at clothes."

"For you?"

"For you."

"What's wrong with my clothes?" I asked, surprised but not really.

"You're adorable, Mo," Brittany said, using the name she'd called me from the time she could talk but was unable to say the name Morgan. She tugged me along and into Macy's. "But the mom jeans have to go. Just come with me."

"Mom jeans?" I blinked as she pulled me through the store. They were that bad?

Half an hour later, I was standing in a dressing room in my underwear, trying on pants that Brittany handed over the door.

"These are stretchy," I said as I stepped into a pair so impossibly soft there was no way they were denim.

"Where have you been?" Brittany asked, disbelief clear in her voice. "Under a rock? This is how jeans are made now. When was the last time you bought a new pair?"

"Um…" I fastened the button and decided not to give her any more ammo—specifically that the last time I'd purchased jeans had literally been years ago.

A loud sigh. "You're like sixty years old in a thirty-three-year-old body. A thirty-three-year-old *hot* body, by the way. I don't get it."

"How dare you?" I feigned horror, but she was absolutely right about me dressing older than I was, so I blew out a breath and said in defeat, "I know. Fashion hates me. Which makes sense because I'm not exactly fond of it either. Help me. Please."

"Doing my best out here." She was back in a few minutes with more pants and a few tops.

"I like the way these feel," I said, studying myself in the mirror.

"Lemme see." The doorknob rattled, and I stepped out so Brittany could see.

"I think they look pretty good."

"Are you kidding me? They look great." Brittany spun me around, scrutinizing every inch. "You have a great ass. I don't know why you hide it."

"Really?" I turned so my back was to the mirror and looked over my shoulder. "Huh. Not bad."

"Not bad? I'd kill for that ass." She handed me a shirt. "You also have amazing boobs. Try this, and leave those pants on."

Back in the dressing stall, I took off my shirt and put on the one Brittany gave me. It was red—a color I didn't wear very often—and had a V-neck that dipped a bit lower than I was used to. I felt the tiniest bit exposed, and I told her so when I opened the door.

"Oh my God. Are you kidding me with that shirt? It's amazing."

"Really? But…" I glanced down into more cleavage than I was used to seeing. Or showing.

"It's just the angle you're seeing. You're looking down. Trust me, you're revealing very little. I wouldn't let you show too much skin, I promise." Her voice was soft, genuine. "But please look in the mirror 'cause"—she spun me again, stood behind me with her hands on my shoulders—"you're a hottie, Mo. You just hide it really, really well."

It was kind of amazing what a good outfit could do. Not only for your outside appearance, but for your internal confidence level. I can admit that mine has never been high. It's why I admire Brittany so much—and envy her a little, if I'm being honest. But looking in that full-length mirror just then? In the horrible dressing room lighting? I could feel my confidence kick up a little bit. I felt my body straighten. I lifted my chin just a bit.

"I like this. A lot." I met Brittany's eyes in the mirror, surprised she was looking at me and not her phone.

"Me, too. You look amazing. Buy it."

"Yeah?"

"All of it."

I did.

❖

Wednesday had my head spinning.

I'm good at my job. I'd even venture to say that I'm very good at my job. But every once in a while, there'd be a day filled with every possible thing that might take up extra time, overload Perry's schedule, confuse the hell out of me, or whatever. They were rare, but they happened, and that Wednesday was one of those days when they *all* happened.

On a day like that, I would turn a pharma rep away in a heartbeat. Phones ringing off the hook, waiting room filled to capacity, I'd hold up a finger or make a dismissive gesture with my hand. "Come tomorrow." "Come next week." I didn't care when they came back, but I couldn't handle them that day. Early on in my job, I'd feel bad putting them off, telling them there just wasn't time. But they were rarely insulted. Pharma reps understand the business.

Zoe was a different story, though, and I realized it on that Wednesday. The ceiling could've been falling down on my head, walls crumbling, floor opening up beneath me, and I still would've waved her in.

She smiled at me while I was on the phone, gave a little wave, and took a seat. I looked at her while trying not to look like I was looking at her. Yes, it was as confusing as it sounds. She was more casual than usual, in simple tan dress slacks, a black top with three-quarter sleeves, and black heels. Sunglasses were perched on top of her head, and her hair was down and all kinds of wavy, and I seriously thought about telling the lab tech on the other end of the line to hold on for just a moment while I went and dug my fingers into it.

Ugh. Stop it.

Luckily, my silly hair fantasy was shoved into the background by more ringing of the phone, along with a patient and the mailman coming through the door at the same time. I spun in my chair to look at a file on the other part of my desk and give the person I was talking to what they asked for, and when I turned back, Zoe was gone. I had no idea if she'd left or been taken back by somebody, but I didn't have time to find out.

My attention was yanked back to my job. Which was where it should've been anyway.

I had no idea how much time had passed, but as I was checking out Mrs. D'Angelo, I heard Zoe's voice. I glanced up and she was at the front door.

"See you next week." Then she grinned, waved, and was gone.

As I waved at her retreating form, I didn't like the wave of disappointment that washed over me at not getting the chance to even say hello, and I tried to push it away. I made a follow-up appointment for Mrs. D'Angelo and sent her on her way just as Perry came up to my desk, in his white lab coat, stethoscope around his neck, sandy hair dashingly tousled.

"You look like you should be on *General Hospital*," I told him, not for the first time.

"In my next life," he replied, closing a file and handing it to me. "I bet it'd be less stressful."

"Probs." The phone rang, but Joanne snatched it up.

Hands empty, Perry continued to stand there, staring at me with a weird grin on his face.

"Why are you smiling at me like a serial killer?" I asked.

"Guess who's got two thumbs and a date with the sexy pharma rep." Before I could say anything at all, let alone guess—which was unnecessary, duh—his smile burst across his face like the sun coming out from behind a cloud. Big and bright and full.

"I'm gonna go out on a limb here and say...this guy?" I pointed at him.

"This guy!" Using both thumbs, he indicated himself.

"That's great," I said, happy to see him so happy, but a little confused by the weirdness that had settled in my belly. "When?"

"Well, I asked her to dinner Friday, but she said she'd rather do lunch." One corner of his mouth went down, and he said, "I know that's a safety thing. Something with a time limit in case we don't hit it off." He'd done enough online dating to get the gist of some of the rules. "But it's okay. We're on our summer hours, so I won't have to hurry back here. I'll make the most of my time." And just like that, his excitement was back. He was like a teenager, and the girl he'd been crushing on for years accepted his invitation to the prom.

"That's great, Per," I called toward his retreating form. Adorable. My big brother, forty-three years old, was adorable, there was no better word. I didn't have to force myself to be glad for him. Despite my own strange emotions, I really was.

"Oh," he said, turning back to me, "she *loved* that stupid poem. Can you do another one for me? Please?" He disappeared around a corner before I could answer.

Later that night, I sat in my chair next to the fire—again, it was really too warm for a fire, but I liked the ambiance of it—and sipped from my glass of Malbec. My poetry notebook was open on my lap, and I racked my brain for some words, but I was so tired from the day that I felt like a gummi bear sitting there, all pliable and soft with not much possibility of arm movement. As if surveilling me through spy cameras in my house, Perry pinged my phone.

Don't forget my poem!

I was now a poet-on-demand. Was that similar to being a poet laureate? A poet-in-residence? Another ping.

Less goofy this time…

I squinted at my phone, then typed back, *Beggars can't be choosers, you know.*

The gray dots bounced for a few minutes before his message came. *I know…just trying to impress.*

Ugh. I felt bad then, because I knew that was the truth. He was my brother, and he'd always been there for me. Now he was asking for my help with impressing the girl he liked. How could I refuse?

Fine. Give me a little while.

He sent back a bitmoji in a lab coat that looked so much like him, it made me chuckle. I took another sip of my wine, picked up my pen, tapped it against my lips. That seemed to be my poetry-writing stance.

"All right, you guys," I said to the cats. "I need less goofy. But not too serious. Don't wanna scare her away, right?" Ross seemed very interested in my words and watched me carefully. Rachel lifted her head, blinked once, set her head back down. Big help she was.

I scribbled, scratched things out, scribbled some more. I kept thinking about the first time Zoe walked in, how Perry and I stared.

Time plays tricks
I can't always tell
If it's moving fast or moving slow
But when you walked in
It stopped
Just like that
You smiled
And I knew I wanted to know more

Done. Not my best work, but not awful. And Perry-passable, I thought. I figured that should do it, should help my brother with the impression making and the wooing. I typed it into my phone and sent it off to him and felt good for helping and unsettled for…I didn't know why.

I set my notebook aside, picked up my wine, and sipped, staring into the fire.

The blue flames offered up no answers.

Chapter Nine

Summer hours at the office were the best. Everybody on staff held their collective breath until mid-June arrived. Then we all got to leave at noon on Fridays. Sometimes, Perry would take us all to lunch as a thank-you for the hard work all year long. Other times, we'd all just skitter off in different directions like kids getting let out on the last day of school.

That Friday boasted gorgeous weather and no emergencies at all. Nearly unheard of. At noon, I clicked the switchboard over to the answering service and watched Joanne, Martha, and Diane scoot out the door like they'd stolen something. I wasn't going to be far behind them, just had a few things to deal with.

I'd expected Perry had left through the back entrance, his preference, but he walked up to my counter. No lab coat. He'd changed into jeans and a navy blue designer polo shirt. His hair was freshly combed.

"Look at you," I said. "Lookin' damn fine, my bro. And you smell amazing."

"Yeah?" He ran his hand through his hair, then made a face and tried to smooth it back out.

"Come here," I said and stood. He leaned toward me, and I finger-combed his locks until they were all back in place. "You're nervous."

He took a deep breath, then let it out. "I am. I'm not usually."

"Just be your charming self." I pointed at him as I sat back down. "And ask her questions. Don't just talk about you."

"Yes, ma'am." He straightened his collar, rolled his big gold watch around his wrist to check the time. "Gonna meet her at Bergman's. They're doing a steak special, grilling it outside."

I almost said, "Let's hope she likes steak," but I didn't want to send him into a panic this late in the game. And Bergman's was a nice joint. Not too casual, not too fancy. Perfect for a lunch date.

"Hey, she really seems to get a kick out of the poems...can you jot a couple more for me? Just to have in my back pocket?" His eyes were pleading, and he gave me that big brother smile that he always gave me when he wanted something from me. It was a combination of *I love you so much* and *Don't forget I kept Timmy Jacobs from beating the crap out of you when you were eleven.* Both very true statements.

"Sure."

"You're the best." He used his arms to prop himself over the counter and kiss my cheek. "Wish me luck." And he was off toward the back of the building.

"Good luck," I called out. Inside, though, I felt weird. It's not that I couldn't pinpoint why—it's that I didn't want to pinpoint why. I knew I had a little crush on Zoe myself. I'm not an idiot. And that made me laugh at myself for several reasons. The biggest of which was the idea that somebody like Zoe—stunning, charming, successful— would even think twice about somebody like me—regular-looking and unexciting, like white bread or an apple.

"Oh, I'm making food analogies now. Perfect." I shook my head as I finished up a couple final things and gathered my stuff. I would write more silly limericks for Perry so he could continue to woo my crush, and I vowed to get myself past that. Perry had been through the wringer with Christine, and he deserved somebody special like Zoe. If I could help him achieve that, I was going to.

I had a lunch date with my mom set up, so I texted her to see if she was ready for me. In response, she sent me a picture of her outdoor table, fully set with two place settings and a bottle of white wine in the ice bucket chiller I'd given her for Christmas.

I sent her back a GIF of a speeding car and typed, *On my way!*

❖

When my mom retired from teaching a few years ago, she'd had trouble finding ways to occupy her time. Which was surprising because I thought it would be my dad that struggled. He didn't. He golfed. He met his buddies for poker night. He started going to the gym.

My mom, on the other hand, sort of wandered aimlessly around the house, cleaning various rooms. About six months into her retirement, me and my brothers all got calls from her, telling us to come and get our stuff out of her attic, since we all had houses of our own now. We had quite the group text going around that. Mom dabbled in a few things here and there, but we were all surprised when she basically decided to become Ina Garten, the Barefoot Contessa. She started trying new recipes. Tons of them. She began stocking up on table decor and place settings and fancy napkins. My dad watched with wide eyes as she kept adding to her collection. But she was happy, and she was entertaining her friends and family, and that's why we worked so hard at our jobs for thirty, forty, fifty years, right? So we can do that? So he wisely kept quiet and let her do what made her happy.

I entered the yard through the back gate. The day was gorgeous, and I didn't want to miss one moment of sunshine. Mom was pouring water into glasses, bright yellow circles of lemon floating in it.

"Hi, honey." She looked up at me and smiled that smile that made everybody fall in love with her. My mom was the most openhearted, open-minded person I knew. She'd barely blinked an eye when I came out. She smiled, said she'd suspected, and told me as long as I was happy, she was happy. My friends adored her. Brittany thought she'd hit the Grandma Jackpot, and she was right. "I made turkey avocado finger sandwiches and a strawberry salad." She indicated the back door with her chin, sign language for me to go in and grab.

I went inside as I felt my phone ping in my back pocket. I took it out to see a notification from Instagram. Perry and Zoe, smiling at the camera, thick, juicy steaks on their plates. They looked like they were having fun. My stomach clenched a bit, and I quickly put the phone away and mentally scolded myself for not being happier to see my brother so happy. I sucked. It was that simple.

With a sigh, I grabbed lunch off the counter.

Ten minutes later, my mom and I were seated at the outdoor table. It was covered in a festive green tablecloth. All the dishes were white, the napkins were green-and-white striped, and the glasses were clear with gold rims and fancy raised spots in the shape of flowers, like *bas-relief* in glass. A vase of fresh-cut tulips in reds and yellows sat at the center. I pointed at them.

"You still have tulips? Aren't they usually gone by now?"

"That new fertilizer I used kept them blooming longer." She shrugged and reached to stroke a petal on one. Turning to me, she picked up a finger sandwich cut in a cute little triangle and asked, "How was your day?"

I stabbed some spinach and strawberry with my fork and told her all about my week. I always thought it was so mundane, but I think my mom liked to hear about workdays. They made her feel included. Maybe she lived vicariously, I wasn't sure. I finished it up with, "Perry's on a date right now with the pharma rep."

"Oh, is he?" Her eyes lit right up. "He mentioned her the last time we talked."

He did? He mentioned a girl to our mom? I didn't think he'd mentioned anybody he'd dated for a while now because Mom tended to get way too excited. His mentioning Zoe only solidified his very deep interest to me. Not that I'd doubted it, but this was kind of a big deal, telling Mom.

"Yeah? What did he say?" I asked, curious how detailed he'd gotten.

Mom gave a little half shrug and picked up her glass of lemon water. "That she was new to the area, pretty, smart."

"All true," I agreed, still amazed he'd mentioned her.

"What do you think of her? I assume you've met?"

"We have. She's nice." My turn to shrug as I chewed my sandwich.

"Pretty?"

"Pretty doesn't begin to cover it," I said, then realized the slightly dreamy quality of my tone and sat up straighter. "She's very… sophisticated. That's a good word to describe her."

Mom seemed to take that in and roll it around a little bit. "Well," she said after a moment, "I'm just happy to know he's found somebody he's taking more than a passing interest in. His drive-by dates are starting to worry me."

I blinked at my mom. This was new information. While I knew she'd been worried about Perry since his divorce, and we joked about his dates, I didn't realize the level of her concern around the subject. "He's a big boy, Mom. He'll be okay."

She sighed but didn't answer.

We ate for a few silent moments. I was just about to change the subject when the sliding glass door opened and Perry walked out, surprising both of us.

"Well, hello there," Mom said and held her arms up for a hug.

Perry kissed her cheek, squeezed her tight. "Hey, Mom."

"How was your date?" she asked him.

He shot me a look I pretended not to see and said, "It was great. Short, but she had an appointment."

I didn't think my mother saw the shadow of disappointment in his eyes, but it was there. I knew what he was thinking, that Zoe had been glad for an excuse to cut things short. As a woman who had done exactly that—made a lunch date or a coffee date rather than dinner to avoid being stuck too long with somebody I wasn't hitting it off with—I knew that was a possibility. But maybe it wasn't. "She's crazy busy, I bet. Remember she hasn't been here that long. I bet she's still got a lot of face time to put in. And I saw your Instagram post. Looked like you guys were having fun."

Perry met my gaze as he sat, and I could see the gratitude in his eyes. I winked at him. "You're probably right."

"Let me see the post," Mom said, holding out her hand and wiggling her fingers.

Perry's phone pinged the second it was in his hand, and he gave a little groan as he took a look.

Mom's curiosity was replaced by her look of pride, the way she always looked when Perry got buzzed while on call. "My son the doctor," she said, sitting up a little straighter.

"Damn," Perry muttered as he read his screen.

"Emergency?" Mom asked.

He sighed, put his phone away, and reached for one of the sandwiches that were left. "No, Gina broke her foot."

I scrunched up my nose in thought just as Mom asked, "Who's Gina?"

"She's a radiologist and is part of my foursome for the Northwood General golf tournament. She plays with us every year."

"Isn't that tournament next weekend?" I asked, trying to remember the flyer in the break room.

"Exactly. Gina's not going to be golfing with a broken foot. Now I need to find a woman to replace her." He groaned. "In a week."

"Well, ask your sister," Mom said, as if it was the most obvious solution in the world, and she couldn't believe he hadn't thought of it.

Perry snorted. "No way. She sucks." He turned to me. "No offense."

I shrugged. "None taken." It's not like he was wrong. And then…a lightning bolt hit me. Well, not really, but an idea did. "Ask Zoe."

He blinked at me. "What?"

"Come on, you guys had lunch, and golf never came up?"

His eyes went wide and his voice cracked like a twelve-year-old's. "No, you told me to stay away from talking too much about sports," he whined.

"Too bad, 'cause she's an excellent golfer." He stared at me and I emphasized my point. "*Excellent.*"

"Seriously?"

"She subs on my league, remember?" Did he listen to me ever? Like, ever in life at all? "She's been playing since she was a kid and is ridiculously good. Plus, I mean, this tournament could be good networking for her, and you'd get to spend more time with her. It's a win-win." I popped the last bite of my sandwich into my mouth.

"Oh my God, you're a genius, baby sis." He stood up, dropped a kiss on my head, and went inside, presumably to send a text. His excitement was obvious. He legit reminded me of a high school kid who found out the girl he likes liked him back.

"Look how cute he is," I said to my mom.

"That was good of you," Mom said as she ate her salad.

"What was?"

Mom shrugged. "Helping your brother like that." She held my gaze, and there was something on her face that was all too knowing. I felt transparent, and I didn't like that. At all.

I forced the nonchalance, hoping it didn't sound that way. "He's my brother."

Mom simply hummed her agreement, and we continued to eat.

Chapter Ten

I think I got the gout."

I inhaled slowly as I blinked at Mr. Wilson as he stared back at me through the Plexiglas window over my desk. There was a ninety-eight percent chance he did not have the gout, but he'd followed protocol this time, had called and made himself an appointment instead of just showing up, as he'd done before. I smiled at him.

"How about we let Dr. Thompson figure out what it is, okay?"

"Yeah, all right." He didn't wave dismissively at me, but I was pretty sure he wanted to.

"Have a seat and Martha will call you in shortly."

He sighed and headed for a seat, and I did my best to hide my smile. *God help me to not become a hypochondriac in my old age*, I silently prayed.

The end of June had gotten hot, and Perry had the air conditioning set at Arctic Tundra. As if reading my mind, Joanne bustled toward her desk from an exam room and muttered, "Why is it that I'm colder here in the summer than in the winter? How does that make sense?"

I shook my head and pulled on the zip-up hoodie I kept draped over the back of my chair for days like this. "I think it's a guy thing. I remember my dad telling me how he and his secretary would fight over the air conditioning in his office. He'd turn the temperature cooler, and as soon as he closed the door to his office, his secretary would get up, run to the thermostat, and kick it back up again. It went on for years."

"Well, it's ridiculous."

It sounded like Joanne was only half joking, so I got up and went down the hall to where the thermostat hung on the wall. There was a small note taped next to it that said *Do not adjust*. I snorted and shook my head as I flipped open the plastic cover. None of the staff would go against Perry's orders, but I was his sister. What was he gonna do, fire me? I clicked the buttons to a temperature that was warmer than Santa's Workshop, closed the plastic lid, and headed back to my desk.

"Those jeans are *so* cute." Zoe's voice startled me. She stood at the window, one forearm on the small slice of counter there, and craned her neck so she could see me. "They look like they were made for you."

Why can't we control our own blushing? Why isn't that a thing? I felt mine crawl right up my neck and cover my cheeks, my face, like I was being submerged in very warm water. I swallowed and made myself smile. "Thank you. They're new. My niece and I went shopping and she helped me pick them out." *God, Morgan, why don't you tell her your entire life story now.*

"Well, they look fantastic on you." She held up the doughnut box in her hand. "I have some samples for you, and I brought snacks."

"God bless you," Joanne said and jumped up so fast to let Zoe in through the door that we both laughed.

"Somebody's hungry," I commented.

"Chewing will help warm me up," Joanna said as Zoe opened the box.

"It *is* kind of chilly in here," Zoe said, furrowing her brow. Summer had blasted in with a heat wave that I wasn't ready for, but Zoe seemed to be. She wore a lightweight dress today, a yellow and red pattern that was a bit brighter than her usual work attire. Her hair was pulled back into a ponytail, and I noticed her skin had darkened a bit from the sun. It also was covered in tiny goose bumps.

Joanne snorted, then shoved a powdered doughnut into her mouth, presumably to keep from saying anything else.

"It's a seasonal battle we have with Perry," I told Zoe with a grin, as I grabbed a Boston cream from the box and took a delicious bite.

"I know exactly what you mean. In my last office, I fought with the guys. Why do they always want it to feel like we work in a morgue?"

"No idea, but Joanne and I were just discussing how we wear more layers here in the summer than in the winter." I set my doughnut down and said to it, "Don't go anywhere, favorite doughnut of mine. I'll be back, I promise." I grabbed my keys and led Zoe to the sample closet.

"Those really are great jeans," she said as she followed me down the hall, reiterating not only her point, but also my blushing, because the only conclusion to come to from her words was that she was looking at my ass. "You always look so put together."

"Me?" I asked, then laughed. Probably too loudly. But seriously, had she seen a mirror? Like, ever? "Well, thanks. I couldn't pull off what you do, though. Your wardrobe is amazing." I wasn't lying.

"Thank you," she said, and I wasn't quite sure, but there might have been a slight tint of pink on those high cheekbones. She opened her bag and began to stock the sample closet as I watched.

I could've left her alone. Just like last time, there really was no need for me to hover. But I liked standing near Zoe. She smelled good. "I heard you're going to play golf in the tournament this weekend."

"I am. It was really nice of your brother to ask."

"He's a good guy." I don't know why I said that. Why I let it slip out. I didn't want her to think I had anything to do with their pairing.

"He is." A slight grin crossed her face as she said, "And quite the poet. He's a funny guy. A good guy and a funny guy. That's a pretty great combination."

Something warm settled in my core. Pleasant. I smiled back at her, knowing that it was my words that she found amusing, even though we were talking about my brother. "I hope you don't mind that I suggested you for the tournament."

"I was a little surprised he didn't ask you." She glanced at me, then went back to stocking and counting.

"Oh God, no. He knows I'm terrible." She made a face at me, and I scrambled to add, "Plus, I work with him every day. I gotta spend Saturdays with him, too?" That made her laugh, and I soaked it in, the surprisingly gentle musicality of it. Then I shrugged and said as nonchalantly as I could, "He likes you."

"Well, I like him, too." It was interesting—I noticed there was no dreamy quality to her words or her tone. Nothing that said, *I so want to get to know more about this guy!* It was more like she was talking about a friend. Or hell, a brother. She didn't ask me for details about him, didn't want to know his likes and dislikes or if he talked about her. Which was a little bit surprising. I mean, I didn't mind not having to educate her on all things Perry, but I was a great source, and she knew it. Still, she didn't probe. Instead, she finished up, closed the closet door, and took out her tablet for a signature. "You know," she said, and this time, there was a bit of wistfulness in her voice, "I would never have expected him to be a words guy." She shot a quick glance at me. "I don't mean that to be offensive at all. I just…the poems are so cute and sweet, and they got me thinking of my mom and how much she loved words. Has he ever written any that are a little deeper? More serious, maybe? He could be good."

I blinked at her twice before I could find words. "I actually think he has, but I'm not sure. I'll hint around about it." I shot her a wink and hoped it didn't look like I'd had some kind of twitch in my face.

"I was reading E. E. Cummings again last night. Remember the book I bought from Sylvia?"

I nodded because of course I remembered it. I'd reread a bunch of his poems after that.

"'I Carry Your Heart With Me' is just so beautiful."

I was familiar with that one, of course. She'd mentioned it before, and I completely agreed with her. "I mean, right? There's this combination of"—I squinted, trying to find the best description—"love and *longing* in the words. Such longing. You can feel them in your soul." Things I strove for in my own writing. I noticed Zoe looking at me with this gaze that could only be described as heavy. Okay, so maybe I'd gone a little overboard with the whole stirring my soul thing.

"Yes," she said finally, softly, and nodded. "That's exactly it."

That gaze held. I'm not sure which one of us was the holder, but it held for several seconds before I somehow managed to yank myself back to reality. Because it felt too good. Too…dangerous.

"Let's get you a signature," I said and inwardly cringed at my own overcheerfulness. God, I was so the opposite of smooth. I turned and led her down the hall, back to my desk.

Perry came out just as the phone rang. Joanne was already on a call, so I answered, which was probably a good thing. Something else to focus on. As I listened to the patient on the line, I tried to eavesdrop on Perry and Zoe, while also trying not to. Believe me when I tell you, this was no easy feat. I watched Perry sign the tablet and smile the smile he reserved for women he was interested in. I'd been told it was his sexy smile, but he's my brother and I can't—and don't want to—think of him that way. So, he smiled, and Zoe smiled back as she collected her things. Perry said he'd see her on Saturday, and damn if he didn't look like an excited teenager. I wondered if Zoe noticed, but if she did, she hid it well. She was way more chill than he was. She told him she was looking forward to it and waved at him as he headed back toward the exam rooms, but she didn't leave.

My call took another seven minutes at least, but Zoe waited near my counter, scrolled on her phone, and never said a word until I finally hung up.

"Did I forget something?" I asked her. Much as I loved that she was still there, I wasn't sure why.

"No." She shook her head and smiled. "I just didn't want to leave without saying good-bye."

Well.

A repeat of the warmth settling in my core happened. I'm pretty sure the grin that spread across my face was a stupid one. I didn't care. "I'm glad you didn't."

Zoe shouldered her bag and slid the box of doughnuts my way. "Have another one. Doughnuts bring joy. See you again soon." This time, she waved and headed out.

"Bye." I waved back and kept watching her until she closed the door behind her. Then I watched through the front window of the waiting room until she walked by.

"She's so nice," Joanne said, and I flinched a tiny bit in my chair because I'd forgotten I wasn't alone and felt like I'd been caught staring. Though I hadn't been. Caught, I mean. I was definitely staring.

I nodded, not trusting myself not to sound like a lovesick schoolgirl. My crush was growing, and as I heard Perry chatting with a patient, I scolded myself as one thought echoed through my head.

She's not yours, she's his.

❖

I love thunderstorms.

I know lots of people don't. They can be unnerving and scary and so, so loud. But there's something about being inside, in my house, safe with my cats and my books and just watching, that I love. I think that joy was also rooted deep in me because of my mom. She loved to watch the rain, and when I was a girl, I'd sit on our open front porch with her and just watch and listen as the raindrops fell from the sky. Watching the sky change colors, the leaves rustle in the wind, people in the neighborhood scatter to get inside, water rushing down the street toward the sewer grate. There was something peaceful about it.

Now that I have my own place, I still feel that way. I still long for that peace. My house has a small, screened-in porch on the front and a rocking chair where I can sit and watch my neighborhood as it lives and breathes. And I can watch the rain as it moves through. Ross is a big baby and stays in the living room when it thunders, and that Thursday night was no different. He watched through the window to the porch as Rachel sat in my lap, and we rocked slowly, listening to the rumbling as the storm got closer.

Golf had been canceled, and we'd played enough weeks now that I was actually disappointed. I'd been looking forward to seeing my friends, having a few drinks, grabbing some munchies, the golf itself really just a vehicle to get me to the clubhouse. Plus, it had been a beast of a week, and I wanted to blow off some steam.

Instead I sat on my porch with my cat, a glass of wine, and my notebook and watched it rain. I bet you're pretty jealous of my life right about now.

I had told Perry about Zoe's comments with regard to his poetry, so it came as no surprise when he practically begged me to write more. He liked the idea of making her laugh, so he told me to get all rhymey again. I did not tell him about how she'd asked if he ever wrote deeper poetry, and I wasn't sure why. Or maybe I was and just didn't want to actually admit it to myself. I wasn't certain. I'd whipped off a silly four-liner about golf the day before, since they'd be golfing together on Saturday, and sent that to him. But then, as I sat there watching the rain, feeling the cool summer breeze as it softly passed through the porch, I started to jot down lines as they came to me.

The rain
I think it knows things
As I sit and watch it fall, can it tell?
It whispers against the leaves
Gently taps the pavement
Rolls along the rooftops
Can it sense my secret?
That you're on my mind
That you are *my mind, my only thought*
When it visits your house, will it tell?
Will it whisper that to you?
Will you know?

I wondered what Zoe was doing. She'd said she was walking distance to Happily Ever After, as was I, so it occurred to me right then, that if she was home, she probably wasn't all that far away. And that was kind of cool. And then it was weird, because here I was again. Thinking about a woman my brother hoped to make his girlfriend. Again. I groaned, startling Rachel in my lap. I laid a hand on her back to calm her and apologized. Then I set my notebook and pen aside and replaced them with my wine.

I took a sip. "Much better," I said quietly. I glanced down at my black Under Armour shorts and the red T-shirt that I'd had since I was a senior in high school and shook my head. "It's not like somebody as sophisticated and put together as her would ever even look twice at Gym Shorts Girl, right?" I asked Rachel. "Which doesn't even matter anyway because my brother called her first." Then I snorted because Zoe wasn't the front seat of the car. She wasn't the biggest piece of cake. She was a woman. An amazing, super sexy, beautiful woman. "Oh, Rach, I need to stop this." To my cat's credit, she did seem like she was listening intently to me, but she offered no comment. Then I shook the whole train of thought right out of my head. "Okay. Enough. That's enough. We're good, right, sweet pea?" I leaned down and dropped a kiss on my cat's head, then sat back, sipped my wine, and watched the rain.

Yeah. I was fine.

Before I went to bed that night, I texted the poem to Perry and told him to keep it in his back pocket for a little ways down the road, when he felt it was right to try to take things a little deeper with Zoe.

Your the best, Morgs! TY!

I cringed a bit at the misspelling but didn't correct him and tease him about it like I usually would. I just set the phone aside, crawled into bed, and reached for the remote. For the next hour, I channel surfed, my cats bookending me as I did my best to just quiet my mind.

Yep. I was totally fine.

CHAPTER ELEVEN

"One more week to go," Diane said on Friday morning. "And then a long weekend."

I felt my brows rise up in surprise, and I glanced at my calendar. She was right. The following weekend was July Fourth, and we'd have a three-day weekend. "And it's Friday. Half day."

She gave a little fist pump and headed back to her office where she'd go over the day's schedule and get ready for her first patient, who I knew would walk in any minute. Janie Crowe was up first, and she was never less than fifteen minutes early for her appointment. Always. I envied her punctuality.

I'd seen Perry walking around near the exam rooms but hadn't talked to him since my arrival at work. Next time he passed by, I waved and said good morning. He surprised me by coming toward my desk. Joanne wasn't in yet, so it was just him and me. He stared at me, took a big breath, blew it out hard enough for his shoulders to drop dramatically.

"Tourney's tomorrow," I said, assuming that was why he seemed so jittery. "Nervous?"

"Very." He swallowed, studied me, then said, "I sent the poem last night."

I grinned. "The golf limerick thing?"

"Well, yeah. But then last night, I texted her to tell her again that I was really excited for Saturday, and then I sent the other one."

I gaped at him. "The one about the rain? No..."

A quick head shake and a half shrug combined with a somewhat blank expression. "I guess? Was it about rain?"

"God, Perry, did you even read it?"

He grimaced and looked down at the tablet he held, hit a few buttons, and scrolled as he read. "Not really."

"Oh, man." I pressed my lips together into a thin line.

"What?"

"It was kind of..." How to describe the words I'd written, the way I'd felt when I did. "Intimate."

Sandy brows flew up. "It was? Now I need to read it." He laughed.

"That's why I told you to wait."

He lifted one shoulder and seemed completely unfazed. Because men knew zero about women. "I mean, she'll like it or she won't, right?" He headed toward the exam rooms.

Or she'll fall in love with you, or she'll think you've gotten way too intense way too fast. My money was on the latter. God, I hoped I hadn't sabotaged my brother's chances with Zoe. No, it wasn't my fault that he'd sent the poem sooner than he should have, but still.

Janie Crowe walked in the front door at eight forty, as predicted, and my Friday began.

And for the rest of my workday, all I could think about was Zoe reading my words, and I wondered how they made her feel.

There's something about the peace and quiet of the early morning that I love. Not early, early. I'm not up at five a.m. But I'm almost always up by seven. Even on weekends. I'll come downstairs, feed the cats, make my coffee, and just sit at my little table, watching out the window. A cardinal came and sat on the railing of my small deck, his red feathers a bright spot in the brown and green of my backyard. My mother once told me that cardinals represent spirits visiting us, and I absently wondered who might have stopped by to say hi to me.

At least Perry had let me get in one sip of coffee before he rang my bell.

"It's open," I called out.

"Hey there." He walked into my kitchen and I gave him the once-over. He wore nicely pressed khakis and a white Ralph Lauren polo shirt. On his head was a navy-blue visor with the Northwood Medical logo on it. This was a charity event after all, and the participants almost always wore some kind of attire with their logo, so people would know which companies and organizations had donated.

"You scream, *I'm a doctor playing in a golf tournament.*" He really did.

"And I am okay with that." He looked down at himself, then back up at me, and wrinkled his nose. "Seriously, though. Do I look okay?" And there were those nerves again. Such an uncommon occurrence in my big brother, though I suspected that's why I could see them so clearly.

"You look great." It was the truth. "And you smell amazing." Also true. Kind of woodsy with a little musk mixed in. "Aftershave? Cologne? What is that?"

"It's a men's body spray I read about." His eyes darted away, and I smiled internally at the adorableness of my brother's embarrassment.

"Well, it's awesome." I gestured to the corner by the door to my garage. "Wedge is right there." He'd broken his sand wedge last time he played and forgot to buy himself another one, so he'd asked to borrow mine.

"Great. Thanks. You've saved my bunker game." Then he pulled out a chair and sat. "I don't have a ton of time, but give me some pointers."

"On golf? I wondered when you'd realize my prowess and ask for my help."

A snort. Then he took my mug and a big sip of my coffee.

"There's more in the pot. You can actually have your own."

"No time. Gotta get to the course. So? Tips?"

"For?" I knew what he wanted, but it was fun to make him spell it out.

"For talking to Zoe, dumbass."

"Oooh," I said with a grin. "That."

He made a go-on gesture with his hands and stood. "Bullet points. Hit me."

"Okay. Number one, don't talk about you all the time. Ask her questions about herself. Number two, don't get pushy. She's there to network, so keep that in mind. This isn't a date, so don't treat it like one."

"It's not?"

I faltered. "I mean, is it? There will be lots of work peeps there. Don't get possessive."

"Good point."

"Three, you can compliment her. Go easy, 'cause of what I just said, but compliments are always good."

"Compliment her?" He blinked at me. I blinked back. How was it possible that my brother could look confused at this directive?

"Yes. Tell her she looks nice. You like her shirt. Compliment that hair—for God's sake, have you even seen it? Don't you wanna dig your fingers into it? How about those cheekbones? When she smiles and they sharpen right up? Man. Her eyes are the coolest shade of blue I've ever seen, you know? She's got a great voice. I love when you expect her to talk quickly, and she doesn't, just keeps that steady, calm tone…" Perry was looking at me with an odd expression on his face, and I gave my head a mental shake. "And her golf game. Definitely compliment that, because you're gonna be shocked when you see how good she is. Trust me."

Perry nodded, his eyes still on my face, and he studied me for a moment. It took every ounce of strength I had not to squirm in my seat. I *think* I stayed still. I *think* I did.

And then, just like that, he broke eye contact, and I felt released. Palms on my table, he pushed himself to his feet. "All right. Gotta go. Thanks for the info." He shot another look in my direction, narrowed his eyes a bit, and then he grabbed the sand wedge and touched it to his visor. "Wish me luck."

I held up my mug. "Don't whiff."

He snorted. "Please." He headed out.

I stayed at my table, sipping my coffee, my house silent. Silence was underrated. I realized that it made me seem older than my thirty-three years to say such a thing, but I loved the quiet. Make no mistake, I loved television and music very much. But there was something about silence. I could hear the birds outside, the cardinal scolding some other bird or squirrel. I could hear Ross's little squeaky snores coming from the cat tree by the window. The world is such a noisy place, in constant motion with a never-ending soundtrack of voices and ringing phones and text notifications and Alexa offering unsolicited advice, and sometimes, I found it shockingly peaceful to simply sit in silence. Every time I did it, I wondered why I didn't do it more often. I suppose it would be classified as meditation, but I just called it peaceful.

Except for right then.

Because the silence in my head was suddenly filled with me blathering on and on about Zoe to Perry.

"Oh, her hair, her eyes, those *cheekbones*," I said aloud in a whiny, unflattering impression of myself. It was one thing to crush on your brother's love interest. It was quite another to let him know about it.

I could only stand my own ridiculousness for another few seconds before I said, "Alexa, play Taylor Swift."

Sometimes, silence needs to be silenced.

Salon Stefan was crazed on Saturdays. Always. I didn't usually make my hair appointments on the weekends for just that reason. I usually tried to go during the week on my lunch break, but Stefan had an opening that Saturday and asked me if I could come then.

It's not like I had a golf tournament to play in or anything.

Salon Stefan is right in downtown Northwood in the midst of the most eclectic part of the city in the very middle of Jefferson Square. It was a fantastic location, in the center of everything, the hustle and bustle in the summer did nothing but help business, and Stefan's clientele ran the gamut of genders and sexualities, one giant mix of everybody. Initially, he'd started out renting a chair at a small salon. That had lasted several years until he built up his own clientele. Then he opened Salon Stefan, just him and one employee. Now, five years later, he had nine hairstylists and five staff members working for him. He was well-known and sought after now, my high school bestie, and I was incredibly proud of him.

The salon was in what used to be a huge house. Possibly Victorian, but I'm not well-versed enough in architecture to know for sure. But you walked in the front door to a grand foyer. To the left was the front counter and waiting area, and back when it was a regular house, it would've been the living room. Or sitting room. Or parlor. Or whatever it was called back then. It was painted a very pale pink and came complete with a pristine, white-bricked fireplace and oak hardwoods. Stefan had done a lot of work on the place but tried to keep as much original charm as he could.

I checked in with Dominic at the front desk, a man so good-looking I often found myself wondering if he was an android of some kind. Because really, could any human have skin that flawless? I was pretty sure Stefan had had a fling with him before he met Justin, and I couldn't blame him. Hell, I'd have a fling with him, and I was unequivocally into girls. He called me gorgeous and told me to have a seat.

I sat in a lovely wingback chair and gazed out the window as I waited. It was a beautiful summer day. Sunny and warm. Light breeze. Perfect for golf. I absently wondered how Perry and Zoe were doing.

Perry and Zoe.

Zoe and Perry.

I said it in my head several times. Let it roll around. Got a feel for it. I mean, they could end up—

"Morgan?" Dominic's voice hauled me out of my own head. "He's ready for you, love." He pointed with his pen because he knew he didn't have to show me where to go.

"There's my favorite lesbian," Stefan said loudly as I turned the corner into the main work section of the house. I just shook my head because he said the same thing every time I came.

"It's a good thing I'm out," I said, which was also the same thing *I* said every time I came.

"I just want to make sure any available lesbians who happen to be here know there's another one right here." He led me to the sinks. He had shampoo boys for such things, but Stefan always took care of me himself. "Pretty soon, I'm going to start announcing you as my favorite *single* lesbian."

I sat back and set my neck in the U-shape of the sink. "Don't you dare," I warned him.

He grinned down at me, and as he was wetting my hair, he tipped his head from one side to the other. Clearly thinking.

"What?" I asked.

"Do you trust me?"

"Nothing good ever comes from a conversation that starts with that."

"Except for today."

I sighed and closed my eyes as he massaged my head. "Yes, I trust you."

"Good. We're gonna give you some highlights today."

"We are?"

"Yep. And we're gonna alter the style a bit."

"We *are*?"

"Yep."

I'd had lots of debates and disagreements with Stefan over the years of our friendship, but one thing he never, ever steered me wrong on was my hair. I'd refused his suggestions of cuts in the past, but each time I'd agreed to let him loose, I'd been very happy with the results. Not only was Stefan an excellent stylist when he knew what you wanted, but he was excellent at deciding what would look best on you, even if it was radically different from what you had.

"I draw the line at a Mohawk."

"Oh, honey, Mohawks are so nineties." He wrapped my head in a towel, and I sat up and walked to his station.

A few minutes later, he was painting my hair, wrapping it in little foil sheets. "You got plans for next weekend?"

It always amused me that we spoke to each other's reflections while he worked. We rarely actually looked directly at each other. It was all mirror talk. "What's next weekend?"

Stefan stopped what he was doing and sort of sagged to the side with a very put-upon sigh. "July Fourth, duh."

"Oh!" That was the second time this week I'd needed a reminder of the upcoming holiday. "Right. Right. No, I don't really. I'll go see the fireworks like always."

"There's a July Fourth drag show at Mix on Saturday night. You should come." Several local drag queens were Stefan's clients, and he always helped with their hair and makeup for a show. I think he had a secret drag queen inside him just itching to come out, but he always told me his downfall was that he couldn't manage to walk in heels without stumbling and that they made his feet hurt. I told him welcome to being a woman.

While I loved the drag shows, I didn't love going by myself. But supporting them was important to me, so I mentally shuffled through my small catalog of friends. "I'll see if Bridget or maybe Adriana is around. Or maybe Brittany wants to come." I took my niece to her first drag show when she was eighteen, and she'd loved every second of it. I was pretty sure she'd go with me.

One of the things I liked most about going to Stefan's place of work was simply watching him with his clients. Once my highlights were on, and I found a different chair to let them set, he moved on to his next client, an older woman, maybe in her sixties. I was always amused to watch Stefan dial his gay up or down, depending on who he was dealing with. And to be clear, his lowest gay setting was still pretty fabulous. He made the woman laugh, and I grinned and just sat there and watched my BFF in his element.

About ninety minutes later, Stefan finished drying my hair, and we both looked at my reflection. I stared. Blinked. Stared some more. Who was this girl?

"Oh my God, Stef, I love it." It was the absolute truth. The color hadn't changed much. He'd simply brought out some of the blond. My hair tends to lean more toward ash blond or, as my grandma used to call it, dishwater blond. Seriously? Why? There was now definite gold, more than one shade of it. He'd trimmed and layered and styled, and even I was impressed. It was casual, breezy, and a little wavy, and it skimmed my shoulders—shorter than it had been, but still long enough to pull back if I wanted.

"I have been wanting to do that to your hair for months now."

"Listen, I'm not good with change."

"No kidding." He rolled his eyes at my reflection.

"Well, I love it." I said it a second time just to make sure he knew.

"Good." His face softened, though, and he took the cape off me. "See you next weekend?"

I nodded because you know what? It was time I started getting out more. My new haircut and my new jeans gave me an unfamiliar boost of confidence, and it felt like they were pushing me toward something.

I just had no idea what it might be.

CHAPTER TWELVE

Monday was gray and gloomy, like all Mondays should probably be. Dark clouds moved quickly, spurred on by the air that walked the fine line between breeze and wind. Rain made cameo appearances all day. It stayed fairly warm, but it was damp and a little depressing, not peaceful like the storms I enjoyed so much.

The office wasn't crazy busy, but steady, and I kept myself occupied with emails and phone calls and labs and referrals. Perry was quiet, almost studious. Every time I saw him, he was looking down at his tablet, and I imagined him analyzing charts, searching for solutions to whatever was ailing his patients. He seemed to be in the same work mode I was in. Head down, checking things on his list.

It wasn't until the end of the day that I finally got to have a conversation with him. I locked up the front. Everybody had gone home, and he and I were the only ones left. I found him in his office in the corner of the building, sitting behind his enormous mahogany desk.

"Hey," I said.

He glanced up from the monitor he was looking at. "Hey."

"I haven't talked to you since the tournament." I took a seat in the chair off to the side. Collapsed into it is more accurate. "How'd it go?"

"We won." He said it very matter-of-factly, no inflection, and kept his gaze on the monitor.

"What?" I sat up. "That's amazing. Why didn't you tell me? I didn't see an Instagram post or anything."

A shrug.

I narrowed my eyes. "What?"

Perry shook his head. "Nothing."

I tipped my head to the side. I hated this game. This was a girls' game, and I'm not saying that to be a sexist jerk. It was true. *I* was the one who was supposed to make my loved ones pry out of me what was wrong. Not my brother. I sighed. "Come on, Perry. I'm tired. You're tired. Something's bothering you. Just tell me what it is."

He took a deep breath. I saw it more than heard it. He opened his mouth, then closed it again, and his shoulders sagged.

"Is it Zoe?" I asked gently. Because what else could it be? "Did something happen?"

I could see the exact moment he decided to give up and tell me. His shoulders dropped a bit more, his face slackened, and he just seemed...resigned.

"Well, we had a great time playing. And you weren't kidding— she's a fantastic golfer. Holy shit. She surprised everybody. We talked. I did everything you told me to. I didn't talk about myself a lot. I complimented her, asked her questions." He inhaled and let it out slowly, as if the story was taking a lot out of him. "I think she met quite a few people she can call on for work. It was good all around."

There was more, and I knew it. I hated seeing what could only be referred to as disappointment on his face. Zoe must've let him down easy. Or not so easy? I waited until he picked up a pen and toyed with it as he continued.

"After the tournament, we went into the clubhouse and celebrated our win. Cocktails and food and conversation. It was great. I looked at her at one point and said that we made a great team. And her reply was that we made a great *golf* team."

Oh, ouch. Okay, I saw where things were going. She had let him down easy.

"And I said, We make a great *team*. And she said again, We make a great *golf* team. I was getting a little frustrated because I didn't think she understood what I was trying to say, so I tried one more time. We make a great *team*, you and I. And she said, But I play on a *different* team. And then she just looked at me and waited for me to finally get it." He sighed. "I'm embarrassed to say that it took me longer than it should have."

Oh, I thought. Furrowed my brow. And then it hit me, and *I* finally got it. "Oooh." Holy crap.

"Yeah, I think the woman of my dreams actually plays on *your* team." He fell heavily back into his chair. "I mean, what are the fucking chances, huh? I finally find somebody who really gets to me, and she's fucking gay." He glanced quickly at me. "No offense."

I held up my hands in surrender. "None taken." I couldn't even absorb the words he was saying, I was so shocked. Zoe was gay? Zoe? Was gay? How had I not picked up on that, like, instantly? I needed to have my gaydar checked, clearly.

"So. Yeah." He shook his head and tossed his pen to the desk. "What the fuck ever."

I opened my mouth to say…What? Something. Anything to make him feel better. There are plenty of fish in the sea? This just means it wasn't meant to be? Before I could come up with something, he held up his hand, traffic cop style, like he'd read my mind.

"Just, spare me the platitudes, okay? I know you mean well, but just let me wallow. I'll be fine."

Much as I wanted to help him somehow, I understood a good wallowing. "Okay." I stood. "For what it's worth, though, I'm really sorry." I waited until he met my gaze.

"Thanks, Morgan."

I let a beat or two pass before I made an attempt at a subject change. "Going to Mom and Dad's for dinner?"

"Yeah. I'll have to let Mom down easy." He sighed and looked so completely dejected, my heart ached.

I wanted to add something about what a catch he was or how lucky some girl was going to be, but he'd just told me he didn't want to hear any of that. I didn't think he wanted to talk much more at all, so I gave him one nod and left him alone.

Back at my desk, I dropped into my chair and just sat there. Absorbing. Replaying the conversation. Absorbing some more. *But I play on a* different *team.* Zoe had actually said those words. I couldn't believe it. And in the next breath, I was again annoyed with myself for not assuming that it was a possibility, my own biases making an embarrassing appearance.

And what difference did it make anyway? It's not like I was going to ask her out or something. I wouldn't do that to Perry. And Zoe likely had no idea I was gay. *Unless her gaydar is way better than mine, which clearly wouldn't take much.* I assumed Perry would've said something to me if he'd told her. And I didn't think she'd look twice at me anyway, so what was I all twisted up about? Nothing had changed in my world. Nothing at all except my brother was feeling flattened by a woman. Again.

I wished I could help him. But there was nothing I could do.

Mix wasn't really big enough to host a huge drag show, but they did it anyway, on a regular basis, and maybe that's what made it so awesome. The stage was crammed into one end of the dance floor, and a curtain was hung to create a makeshift backstage, even though backstage consisted of about four square feet plus the manager's office, which was directly behind the stage. I had no idea how they made it work, as several of them were six feet or taller, *and* Stefan was back there to help with hair and makeup, but they did. And it was glorious.

What is it about a drag show that's so exciting? I mean, it's essentially just people lip-synching. But add in the glitz and the sparkle and the sky-high heels and comic stylings and dance moves, and it was a damn extravaganza. I loved drag shows, and that night, I was grateful Stefan had reminded me.

It was the Saturday of the long July Fourth weekend, and the place was packed, people crammed in like sardines to watch Bella Vista, Butch Dunn, Helena Handbasket, Justin Time, and more give everything they had and leave it all on the stage floor when they finished.

We'd gotten there early enough that we somehow managed to secure a spot at the end of the bar. Just one spot, which meant Brittany, Adriana, and I had to take turns leaning or sitting on the one stool we'd commandeered, but that was okay with us. We were there and we were ready.

"Ladies." The bartender was a solidly built woman with a buzz cut, two sleeves of tattoos, and ice-blue eyes. When she smiled, her dimples went deep. I knew her name was Dutch, as I'd been there many times before. I also knew Dutch made a kick-ass dirty martini, and my mouth watered in anticipation as she slid mine—extra, extra dirty with three olives—across the bar to me. Brittany had a cosmo, and Adriana, a 7 and 7. Dutch winked and was off to take care of her next customer.

"She's handsome," Brittany commented. "I don't think I've ever described another woman that way, but she really, really is."

"Agreed." I raised my glass, and my niece and my dear friend touched theirs to mine.

"I haven't been here in ages," Adriana said as she looked around Mix. "It hasn't changed much." Adriana and I went all the way back to elementary school when she and her family lived next door. From five years old to ten years old, we were the best of friends. We played together, went to summer day camp together, discussed the variations of yucky that boys covered. Which we laugh about now because our little ten-year-old selves had no idea we were both gay. Life is weird, isn't it? Just before Adriana's eleventh birthday, her father got transferred, and they moved to New Hampshire. My youthful heart was broken, and I missed Adriana terribly. But as it happens, we both made new friends and went on with our lives, until seven years ago when Adriana got a job at a large payroll firm right here in Northwood and moved back. When we met again for the first time in more than twenty years, it was like we'd never been apart. Some friends were like that. We had our own lives now, but if one of us needed something, the other would drop whatever she was doing and show up to help. I was grateful to have her in my corner.

I have never been a fan of the bar scene. I didn't like the noise, being crammed close to strangers, the weird and sometimes inexplicable smells. I realize this all makes me sound inches away from shouting for all the kids to get off my damn lawn, but what can I say? I'm just me, and it doesn't thrill me to have strangers in my space.

But the drag shows? I made an exception for those because it was totally worth it to be crammed in like people at the Apple Store waiting for the next iPhone in order to see some of my favorite acts. There was something about the energy and the excitement of the crowd, and as the lights in the bar dimmed and the spotlights went up, that energy only grew, shouts and applause increasing in volume and intensity. Brittany, Adriana, and I all turned to watch the show.

Five acts and about forty-five minutes later, the lights came back up, and the drag queens and kings took a short break. They'd be back quickly, and there was a sudden surge at the bar of people wanting refills. Luckily, I'd caught Dutch's eye the second she could see me, and she slid three refills our way.

"This is amazing," Adriana said, raising her voice to be heard over the crowd, then took a sip of her drink. "I haven't been to one of these in forever. I forgot how much I like them."

"That's because you and Shayna are bigger homebodies than I am." Shayna was Adriana's wife of five years. They'd been together since college and were an incredible pair. I loved them dearly and, I was ashamed to admit, often had trouble being around them because the envy I had of their life could be palpable for me. I know that's terrible—Adriana had never been anything but a terrific friend—but it was the truth. I badly wanted what she had, and I just didn't like to admit that to myself. I was fine on my own. Somebody would come along eventually. I didn't need a partner to be happy. All those head-patting clichés ran through my mind.

Brittany had discovered a college friend and sidled over to talk to him while the couple next to Adriana chatted her up, so I sipped my martini and scanned the crowd. It was one of my favorite things to do anyway, people watch.

Straight ahead were a couple of gay men. I watched them, their body language. They knew each other well, but there was space between them, and I concluded they were together but mad at each other for some reason. To their left was a group of four women, middle-aged-ish, most likely straight. Girls' night out, maybe? Next to them was another foursome, two straight couples. The drag shows always pulled them in, because they weren't about sexuality—well, they were in a strictly entertainment capacity—they were about the performances. The glitz and the glamour and the music. So when there was a drag show at Mix, the bar truly lived up to its name.

I took the pick out of my drink and pulled an olive off with my teeth as I continued to scan the bar area. As I chewed, I noticed Mia from my golf league at the other end. She was leaning one forearm on the bar and talking to a woman whose back was to me. All I could see was dark hair, and I waited to catch Mia's eye so I could give her a wave. It only took a few seconds before she turned to signal the bartender and saw me. Her face lit up with a smile, and she waved. I was in the midst of waving back when the person she was talking to turned around and my wave froze. I kept my unmoving hand up in the air like a student waiting to be called on as my eyes locked with Zoe's across the bar.

It was a jolt, to say the least.

I felt it deep inside me. Like my entire being was startled awake. Like I had touched a live wire and gotten zapped. Zoe had that kind of effect on me, I was realizing. She smiled, those cheekbones waving hello to me even from a distance, but there was also something in her expression. Something uncertain. She widened her eyes and used them to indicate Mia, and I understood instantly.

Have you ever had the golden opportunity to be somebody's proverbial knight in shining armor? Because if you ever have, you know what I mean when I say I jumped into action. I grabbed Adriana and told her to guard our spot at the bar and my martini, that I'd be right back, ignoring her surprised confusion. And then I plunged into the crowd like I was diving into a raging ocean, fighting crashing waves and a brutal undertow, using the bar as my coast to keep from getting pulled out to sea. I swear to God it felt like that's exactly what I was doing as I sidled between bodies, ducked under arms, gently nudged people so I could get through. The whole time, I was sifting through ideas in my head, things I could say to draw Zoe away from Mia without being a jerk about it. Mia wasn't a bad person. She just didn't understand subtlety. Or read signals very well. I remembered when Zoe had told me that Mia wasn't her type. I had assumed she meant because Mia was a woman, but I realized then that it was more specific than that.

I wondered what her type was. Because I knew it wasn't men, and I knew it wasn't Mia.

"Hey, you guys," I said once I reached the other side of the bar. I plastered on a big smile and hoped I didn't look deranged. "Great show, huh?"

"Seriously good," Mia said. "I know Butch Dunn and he's always amazing."

"He is," I said, nodding, being a pal to Mia before I slid in and stole away her target. "And Bella Vista was stunning. That sparkly green dress? Wow."

"I came with some friends, but then I saw this one"—Mia indicated Zoe by rubbing a hand up and down her upper arm—"at the bar alone and thought, I can't let a beautiful woman drink all by herself." Mia was obviously proud of her chivalry. Also obvious were her intentions, if the ogling glances from her group of friends a few feet away were any indication. Zoe was obviously trying to be kind while looking for the nearest escape route. I could tell by the fact that her blue eyes were slightly wider than usual—not quite a cornered animal, but not far off.

"Well, listen," I said, easing in, pretending my intention was not at all to rescue Zoe from Mia. "If you want to get back to your friends, my niece is here with me, and she's about to start a new sales job. I'd told her that she could pick Zoe's brain." I looked at Zoe, raised my eyebrows pointedly. "Remember?"

She picked up her role immediately, stood up straighter, and finished her drink. "Yes! Yes, of course. I've got so much to tell her, too." Laying a hand on Mia's forearm, Zoe leaned toward her. "Thank you so much for the drink and the company."

Mia blushed. I watched the red climb up her neck, cover her face, disappear into her close-cropped hair, and honestly, it was kind of adorable. "Anytime," she said.

"Shall we?" I held out my hand to Zoe—a very bold move on my part, thank you very much—and she took it without hesitation.

"Your hair looks amazing," she said. "Not that it didn't look great before, 'cause it did. But the highlights really bring out your skin tone and your eyes."

I knew I was blushing, could feel the heat, and for a second, I understood Mia's blushing perfectly. "Thank you," I said and hoped she felt the sincerity in my voice.

I led her back through the crashing waves and riptides of people, doing my very best not to notice or dwell on how warm and perfect her hand felt in mine. And also, doing my very best to not let go of it. Because, yeah.

"And who do we have here?" Adriana asked upon our arrival at our end of the bar.

I blew out a breath like I'd just run a race, and Zoe looked like she felt the same way. Reluctantly, I let go of her hand as I said, "Adriana, this is my friend Zoe. Zoe, Adriana."

They shook hands, and I watched Zoe's charm settle over Adriana like a warm blanket. "How do you two know each other?" Zoe asked.

Adriana looked to me, but I waved my hand, giving her permission to tell the story. Mostly because I needed a moment or two to get my shit together. As she began to speak, I tried to be very subtle about taking in Zoe, who looked as amazing as always, a fun combination of dressed up and casual. Dark skinny jeans and black sandals with a slight heel, a black tank top that clung to her figure, and a short, lightweight black jacket. A silver heart dangled just below her breasts on a black necklace, along with that familiar shorter necklace with the two red stones that still hung near her collarbone. Silver hoops were visible through her dark hair, which was down and to the side and wavy and full, and I wanted nothing more than to bury my nose in it and inhale what I suspected would be strawberries and vanilla.

"And the rest is history," Adriana said, and I blinked because… she was done already?

"That's an awesome story," Zoe said. "Not many people still have the same friends from their childhood."

"We definitely got lucky," I said, and it was true.

"Do you need a drink?" she asked. "'Cause I do." Then she leaned close to me, hand on my hip, her lips so near my ear I felt goose bumps tickle along my spine. "Thank you for rescuing me. I owe you."

I shook my head as I reclaimed the drink I'd left on the bar. "Well, your eye language game is very strong."

Zoe barked a laugh as she signaled to Dutch. "Were they screaming for help?" She ordered herself a rum and Coke.

"From way across the bar, yes."

Adriana had been following along. "Oh, did you have to save her from Mia?" I nodded, and she gave a little shrug. "I've had to be saved from Mia before, too. She's nice enough but comes on immediately and *strong*." She glanced at me. "Remember when I first got back, and we went out and ran into her?"

"Oh my God, I forgot about that. She set her sights on you and was like a heat-seeking missile."

Zoe got her drink and turned to us. "She really is. It started the second I set foot onto the golf course that first night. She was just... *there*. I mean, I didn't want to hurt her feelings, you know? She's very nice. But wow, she likes to lay claim."

"Claim that ain't hers," Adriana said with a snort, and I could tell by her slang that the alcohol was setting in. She was one of those people who just got funnier the more she drank. I was glad we'd both Ubered.

I looked across the room toward where Mia stood with her crew. She clearly still had eyes for Zoe because the whole group was sending glances our way.

"Sometimes," Adriana said, shooting me such an intense stare that I squinted at her, "the only way to combat the Mias of the world is to pretend you're with somebody else."

Zoe pointed at Adriana. "She makes a good point." And with that, she sidled up next to me. I mean, close. Like, super close. I'm talking her hip pressed in my stomach, very much in my personal space, and when I said earlier that I didn't like people in my personal space? Yeah, Zoe didn't count because I very much liked her there. *Very* much. I didn't move. Then she turned her head, and her lips were back to practically brushing my ear, and she whispered, "You don't mind, do you? Save me one more time?"

Jesus God in heaven.

"Happy to," I said before I could even think about it. Before I could go over things in my head and figure out what to say. But it didn't matter, right? Because I was simply doing her a favor. That was all.

The lights dimmed, and the spotlights came on, and Bella Vista took the stage in a new dress that was just as sparkly and gorgeous, but red this time, to introduce the next wave of performers. The three of us stood and watched, Brittany still across the bar with the friend she'd spotted. Zoe put her hands on my shoulders and moved me so I was in front of her taller form, but I could feel her behind me. Every inch of her that was within an inch of me, I could *feel*. I have never been so painfully aware of another woman's presence the way I was that night. Honestly? I never wanted to move. Ever again. I'd have been perfectly fine standing just like that, Zoe's warm body pressed against my back, for the rest of my damn life. A woman who had just breezed into my world, completely unexpected. A woman who was in a class by herself as far as I was concerned. A class way, way above mine, but still, she was here with me. A woman who—

The logical part of my brain interrupted the dreamy, unrealistic part.

The woman my brother had wanted. Had tried for. Had been crushed by.

That woman.

I pictured Perry's face on Monday, how defeated he'd seemed.

God, what was I doing?

I was pathetic.

CHAPTER THIRTEEN

So I guess I'll see you at the fireworks then."

Those were Zoe's parting words at the drag show the night before, and as I lay in my bed on Saturday morning, I heard them over and over again. The mix of emotions they caused was real, let me tell you, and I had no idea what to do with them, so I just tossed them on the pile with last night's. I could have myself a nice emotional bonfire with the heap I was making.

Brittany and Zoe had hit it off, even though they'd only spent a handful of minutes together by the time she made it back to us at the bar. Must've been a salesperson thing, but they chatted nonstop as we finished our drinks once the show was over. As we stood waiting for our Ubers, they exchanged numbers, and Brittany had asked Zoe what she was doing the next night, which would be the Fourth of July.

Zoe had shrugged. "No idea. I think I might wander around, see if I can find a good place to watch the fireworks."

I knew it was coming before Brittany even opened her mouth.

"Oh, you *have* to go to Ridgecrest Park! It's up on a hill, and it overlooks the city, and you get the most amazingly clear shot of the fireworks. And they have vendors set up with food and drinks. It's awesome and so much fun. We go every year, right, Aunt Morgs?"

I nodded. Smiled.

"Ridgecrest Park." Zoe took out her phone and typed something in. A note, I guessed. "Perfect. Thank you." And she'd turned those eyes on me, hit me with the cheekbones, and I felt my knees go all jellylike, damn traitors that they were. And her Uber had pulled up then and she'd said softly, "So I guess I'll see you at the fireworks then."

I think I nodded some more. I honestly don't remember saying actual words, just nodding like a bobblehead on a dashboard. Because I was clearly a fourteen-year-old boy with a crush.

And after Zoe's Uber had driven away and Brittany had leaned into me with a knowing smile and said, "A little crush going on there?" I kind of snapped at her.

"*No*. There's no crush, and even if there was, it doesn't matter. She is off-limits, okay? *Off-limits*." And I karate-chopped my hand sideways through the air to punctuate my point. And then I stood there blinking, because not only was I surprised at my own outburst, but I was surprised by what I'd said. And I was angry about it. No mention of Zoe being out of my league. Not a word about her being too good for me and wondering why on earth anybody would think she'd be interested in me. Because I was pretty sure she was. She'd stood with her entire body pressed up against mine for the better part of an hour. Seemed like a pretty big clue to me. Friends didn't do that. I couldn't imagine standing that close to Adriana, even if we were packed into a room like sardines. This was *all* of Zoe's front to *all* of my back and it was…sensual. Warm. Thrilling. And sexy as hell. The anger had surged in, and I'd tossed it onto the emotional bonfire pile. Brittany held up her hands and just looked at me, got that expression people her age get that basically says, *Fine, whatever*. She took a small step away and muttered, "Sorry," stressing each syllable.

Maybe I should've told her the truth about Perry and his interest in Zoe at that point, but I didn't feel it was my place, so Brittany really had no idea why I'd gotten so freaky, why Zoe was off-limits.

I could never do that to my brother.

I stared at my ceiling as the rays of the rising sun moved slowly across it, my legs bookended by Ross and Rachel.

I could just not go tonight.

The thought slid into my head, rolled around a little bit like a puppy in the warm summer grass. I'd gone every year I could think of. It was tradition. Not everybody in my family did, but sometimes. My parents would make the trek if they had nothing better to do. Perry and Christine used to go, so I imagined that Perry probably wouldn't go that night. Brittany always did, usually with her mom because my brother Carter was afraid of fireworks, though he'd never admit it. Adriana said the night before that she and her wife would probably show up.

And Zoe would be there.

It was a very good reason to go.

It was also a very good reason not to go.

Goddamn it.

I sat up in my bed and each cat lifted its head. Blinked. Yawned. It was barely six in the morning, and I didn't blame them, but I just couldn't sleep.

"I'm an adult," I said to them, looking from one to the other. "I am in full control of myself. My actions. Right?" Neither cat commented, but they both looked intently at me. "Which means I can certainly go to Ridgecrest Park, enjoy the fireworks, be sociable and friendly, and it'll be totally fine. I like Zoe. I can be friends with her, can't I?" As if in some unspoken agreement, the cats looked at each other, then rested their heads back down on the bed. "Right. Yes. Exactly." I lay back down, feeling so much better, so much lighter, like I'd had a gravity blanket on, and somebody came by and pulled it off me.

I would go to the fireworks.

I would socialize with Zoe.

I would be a normal person.

How hard could it be?

Is there anything better than a vendor hot dog? I mean, maybe the sausage with peppers and onions, but it's a close call. And nothing goes better with both of those things than an ice cold beer in a plastic cup. I stood in Ridgecrest Park at the top of the hill where most of the night's crowd had gathered, eating, drinking, anticipating the fireworks display that would start in about a half hour. It wasn't fully dark yet, and I loved the long summer days when the sun didn't set until close to nine, and it felt like you had all the time in the world. I squirted a bunch of mustard on my hot dog and took a bite.

"Good?" Brittany asked. "You're humming."

"So good."

Stefan once gave me boatloads of crap about eating hot dogs. "Do you know what they're made of?" I didn't know, and the horror on his face was enough to tell me that I did not *want* to know. He'd watched a documentary about the making of hot dogs and vowed never to eat one ever again. I made him promise never to tell me what he'd learned because I didn't want them ruined for me. He's kept that promise but gives me a look and a disgusted shake of his head anytime I eat one.

Brittany got the sausage, and once she had it in hand, we allowed each other a bite, and then we were both humming.

"I'm also going to need cotton candy and a funnel cake before this night is over," I told her, feeling a slight buzz as beer number two kicked in.

"Duh." Brittany craned her neck and looked around. "Are Grandma and Grandpa here?"

"I think so." The gorgeous weather definitely brought out the people, and it was more populated than it had been in a couple years. "Remember how muddy it was last year?" I asked Brittany as we wandered, looking for my parents.

"And it cleared up, like, half an hour before the fireworks display was scheduled."

"Yes. It was so weird. Oh, there they are." I saw my mother and did that thing where you wave at somebody who absolutely doesn't see you, but you think you should wave anyway, and then you just look like a giant dweeb.

We finished our food and headed in that direction, beer raised to avoid spillage as we sidestepped people and dodged little kids, until we met up with my parents. My mom was eating a funnel cake. I handed Brittany my beer to hold, then tore a piece off and popped it into my mouth. Brittany gave me back my beer and hugged my parents.

"I was going to get one of these later, but I might have to step up my schedule," I said, savoring the hot dough and the powdered sugar.

"I think you should go get your mother another one," my mom said as Brittany mimicked my move and took a hunk for herself.

"You got it." I laughed, told them I'd be right back, and headed toward the truck with the massive Funnel Cakes sign, giant light bulbs all around it. There was a sizable line, so I took my place and waited. I finished my beer, tossed the cup in a nearby trash can, and enjoyed the pleasant buzz that sizzled through me. I was just at the perfect stage of not quite drunk but not quite sober, so I sucked in a deep breath and decided to people watch as I enjoyed the feeling. Folks milled about, and I caught snippets of conversations, noticed facial expressions, nodded and smiled if somebody made eye contact with me. As I did all of this, words began to float through my head.

Indigo dusk carries the joyous shrieks of children
As it moves over the park
Readying the crowd
Anticipation is tangible, like something you
could hold
Touch
Feel

I squinted as I took a few steps forward in line, trying to find the rest of the poem, but the beer made it a little harder than usual. The Notes app on my phone got a workout as I typed furiously, so I wouldn't forget what had come to me, what had drifted to me like dogwood blossoms on the breeze of a summer afternoon.

"Who's in trouble?" The voice came out of nowhere, startling me and not startling me at all. I knew she'd be here. I felt it in my bones, and I wonder now, looking back, if I'd actually felt her *presence* somehow before I'd actually heard her. The mixture of happy relief and irritation that surged through me was confusing as hell.

Except it wasn't really. Not at all.

"Hi," I said, and I could hear that relief coming to the forefront, shoving the irritation down the basement stairs and slamming the door on it. "Trouble? What do you mean?"

Zoe must have noticed the tender softness in my voice, too, because her smile went wide, her cheekbones saying hello to me. "That was some very intense typing." She indicated my phone with her chin, then took a sip from the plastic cup of white wine in her hand. "I wondered who was in trouble."

"Oh. Oh…no. Nobody's in trouble. I was just looking at Instagram." I slid the phone into my back pocket, and that right there sent me veering onto a different path than I'd originally been strolling down. I shrugged, glancing off into the distance, trying not to be obvious about how nervous and jerky she made me. Except at the same time, I was completely relaxed. Yes, I know it makes no sense. It didn't then either, but there you have it.

"I can lose so much time on Insta," she told me, and her smile said she hadn't missed a beat. "I'll think, lemme just take a quick peek, and the next thing I know, two hours have gone by."

"Right?" I said, my nerves evaporating as I slid easily into conversation with her. "I don't post as much as I'd like. I should take a photo at some point." I looked around. "It's just a really great night. It feels and looks so *vast*. With the people and the colors and the smells…" I shook my head, pretty sure I sounded like some woo-woo hippie chick, as my dad would say, who should be decked out in flowing clothes and lots of beads and peering at crystals. But Zoe surprised me with her next words.

"It really does. What about over there?" She pointed to her right. "I bet if you stand there and turn back, you'd get a great shot of the whole festival."

I followed her hand with my eyes, then turned around to see behind us, and damn if she wasn't right. With a nod, she held my spot in line, and I headed in that direction, turned back to face the festival, and I raised my phone in camera mode up over my head. The lights from the food trucks and vendors against the indigo sky created a beautiful shot, and I took photos from several different angles.

"Let me see," Zoe said as I returned to her. She moved closer, and we stood with our heads nearly touching as we scrolled through the shots, pointing out our favorites, which were the same. Because of course they were. "Amazing."

"Thanks," I said, feeling that wash of joy and happiness you get just from standing near somebody you kind of adored. Even if you weren't quite ready to admit it to yourself.

"Did I tell you I finished *Pride and Prejudice*?" Her question came as my cakes were finally handed through the window of the food truck, and I silently gave her one plate while I grabbed the other.

"You did not tell me this. And?"

"It was fantastic, just like you said." She fell in step with me, never asking where we were going and, more impressively, never touching the funnel cake she carried. "Jane Austen was so ahead of her time. And her *humor*. I can't tell you how many times I found myself kind of laughing quietly as I read."

We went back and forth a few times about the book until we reached my parents. My dad was chatting up a vaguely familiar-looking man, and my mom was talking with Brittany, who was still hanging with them. I introduced Zoe to my mom and dad.

"Hey," Brittany said, her eyes sparkling with some kind of knowledge I pretended not to see.

"I thought you'd be off with your peeps," I said to Brittany as I handed my plate to my mother.

"Just about to bounce. I saw Madison over that way." She pointed absently to her left. "Later." And she was gone.

"God, can I bottle, like, a third of her energy?" Zoe asked, her eyes still on Brittany as she zipped through the crowd.

"Right?" my mom said. "That girl never stops." She popped some of her funnel cake into her mouth as she said, "So, Zoe, tell us about yourself. What do you do?"

I reached toward the plate Zoe still held, ripped off a piece, made a gesture to Zoe to help herself. My mother's question didn't even register in my head until I was chewing and heard Zoe answer.

"I'm a pharmaceutical rep. I actually met Morgan when I called on Dr. Thompson—err, Perry."

My mom's a smart woman and she pays attention. My dad was oblivious, still talking to his buddy, but I could see exactly when Mom made the connection. Thank God Perry had already told them that things didn't work between him and Zoe, or she'd have been sticking her nose right into that, prepping Zoe to be her daughter-in-law. I didn't realize Perry had told them *why* things didn't work out until Zoe turned her focus to the funnel cake, and my mother gave me a *look*. So many messages wrapped up in that one expression, but the biggest one was *Don't even think about it.*

I shot her my own look back that said, *I can't believe you* think *I'd even think about it.* And the Universe snorted sarcastically at me because I was *absolutely thinking about it,* and I had been since she'd first come up to me. I couldn't help it. Zoe was dressed so cutely in a simple black T-shirt and shorts that I couldn't look at because there was way too much sexy leg there to feast my eyes on. She'd pulled all that thick, dark hair back into a low ponytail, and that only made her cheekbones more prominent and her eyes seem even bigger. Goddamn it, how was I *not* supposed to think about it? I was only human.

"I always thought that would be such a fun job," Mom said, and I saw she wasn't going to mention anything about Zoe and Perry. I sent her a thank-you with my eyes, and she gave a slight nod back. An entire conversation between my mother and me had taken place without a single word, which I found amusing. Kind of. "I mean, aside from the sales part, which I'd be terrible at," Mom was saying. "But I bet you get to meet lots of people, and you're not stuck in an office all day, right?"

"That's a huge perk," Zoe said, and I let her and Mom converse a bit about the ins and outs of pharma rep life. Weirdly, I didn't feel a need to participate. I was perfectly content to stand next to Zoe— God, why did she always smell so good?—and, yeah, just do that. Just stand next to her. Listen to her voice. Be in her presence. I'd sobered up very quickly when my mother had put together who Zoe was, and now I itched for my buzz to return. As if reading my mind, Zoe suddenly looked at me and said, "I think I'd like to grab another drink. How about you?"

Skillfully avoiding eye contact with my mother, I responded, "Love to."

"Your mom's nice," Zoe said as we walked. It had grown fully dark by that point, and people were starting to find spots to watch the fireworks display that would begin soon.

"She is. I kinda hit the mom jackpot with her."

"We both got lucky with that then, huh?" She glanced at me, a mix of happiness and sadness in her eyes that I didn't think was possible.

"Tell me about your mom."

We found the beer and wine truck and got in another lengthy line. Which I didn't mind because, again, I was perfectly content just to stand next to Zoe. If the line never moved, I'd have been okay with that.

"She was a force," Zoe said and laughed softly as her eyes got a faraway look in them. "You didn't mess with her. She was really nice, super kind, but you did not cross her. She could hold a grudge like nobody's business. But she had the biggest heart of anybody I've ever met. She couldn't stand seeing anybody in pain or in need. She always did whatever she could to help."

"She sounds incredible."

"She was."

"Siblings?"

"No. Just me. It was just me and her for most of my life. I never knew my dad, and Mom was an only child. Her parents were older and passed away when I was very young. I barely remember them."

The idea of Zoe being completely without family after her mom died was like a giant concrete fist that just grabbed my heart and squeezed. "Her death must have been so hard for you." I said it softly. Swallowed hard. Felt my eyes well up and clenched my jaw to will that away.

Zoe noticed, and she tipped her head, smiled tenderly. "Oh, look at you, tearing up." She reached her hand toward me and wiped away one stray tear with her thumb. "You're so sweet." We moved up a few steps in line. "It was awful, yes. Worst time of my life. But she was sick for a long time, so at least we had a chance to prepare. Got to say everything we wanted to say, you know?"

"Not a lot of people get that."

"Exactly. So while it sucks that I lost her, I consider myself lucky to have had the time I did with her."

"I bet you miss her so much."

"Every single day." Another few steps forward in line. "You know, it's funny. I used to tease her about all the poetry reading she did. But once she was gone, and I made myself read a couple of her favorites, I understood why she loved them so much. They're so... *raw*. Like, cut through the skin and tissue and bone and get right to the *heart*. You know? It's something that I really liked about your brother. His way with words."

I nibbled on my bottom lip and didn't comment.

"He doesn't seem like the kind of guy who'd connect with them the way he did, but some of his stuff was…" She dropped her head back as if she was searching the dark sky for the right word. "Emotional." She turned to look at me. "Does that make sense?"

A nod. "It does." What else could I say? How much did I want to scream, *Those were* my *words, damn it?*

"I assume you know the…details?" Zoe asked the question without looking at me.

"I do. You don't play on his team."

"That's right." Clearing her throat and still not looking at me, she added, "I think I play on yours, though."

A wave of warm arousal shot through me. "You do."

Luckily, there was no opportunity for more, because we were up for drinks. Zoe ordered me a beer without asking and got herself a white wine.

"I always laugh when your options for wine aren't merlot or pinot grigio. They're red or white." She handed me my beer as we began walking again, no discussion about where we were headed.

"Makes it pretty clear about the quality of the wine, right?"

She sipped from her clear plastic cup, grimaced slightly. "Yep." Then she shrugged. "Totally okay. I don't mind. I have wine, so I'm happy."

"To wine, beer, and fireworks," I said and held up my cup.

"I will drink to that."

We had wandered a bit away from the thick of the crowd to a spot where there were some trees and few people. The first firework shot up, startling us both, and as it exploded in bright white, we stopped by unspoken agreement and sat in tandem.

My back and feet thanked me for taking a seat, and I sat back against the solid trunk of a maple tree. Another firework went off, this one in blue, and it shone on Zoe's face. I watched her as her smile widened and her face tilted up, giving me a gorgeous view of her long neck.

I did a lot of hard swallowing that night. I remember that distinctly.

For the next few minutes, Zoe watched the fireworks, and I watched Zoe. I was probably pretty obvious about it because when she turned toward me, there was zero surprise in her eyes to find me staring. Instead, she scooted closer, so our hips and thighs were touching.

I was a mess inside. You know that feeling you get when you're super attracted to somebody, and they're very close to you or even touching you, and you get that fluttering in your stomach that won't stop? And your thighs kind of tingle? And your heart rate speeds up, and your head gets kind of fuzzy, though that was probably the beer? Yeah, I had all of that going on, paired with a voice that was trying to scream really loudly in my head about this being a very bad idea, except it seemed like it could only whisper. Because I'd spent so much time helping Perry woo this woman he was so into and telling myself that I was far from good enough to catch the eye of somebody like her anyway, and I should just stay away from her because of those two things, all of that was a big jumble in my head. But I suddenly realized that, loud as it all was trying to be, it was also completely buried by this other thing, this stronger, bigger, heavier thing.

Desire.

I'd never felt it so tangibly. In my entire life. I felt like I could reach out, scoop it up, and hold it in my hands. Study it.

And when the next fireworks went off, a bunch of them in quick succession, lighting up the sky with red, I looked at Zoe, and she looked back at me, and I could see it. I could see on her face, in her eyes, that she was having a similar internal struggle, and for the third or fourth time that night, we decided the same thing, made a decision without words, as if we could hear each other's thoughts.

I leaned in. I couldn't not. I couldn't *not* kiss her.

Zoe leaned in, too, and our mouths met. Soft at first, just a touching of lips, a test, dipping a toe in. Then she leaned a little more, pressed a bit more firmly and I did the same. My God, her lips were the softest, the warmest, and I deepened things. I knew that I never wanted to stop kissing her, and there weren't even tongues involved yet. What the hell was happening?

And then it didn't matter. The facts, the details, they just blurred and then dissipated like vapor, floating off into some unnamed distance, and I was left kissing Zoe. I felt her hand slide along my face, her fingers pressing into the back of my head and pulling, insisting I move in closer, even though there was no more closer. We were pressed together, as pressed together as two sitting people could be, and it was delicious. Hot and sensual and just delicious. There was no better word for it. I parted my lips when I felt her asking for permission, and then her tongue pushed into my mouth, and I pushed back with mine, and things got hotter. Which didn't seem possible in the moment. It couldn't be any sexier really, the two of us, under a tree, away from the throngs of people, but also completely visible if somebody chose to squint in our direction.

Somebody did.

I don't know if I felt the eyes on us or if there had been a sound or what made me stop, but I did. I pulled back from Zoe's glorious mouth, only for a second. I didn't go far, kept her face mere inches from mine, smiled at her, and turned my head.

There were eyes on us. There was a person watching us making out like high schoolers under a tree while fireworks shot off above us.

"Oh God," I whispered, and my stomach felt like a rock had dropped into it. Because somebody did see us.

Perry.

CHAPTER FOURTEEN

Have you ever felt like complete and utter garbage? I'm not talking, *Oops, I ate my coworker's lunch they left in the fridge*, or even I *got the job my best friend wanted*. I mean super, all-time low, you hate yourself awful. That kind of garbage.

Well, it sucks. Just so you know. Let me steer you far, far away from doing anything that you know will hurt somebody you care about deeply. When you do that, you suck, and you deserve to feel like complete and utter garbage. That's called facing the consequences of your own actions, and I was doing that in a big way on Sunday.

Perry had stomped away Saturday night once I met his eyes. As you can imagine, things with Zoe went from crazy super hot to holy crap we should *not* have done that in about two and a half seconds flat. She felt as bad as I did, which helped. Well, maybe not as bad, but she knew we'd hurt my brother. Tons of whispered oh my Gods and I'm sorrys happened, and we stood up and pulled ourselves together. I left on one more apology, backing away from her and then rushing into the crowd to try to find Perry in the dark. The fireworks were still shooting off above us, but instead of creating an amazing backdrop for my make-out session with Zoe, they seemed to point and yell at me. Scold me. Threaten me.

It was no surprise that I couldn't find Perry. I figured he'd taken off, so I texted him. Again, it was no surprise that he didn't answer me, even after I sent fourteen apologies.

Not wanting to face my mother, who would know in one instant of looking at my face that something was wrong because moms could do that, I walked home. Ten minutes earlier, I'd been slightly intoxicated with my tongue in the mouth of a woman who attracted me like no other in my entire life, and now, I was stone-cold sober and slowly shuffling home like a scolded child, *thinking about what I'd done.*

At home, I dropped back onto my couch and waited for Perry to answer my texts. Which he didn't. I thought about texting Zoe, but my guilt was too heavy, so I set the phone on the coffee table, then picked up Ross and force-cuddled him. My brain would not stop, and thoughts, feelings, emotions rolled round my head like balls in a Bingo cage. Eventually, I guess I fell asleep.

The way-too-early sunshine in the morning felt like it was trying to laser my eyes open, and for a split second, I found humor in the fact that I'd slept all night on my couch, which did happen occasionally. Just like that, though, I remembered the night before and *why* I'd fallen asleep there, and that humor was chased right out of me by way more intense feelings of guilt, longing, shame, and an overwhelming need to fix it all.

I just wasn't sure how.

I sighed as Ross shifted himself so he stood directly on my chest and stared into my face like a serial killer sizing up his prey.

"I feel like you're trying to tell me something."

He made this sound I called his squirping. Ross didn't really meow. He left that to Rachel. Instead he made a sound that was kind of a cross between a squeak and a chirp, and sometimes when he did it, the sound would go up at the end as if he was asking me a question. I swore he was part human.

He squirped again, with the raised inflection at the end.

"I know, I know. You want breakfast." I sighed the deep, bone-weary sigh of a person who has way too much on her mind and shifted him off me. "I need coffee. What do you say I take care of both of us?"

I grabbed my phone as I stood, knowing I needed to plug it in to the extra charger I kept in the kitchen. I was surprised to see there were three texts from Zoe, and my heart rate kicked up a notch. The first had come at 2:17 a.m.

I've been lying here for hours trying to think of the right thing to say. I'm sorry? Well, I am, but only for hurting Perry. I didn't think about his feelings. I didn't think about him at all, to be honest. But he's a good guy and I'm very sorry I played a part in hurting him. Her words were followed by a sad emoji. Just one.

It looked like fifteen minutes had gone by before the second text had arrived.

To be clear, I am NOT sorry for kissing you, though. Not even a little.

I should *not* have been thrilled by that. Electric heat should *not* have sizzled through my entire body as if injected directly into my bloodstream. But I was, and it did. God help me. The third text cooled it right down, though.

Friends?

What could I say to that? No? I don't think so? I have enough friends, don't need any more? I typed the only thing I could.

Friends. And added a smiley for good measure.

Phone plugged in, I set it aside and got the coffee going, then focused on feeding my babies as they wandered around my feet and made sounds like they hadn't been fed in weeks and were about to keel over from starvation.

With the cats fed and a big mug of coffee in my hands, I went out onto my small back deck to watch the sky brighten. The forecast called for a hot day in the upper eighties, but right then, it was lovely out. Maybe sixty-eight degrees. Quiet. I watched the male and female cardinal couple that always flitted around my yard. A chickadee sang his happy little song from somewhere I couldn't see. I heard the buzz of a hummingbird, a sound that always surprised me when I realized it wasn't a bumblebee, and he hovered around the feeder I'd filled with sugar water the day before, sipping carefully. I thought about going in to grab my notebook, jotting down some words, trying to craft them into something that flowed, but I just couldn't muster the energy. Plus, I knew the words in my head were left over from last night, and writing about feelings from last night wasn't going to help anything. Instead, I inhaled the fresh morning air and basked in all that peace and quiet because I knew it wouldn't last, and I'd have to deal with the fallout I'd created by simply kissing a woman I found wildly attractive.

As if scripted that way, I heard the clasp of my gate opening and looked up to see Perry coming into my backyard, a Starbucks cup in each hand and a paper bag in his teeth. He climbed the three steps up to my deck, set down his booty, and took the seat next to me. He opened his cup and sipped, then opened the bag and took out four scones. Two cranberry orange, two blueberry. Set them on napkins on the little table between us.

A peace offering.

I knew my brother well. While he wasn't great at apologies—not that he owed me one—or eating his own words—he rarely did that, ever—he understood that baked goods and a Starbucks grande caramel macchiato were the fastest route to my heart, and he used it often. This time, though, he sat silently, and I knew he was waiting for me to take the lead.

"I'm so sorry, Per," I said, not looking at him. Afraid to look at him, really. I felt more than saw him nod. When I did finally brave a glance, he pushed the coffee and a napkin with two scones on it toward me.

"I know."

"I wasn't really thinking, I just…" Ugh. That was not the right way to start, so I shut up.

"It's okay. I know."

It was such a weird state to be in. Technically, I hadn't done anything wrong. *Technically*. Zoe wasn't his girlfriend. I was completely single. There was a mutual attraction. *Technically*, I was perfectly within my rights to kiss her. And I almost said so but stayed quiet and, instead, watched my brother as he watched my birds. We ate our scones silently. Sipped our coffee. Watched nature. Listened to the neighborhood wake up.

Finally, he turned to face me, and I almost made a sound of surprise at the clear emotion on his face. So much of it. He looked sad and embarrassed and uncertain and tired. All at once. My big brother was very good at hiding his feelings. At being stoic. He was a doctor, he had to do that, he had to be able to remain neutral, and it only made sense that quality would spill over into the nonmedical parts of his life. He was rarely vulnerable, but on those few occasions he was, it was usually with me. He looked at me now, his blue eyes intense, his eyebrows tipping upward, almost in question.

"Look, I know you've been single for a while, and you've been dating here and there. But maybe…" His voice went husky, and he cleared his throat, tried again. "Just…maybe not her, okay?" I watched his Adam's apple bob as he swallowed. "Maybe not her."

It rained all day Tuesday and all day Wednesday and much of Thursday morning but managed to clear up in the early afternoon, so golf wasn't canceled. I was glad because I'd actually been looking forward to playing, seeing my friends, and having a drink or two.

I'd been in a weird mental state since talking to Perry the weekend before. I know that makes me sound like I was losing my mind, and it wasn't that. I just felt like I was in some weird state of limbo. Like I'd been zipping down a path, happy to be on it, certain I'd like the destination, and then a gate slammed closed, a big red No Trespassing sign swinging from it. And I had to choose a different path except there was none in sight. So I stood there like an idiot. Doing nothing. Going nowhere. Limbo.

I didn't blame Perry. Also, I did.

I'd gotten a text or two from Zoe, and I'd responded, and it was all very friendly and aboveboard, but I hadn't seen her. I simultaneously felt glad about that and missed her terribly, and the missing part was weird because I hadn't really been around her all that much. How can you miss somebody you've spent so little time with? At that point, I had so many frustrating questions like that, that it was driving me a little bananas. Add to that Perry's much more cheerful demeanor and my internal war between *I did the right thing* and *Why can't I pursue whatever might be with Zoe?* and I was kind of a mess inside. To combat my whirring brain, I'd thrown myself into my work all week, and now I was ready to set thoughts of Perry and thoughts of Zoe aside and blow off some steam with a seven iron and a martini. Not necessarily in that order.

Imagine my surprise when I hauled my clubs to the course and saw Zoe standing there as part of my foursome.

Why does the Universe hate me?

The mix of emotions that sprinted through me at the sight of her…God. I could barely get a handle on myself. Joy, worry, irritation, a little fear, a lot of thrill. Just so much. But I can honestly say that when she turned her head and met me with those gorgeous blue eyes, and her smile widened, her face clearly lit up, everything left but the joy.

"Hi," she said, and that one simple word went into my ears, through my body, and straight down.

"Hey, you," I said back and set my clubs next to her. I loved that I could smell what had simply become *her* to me. That mix of strawberries and vanilla, all fresh and inviting and warm.

She raised her hand, gave it a little wave. "Subbing again. Looks like we're playing together."

"Looks like it." I nodded once.

Her smile faltered just a bit—I was pretty sure I saw it—and I was immediately hit with a combination of guilt and anger. I hated seeing her expression dim. Worse, I hated being the cause.

"It's a good night for it," I said then, in a weak attempt to bring back the full smile. It sort of worked.

"It really is."

We got ourselves situated as the other two women from our foursome arrived, and then we teed off.

It was the fourth hole. I pulled out my club in preparation to drive next, and Zoe stopped me with a hand on my shoulder.

"Can I show you something?" she asked, gesturing to my hands, then made a face that told me she wasn't sure her advice was welcome.

I held out my club and said pitifully, "Please help me." That made her grin.

"Okay, let me see your grip. Like you're going to drive."

I did as she asked and grasped the club in both hands. Zoe stepped close. Very close. I could feel her body heat—she was that close. And then her hands were on my hands, and every bit of moisture in my body headed directly south.

"Link your forefinger here and this pinky. Gives you more control."

I blinked at my grip, gave myself a little time to reset. "Seriously? I thought that was just some weird quirky thing people did."

That got a hearty laugh out of Zoe. Full and deep and wonderful. "You are so cute. You know that?" Then she turned back to her own clubs without waiting for a response.

I was on a high for the remainder of the round. I wouldn't say I played well. I would say I didn't care how I played because I was on a high. A simple touch and a few kind words, and I was back on the Zoe train, full speed ahead. I pushed thoughts of Perry into a faraway corner of my mind.

The clubhouse bar was buzzing, filled with not only our golf league, but regular members and golfers from other leagues that also played. It was loud, hard to hear Zoe when she spoke, and she finally leaned in close. Again, everything within me fluttered with excitement as her lips pressed close to my ear.

"Wanna get out of here?" She pulled back just enough so I could see her eyes. All I'd have to do to kiss those full glossy lips was lean a teeny, tiny bit.

"Yes, please." I didn't need to think about my answer. Maybe I should have. Maybe I simply should've said no. I did neither of those things. I picked up my purse, didn't say good-bye to anybody, and followed Zoe out into the parking lot.

"There's a cool bar in Jefferson Square I've been wanting to try. Martini's. Care to join me?" She didn't look at me when she asked, and it was only then that I wondered if she was as nervous as I was.

"How about we each drive home and then walk to it? Meet you there in twenty?"

"Perfect."

You'd think I'd have taken the drive home, the quick stop into my house, to think about what I was doing, to remember Perry's words, to feel guilty. But I did none of those things. What I did do was tell myself this was simply friendship. I could be friends with Zoe. That was allowed. Perry didn't get to decide who I liked and who I didn't, who I hung out with and who I couldn't. I was a grown-ass adult. I said many of these things right out loud as I changed out of my sweaty shirt and into a nice clean one, a green camp shirt. I left it unbuttoned one button lower than I normally would. Because yes,

I was always interested in showing my friends a teasing peek of my cleavage. I rolled my eyes at myself. I did not, however, refasten the button.

I tossed Ross and Rachel some treats, told them I loved them and I'd be home soon, and locked my house behind me.

I was familiar with Martini's, a bar that my dad had gone to when he was young. So it had been around a long time. Finding itself in Jefferson Square when things were up and coming and growing more modern and eclectic, Martini's had had to change and adjust to survive. A slow process, I imagined, but they seemed to be doing all right, judging from the decent number of patrons sitting and standing around the large, rectangular bar that sat in the center of the room, when I walked in. I found Zoe right away, seated at one corner of the bar, and my stomach did that flip-flop-flutter thing that I realized was a regular occurrence whenever I laid eyes on her.

Friends. Friends. Friends.

I let the word float through my head, roll around in there, hoping it would find a space and park itself. I was not optimistic.

"Hi," Zoe said, indicating the seat on the other side of the corner from her. "I snagged this spot so we can see each other when we talk instead of being side by side and having to crane our necks." Then she wrinkled her nose in a display of adorable and asked, "Is that weird? Am I a weirdo?"

"I mean, duh, of course you are," I said as I hung my purse on a hook under the bar and took a seat. "But that's nothing new. I could tell the first time I saw you, so it's all good. I will sit in the corner seat and look at you and not crane my neck."

"Perfect." Zoe gave a quick laugh. "I didn't want to order until you got here, but I'm feeling like a martini."

We were on the same wavelength again, and I tried not to focus on that. "Then I think it bodes well that we're in a bar called Martini's."

We ordered from a pretty brunette bartender whose name tag said she was Julia. Pomegranate for Zoe, cucumber watermelon for me. Julia slid them our way, and Zoe slapped down her credit card before I could.

"Nope. I invited you. I'm buying. You can buy next time."

Next time. That was okay. Totally cool. Friends hung out. No reason to think of it as anything more than that.

"Wait," Zoe said as I reached for my glass. She arranged them close together, the small votive candle on the bar behind them, and snapped a photo. "They're too pretty not to document." She put her phone down and picked up her glass. "To summer, martinis, and friendship."

How come when I thought about us just being friends, it was good, but when she mentioned it, something twisted with yuck in my gut?

I swallowed, touched my glass to hers, and we sipped.

"Oh, that's delicious," she said and licked her lips.

"Same," I said of mine, and then without saying a word, we switched glasses and sipped each other's.

"Yours is better," she said.

"You think? I like them both. Wanna trade?"

Her smile was tender. "No, but that's very sweet of you." We were quiet for a few moments, just looking at the bar, the people around us, the bartenders. "I like this place," Zoe said, a wistful quality to her voice.

"Me, too. My dad says it's been here for years and years. He used to come with his buddies when he had his internship right out of college."

"Really?" Zoe looked around. "I think it would be hard to keep a bar in business, making a profit, for so long." She nodded, as if I'd asked her a question. "But yeah, I like it here. Might become my neighborhood hangout. Everybody needs one."

"You have Happily Ever After, too. Look at you with two hangouts already. You're living your best life."

"That will be my non-alcoholic hangout."

"Oh, I see. You're so important that your hangouts serve different purposes."

"Now you're beginning to understand me." She grinned at me.

"You have the most amazing cheekbones I've ever seen." It was out before I had a chance to catch it or even filter it, and I felt my eyes go slightly wide. Which made Zoe laugh.

"A, thank you. B, you should see your face right now."

I groaned, then dropped my head to the bar and let it thud once, twice, as Zoe kept laughing. Picking my head up, I chuckled as I asked, "Friends can say that to each other, right? I can think my friend has great cheekbones, can't I?"

"I have zero problem with you thinking that, as long as I'm allowed to think your voice is super sexy."

My laughter died in my throat as I absorbed her words. "You do?"

"Oh my God, yes. Has nobody ever told you that? It's kind of husky and a little gravelly and..." She stopped talking and let the rest of her thought hang in the air unspoken. I admit to a very pleasant tingle running hotly through my body. "I guess maybe that's overstepping for a friend, huh?"

I shrugged. "I mean, who's to say? Who gets to judge? I'm not judging."

Zoe's smile returned. "Good. Now you know."

Now I knew.

"Tell me about your family," Zoe said, shifting her body a bit as she shifted the subject. "Is there more than you and Perry?"

"Yes, there's another brother. Carter. He's Brittany's dad."

"Older."

"Yes. He's forty-six, Perry is forty-three, I'm thirty-three."

"Were you an oops baby?" Zoe's eyes sparkled with humor.

"I was, and I own that. I also own that I was spoiled rotten and still am. So don't think you can hold any of that over me. I'm already aware, and I'm totally okay with it."

"Spoken like a true baby of the family."

"And only girl." I pointed at her. "Don't forget that. It's key to the spoiling."

"Oh, I bet. So, Carter, Perry, and Morgan. Cool names."

"They're actually maiden names in our family."

"Really?"

I nodded, proud of this little Thompson family tidbit. "My mom's maiden name is Carter. My dad's mother's maiden name was Perry. And my mom's mother's maiden name is Morgan."

"Well, I think it's lucky that her maiden name wasn't, like, Butts or Lipschitz or something."

I tipped my head, made a show of considering. "I don't know. Butts Thompson has kind of a nice ring to it."

Zoe's laugh was one of the best sounds in the world, as far as I was concerned. I've said before that it was musical. Kinda girly. But it was also genuine and seemed to come from deep within her. I wanted to make her laugh. A lot.

"So, tell me," I said, once our laughter had eased up. "What does Zoe Blake, pharma rep extraordinaire, do in her spare time? Besides analyze poetry and kick the behinds of other poor souls on the golf course?"

Zoe pursed her lips, then took a sip of her drink. "I love movies, though I don't go as much as I'd like. I would love to learn mixology, so I could make martinis this good." She finished hers. "Are you going to have another?"

"I mean, I walked, so I'm not worried about getting home safely."

"Good." She pulled the martini menu from its little holder on the bar and held it up. "I'm going to try a different one. Wanna?"

"Mixing it up. I like that."

We went back and forth a few times before I settled on a chocolate and salted caramel martini, and Zoe chose the cinnamon toast version.

"I feel like we just ordered dessert," I said after Julia set about making our drinks.

"I see no problem with that." Zoe shrugged, and we watched as Julia added ingredients into her shaker, lined the rims of the glasses, shook, poured. It was like watching a performance. "It's like artistry," Zoe whispered, as if she knew what I was thinking.

"Right?" I whispered back. Then we looked at each other and smiled big. "I'm cracking up that we're whispering," I said in another whisper.

"Well, we don't want to disturb the artist at work." Zoe whispered as well. And we grinned some more.

Julia didn't disappoint, and when she slid our drinks in front of us, they truly did look like works of art. Mine all chocolaty, drizzled with caramel sauce, a Hershey's kiss in the bottom. Zoe's was white and frothy, cinnamon dusting the rim. We carefully lifted them, touched them to each other, and sipped.

"Oh, this could be deadly," I said of mine. "I mean, I watched her pour in the vodka, but all I taste is sweet and salty chocolaty goodness. This could be trouble."

Zoe's grin was made even cuter by the tiny bit of white froth on her upper lip. I reached over and wiped it off with my thumb.

"And?" I asked.

"Shh. I'm busy drinking the best drink I've ever had in my life. It's so good, I don't want to lose even one sip by letting you taste it."

I gasped in feigned outrage.

"But I will because I like you just that much." The cheekbones. God. We switched drinks. Sipped. Moaned in delight. I caught Julia out of the corner of my eye looking extremely satisfied.

"Yours really does taste like cinnamon toast," I said as I handed Zoe's glass back to her. "My mom used to make it for me when I was a kid." At her furrowed brow, I gaped. "How have you never had cinnamon toast? It's just toast with butter and then some cinnamon and sugar sprinkled on it."

"That sounds like heaven," Zoe said.

"I feel you've been deprived. I'm going to have to make it for you because I now feel like it's my duty to do so."

"Listen, I will not be turning down any offerings of cinnamon toast."

"Noted."

And then we did that thing where we just sat there and smiled kind of goofily at each other, and it held. No words. No movement. Just smiling at each other like two dorks. Or two people who really, really liked each other.

Sigh.

We took our time finishing the second round of drinks, talking the whole time, but it was a school night, and we both had to be up early the next morning. I knew I didn't want to leave. I'd have been completely happy to stay sitting at that bar with Zoe for the rest of time. But even better? I didn't think she wanted to leave either.

"We should probably go," I said reluctantly, just as she opened her mouth to speak.

"I was going to say the same thing. I don't want to go, but we probably should. Work. Responsibility. Blah, blah, blah."

I nodded as she signaled Julia to close out her tab. When she waved off my offer of money, I said, "Then I definitely get the next round."

"Deal. When?" The arrival of the tab gave her an excuse not to look at me as she asked.

"Saturday?" It was out of my mouth before I could even think about it.

"Yes. Love to." Zoe's answer came just as quickly as my question. We were so on the same page. I wasn't sure if that was a good thing or a bad thing. We agreed to work out the details the next day and headed out into the night.

It was still a bit on the muggy side, which felt even stickier after the air-conditioning in the bar. I felt my skin start to perspire lightly as we walked in the same direction toward a small branch of the library that sat on the corner. I knew once we reached the intersection, we'd go in different directions, but I only dreaded it for a second or two before Zoe grabbed my hand and tugged me into the library parking lot, which was empty.

"Are we breaking into the library?" I asked as she led me around the building to the back where a large book depository sat, the size of a public mailbox. "We could get you a card. It's not that difficult. Or are you so desperate for more poetry that we have to steal some?"

Zoe pushed me up against the wall next to the book box, the brick building solid against my back, leaned in close, and whispered, "Shut up and kiss me."

Never one to disobey a beautiful woman, I did exactly as I was ordered, and I was not gentle. My brain really wasn't even a part of the decision when I grabbed Zoe's waist with one hand, the back of her neck with the other, and pulled her roughly against me. I couldn't not. It had been building up since the second I sat down at the bar. No. Lies. Since I'd laid eyes on her at the golf course. I'd wanted to kiss that mouth the entire night.

So I did.

She felt it, too, the insistence, the urgency, if the instant plunging of her tongue into my mouth was any indication.

Time became meaningless. We might have kissed for a minute or two. It might've been a week. I had no idea, and I didn't care. All I wanted was to kiss Zoe Blake for the rest of time.

Eventually, we needed air. Zoe pulled her mouth away but kept her forehead pressed to mine, and our ragged breathing was the only sound for several moments.

"Friends do that, right?" she asked, her breathing finally beginning to slow down. She lifted her head, looked at me with those eyes, and her dark brows rose in question.

I nodded. "Absolutely. I make out with my friends all the time."

"Oh, good. Just making sure."

"Definitely. You're the best kisser, though, gotta say. Way better than Adriana. And Stefan uses too much tongue."

Zoe threw her head back and laughed. Loudly and from deep in her belly. And oh my God, I wanted to fasten my mouth to that throat, run my tongue up and down it, taste her skin, feel the heat radiating from her. But I knew if I did that, we'd go too far down this road to come back, and I wasn't ready for that.

I think she sensed it because her laughter died down and we stood there. Holding each other. Gazing into one another's eyes. I could feel her thumb tracing circles on the bare skin of my side where my shirt had ridden up a bit. I played with her hair, quietly thrilled to finally be able to sift it through my fingers.

"We should get home," I said, forcing the words out because I didn't want to let go of her, didn't want to say good-bye, didn't want to leave her.

"We should." Zoe seemed as hesitant to go as I was, but we made ourselves leave the side of the building and take some tentative steps back toward the street. We held hands as we walked to the corner, and it felt like the most natural thing in the world, like we'd been doing that for years. "I'll see you soon," she said as we reached the spot where we'd go in separate directions.

"Not if I see you first," was my completely eye-roll-inducing comeback, but she smiled anyway. I held on to her hand as she walked away, until our fingers slipped from each other's, and I watched the beautiful, gentle sway of her hips for a moment before heading toward my own house.

That, of course, is when the tsunami of emotions hit because what the hell was I doing? Perry had specifically asked me not to pursue anything with Zoe. Specifically Zoe. Nobody else. Just her. For him. And my response to that was to meet her for drinks and then have a super heavy make-out session with her behind the library like sneaky school kids, all the while knowing that if she'd even started to utter anything about going home with her, I'd have gone. In a heartbeat. No questions asked.

God, I was the absolute *worst* sister on the planet.

I was also very, very wet...

CHAPTER FIFTEEN

*O*kay. *Much as I hate to say it, we can't be doing that.*
I stared at the words on my screen, my thumb hovering over the Send button, for several moments before I added a sad emoji and finally sent it.

The bouncing gray dots of torment appeared, disappeared, appeared again, went away. Zoe was clearly trying to figure out what to say.

I was in bed, snuggled in with Ross and Rachel. It wasn't terribly late, but the day had exhausted me emotionally, and I felt like I'd been mentally beaten up. I'd had an amazing night...doing exactly what my big brother had pleaded for me not to do.

I sucked.

My phone pinged.

Sigh. I know. I'm sorry. I just had such a great time with you...

The dots told me there was more coming, so I tried to be patient while Zoe finished her thought.

I wish I'd met you first.

I smiled because she actually had. Well, she'd met us at the same time. I smiled as I typed, *I wish I'd thought to make a move before my brother did.* I added a smiley to keep it light, even as I gave a sarcastic snort that made Ross lift his head. I never would've made a move on Zoe. Never in a million years. I didn't have it in me.

LOL. Never would've happened. But I wish I'd been more open about my interest in you that first night of golf.

That made me blink at the screen. And blink some more. Two big reveals in that text. One, that she knew I never would've made the first move. I shoved aside how much I wanted to know how she knew that. Two, she was interested in me way back then? In *me*? I wasn't even sure what to do with that. Damn my brother. Damn him.

I guess we're just meant to be friends.

I hesitated for what felt like a long time before I sent that one, because I didn't really believe it. A long time seemed to go by again, no bouncing dots this time, until Zoe replied.

I don't have a lot of those, so I'll take it.

No emoji. I had the distinct feeling she was doing exactly what I was doing—making the best of a situation she hated.

We signed off, and suddenly, I was wide-awake. I sighed loudly, annoyed because I just wanted to go to sleep and end this day. A day of such ups and downs. I'd run the gamut from extraordinarily happy to crushingly disappointed, and all of a sudden, I was mad. Mad at myself for wanting what I couldn't have. Mad at Zoe for being, well, Zoe. Mad at Perry for erecting Stop signs and No Trespassing signs and Do Not Enter signs all around something that I really, really wanted. And then I was mad at myself again for not having the balls to tell Perry to get over his damn self. I picked up my notebook.

> *Who gets to say*
> *No, stay away, off limits*
> *What should I do*
> *About this pull, this want*
> *When will I*
> *Get to live for me, not others*
> *Where does it say*
> *You can only choose from this pool*
> *Why can't I*
> *See, touch, explore her the way I want to*
> *How am I*
> *Supposed to shut it all out*

Yeah, it was terrible. I groaned, closed the notebook, and tossed it to the nightstand. Still wide-awake and annoyed on top of that. I grabbed the remote, clicked on the TV, and found a rerun of *Chicago P.D.*

It was gonna be a long night.

Summer had finally hit full throttle. Late July came with ninety-degree temperatures and humidity that had my hair doing its own crazy dance on my head, refusing to be tamed by any and all product I worked, lathered, or sprayed into it. Ponytails were a very common thing for me during the summer, and that Monday was no exception.

The office was steady, patients flowing in and out at a manageable pace. Mr. Wilson, certain he was suffering from a kidney stone—I wanted to tell him if he was, he'd be on the floor flopping around in pain, I knew this from experience—shuffled his way to a seat in the waiting room just as the door opened and Zoe walked in, doughnut box in hand.

Would there be a time when I could see her and not have my heart rate speed up in my chest? True, I'd only actually seen her once or twice since our first kiss under the fireworks—and one of those was a major make-out sesh—but since then, anytime she came into view, my body did strange things. My hands sweat—my hands never sweat. My heart raced. My stomach got all fluttery and weird.

"Hey," she said, looking absolutely stunning in black pants and a print top in white, blue, and black. The silver bangle bracelet around her wrist caught my eye, and then I was thinking about her wrists. And her hands. And her fingers.

When I finally looked up at her actual face, she was smiling knowingly. That was the only way to describe it. Knowingly. She knew exactly what was happening in my head. I both loved that and was embarrassed by it. This was my work. I needed to maintain some kind of professionalism. And then she spoke, and I saw her tongue, and away went my brain again.

"I wanted to see if Dr. Thompson had a couple minutes for me today," she said, leaning her forearms on the counter. Which gave me a nice view down the front of her shirt. I wasn't sure if she knew that or not but didn't have time to wonder for long because Perry's voice interrupted us from my left.

"Unfortunately, he does not." He handed me a file and leaned forward so he could see Zoe. "Crazy schedule today," he said and smiled his professional smile at her. "I think Friday is okay, though."

I felt relief surge through me because part of me worried he was just going to blow Zoe off from now on. But he apparently had put on his business hat and pushed past any personal yuck that might be hanging out.

"Friday it is, then." Zoe's smile was its usual charming self, no sign of her feeling weird or being hesitant about anything. After all, what had she done? It wasn't her fault Perry wasn't her type.

He rapped his knuckles on the counter. "Okay. Good to see you, Zoe." With a quick wave, he went back to work.

Zoe's face was interesting right then. With Perry out of sight, the smile didn't fade so much as drop off her face for a second. We had texted a bit on and off since our crazy awesome make-out session the previous week, but we'd done our best to keep things light and friendly. We'd decided to skip going out on Saturday, just because it felt safer to have a little distance. We talked superficially about not much. Anytime one of us ventured into the Forbidden Lands, as I started to call it in my head whenever we got close to flirting or anything related to sex, the other would pull it back to the friend zone.

Honestly? It sucked, and I decided a doughnut would help with that. I opened the box Zoe had set on the counter to see that the entire dozen was Boston cream. My favorite. She'd remembered that. I looked up at her, and her smile was tender, even as she walked slowly backward toward the door.

"Until Friday," she said and was gone.

I stared at the door, at the space where she'd stood, for a long time after she was gone.

A little seed of resentment sprouted at that moment. I didn't know it then, didn't realize it, but looking back, I'm sure of it. The poem I'd written about not being able to reach for something I wanted came surging back into my head.

Can you eat a doughnut angrily? 'Cause that's exactly what I did.

❖

Friday was dark and gloomy and rainy, and I didn't love it, not like I usually do with storms. In fact, the weather fit my mood perfectly, so I accepted it as the day's backdrop as I punched keys on my keyboard harder than necessary and knew that my brows were pointing down in a V at the top of my nose and staying that way.

I wasn't this person. I did not enjoy being in a crappy mood. I was usually able to pull myself out of one just by sheer will and the desire to be happy. But since Zoe's visit on Monday, a shadow, a darkness had settled on me. I wrote some angry poetry, went darker than I usually do, just trying to work out why I felt so...defeated. I mean, I knew. Of course I did. But I wanted to analyze it so I could pull myself out of it because being perpetually pissed off was not a good look for me.

Perry, on the other hand, was excessively chipper, and I squinted at him suspiciously all morning. He whistled—literally *whistled a little tune*—as he handed me a file, winked, and went back to the exam rooms.

I wanted to punch him in the throat.

And then Zoe walked in, and it was like the clouds parted, and the sun came out, and angels sang, and all was right in the world, and I just about rolled my eyes right out of my skull at myself, even as I was thrilled to see her.

Jesus Christ, I was a disaster.

She was in a suit that day, navy blue with a light blue top, and she shrugged out of the jacket as she crossed the waiting room toward me. "I don't know what I was thinking, dressing like this in the heat of summer." She shook her head, draped the jacket over her arm, and met my eyes. "Hi." The way she said that teeny, tiny word spoke volumes to me. It was tinted with relief and longing and wistfulness, and it made me think she was in the same boat as I was.

"Hey, you," I said back, my tone the twin of hers.

She glanced around the waiting room where two patients sat, one reading a copy of Time that was woefully out of date and the other scrolling on her phone. Then she turned back my way, looked past me to Joanne, who was talking on the phone, and said quietly, "You look amazing."

I felt that blush I couldn't control burst in like a drag queen taking the stage and color my entire face in pink heat. "Thank you," I whispered. "Looked in the mirror lately? 'Cause, damn."

Her face lit up at the compliment, and I saw a little pink heat of her own blossom on those cheekbones as if dabbed there by a soft brush.

We stayed like that, just looking at each other, for an inordinately long amount of time. Joanne saying good-bye and hanging up from her call seemed to snap us both out of it, like a game of freeze tag we'd just been released from.

"Dr. Thompson said he has a few minutes for me," Zoe said, her professional mask back in place.

I nodded, picked up the phone, and buzzed Perry in his office. He told me he'd be right out, and I motioned Zoe through the door. When Perry appeared at the end of the hall and called out a greeting, Zoe held my gaze for a beat, then turned and headed his way. I watched every step she took, and when I finally pulled my eyes away, I met Perry's.

He was watching me.

I didn't care.

Once they were out of sight, I busied myself with work. There was rarely a time when I had nothing to do, so throwing myself into my job was easy, and I realized that I'd been doing it often over the past couple of months. *Gee, I wonder why.*

The meeting only lasted about fifteen minutes, and then Zoe and Perry were walking my way, smiling and laughing. I knew them both well enough to recognize a slightly feigned quality, like when you want to impress somebody, so you laugh a little too hard at their joke that wasn't really all that funny.

"All right, send me the product, and you could probably check on the sample closet in a week or two," Perry said.

Zoe met my gaze and hers visibly softened. "I'll do that," she said but didn't look at him.

There was a beat, and then I shifted my gaze to my brother, who narrowed his eyes at me just enough to let me know he was aware of what could only be described as sexual tension in the air. I knew it. I felt it constantly whenever I was around Zoe. I shouldn't have been surprised that somebody else would notice, but I was, a little bit.

Good-byes were said, and—in an unusual move for my very busy doctor brother—he stayed where he was and waited for Zoe to go. Once the front door closed behind her, he gave me a look of irritation but said nothing as he headed back to his next patient.

"Your brother moves fast," Joanne said a moment later. "I mean, I don't say that to be a jerk. It's just an observation."

Her words confused me, and I spun my chair around to face her. "What do you mean?"

Joanne shrugged, and I could tell by the way she suddenly started shuffling papers on her desk that she might be worried she'd overstepped. Still, she answered me. "I mean, he was all about Zoe for a while and seemed so bummed when that didn't pan out, but here we are, just a week or two later, and he's already moved on to somebody new."

"He has?" This was information I didn't have, and Joanne's eyes went wide with the realization that she might have revealed a secret. I snorted and waved a dismissive hand. "Please. It's fine. He probably just forgot to tell me. Who's the new person?"

"Some golf buddy's daughter? Jennifer Zimmerman is her name."

I nodded like I had any clue who this person was. "Right. Dr. Zimmerman's daughter." Making it up as I went. I did know who Dr. Zimmerman was, just not that he had a daughter Perry might want to date.

"That's the one." Joanne pointed at me. "They must've hit if off because he had me send her flowers this morning."

Blinking. That was about all I could do. I blinked at her until she clearly became uncomfortable and started to subtly squirm in her seat. Was this true? Had Perry given me the old *my poor heart, you can't date this one because I liked her so much, it would be too hard for me* and then turned around and started dating somebody new? He obviously had, which was why I knew nothing about it. That had been purposeful. I wondered when he thought he'd get around to telling me.

"Well, that explains all the whistling and the spring in his step," I said, doing my best to be nonchalant, oh-that-crazy-brother-of-mine, so Joanne would relax a bit. This had nothing to do with her, and it wasn't her fault that Perry had kept his current situation a secret from me. I chuckled and shrugged and shook my head and grinned. I did everything I could to put Joanne at ease and punctuate how *so* not a big deal this was.

But oh my God, we were going to have words.

All I had to do was get through the rest of the day. Of course, that's when time decided to slow waaaaaay down. It felt like the afternoon was about twelve hours long, but finally—finally—Martha left, and I locked the front door, and it was just me and Perry remaining. I inhaled slowly, filled up my lungs and held the breath in there for a count of seven, then let it out slowly. The buzzing of my intercom seemed so loud in the quiet of the office, and I flinched as it startled me.

"Morgan?" Perry's disembodied voice asked.

"Yup."

"Is everybody gone?"

"Yup."

"Good. Can you come see me for a minute?"

"Yup." Well, that was interesting. Maybe he'd decided it was time to tell me about the new woman in his life. I pushed down my irritation, vowed to give him the benefit of the doubt, as I walked down the hall, around the corner, and into his office.

He sat behind his enormous desk, his white coat draped on the back of the big leather chair, his stethoscope on the desk, curled up like a snake. Elbows on the desk, he steepled his fingers and brought his lips to them as he looked at me. Studied me.

"You're freaking me out," I said, because it was true. It felt weird to stand there and have him staring at me.

He cleared his throat. "So...I noticed when Zoe was here that you two..."

I waited for him to finish his sentence, and he suddenly shifted in his seat, seemingly uncomfortable. I narrowed my eyes at him. "We two...what?"

"You're not seeing her, right? Not after I asked you not to."

I blinked. Stared at him.

"It just seemed like"—he shrugged—"there was something there. I could almost feel it. I feel like a dick for even asking, but it's been on my mind all day."

"So, hang on." I'd had enough. I felt my limit as it rushed up on me like I was running toward a brick wall. I held up a finger and took a moment to get a handle on my anger. "Let me get this straight. You asked me not to see Zoe because her rejection of you was so hard on your poor little ego, and it would hurt you if I did."

Surprise zipped across his face, likely at the snark in my tone, but I didn't care. "You seemed to understand." His voice said he was less sure of himself than he had been just a minute ago.

"Oh, I did. I did exactly as you asked. Because I did understand. Then. But now? I have two words for you." When his sandy brows went up toward his hairline, I said, "Jennifer Zimmerman."

Yeah. His eyes went wide because it was clear he didn't know I knew about her. And then he looked at least the tiniest bit embarrassed. "That's just been one date."

"And flowers."

He chewed his lip. "Yeah. But it's nothing, really. I'm just trying to get out there again."

"Seriously? I can't see Zoe because it would be too hard on you while you're dating somebody else? Really? Explain that to me."

He shook his head, and I saw his Adam's apple bob as he swallowed. "I know. I'm sorry. I just…Zoe turning me down was a blow."

"It had nothing to do with you, asshat—she's gay." My irritation was ratcheting up.

"I know, but still. It stung. You know me, I'm not used to getting turned down. And then to see that she's clearly interested in *you*…"

Oh my God.

The reality of what he'd intimated hit me like a fist to the stomach, taking my breath for a moment as I stared at him with disbelieving eyes.

"I can't even believe you just said that," I said quietly. "It's killing you, isn't it? You can't stand knowing that a girl you were into is into me instead. Your plain, uninteresting little sister."

"No, it's not that at all." But his voice was less than convincing. I knew Perry thought pretty highly of himself. That wasn't new information. He liked to be on top. He liked that he was the guy who won. He liked being first. And he liked that he beat me in just about everything. He got better grades in school and in college. He was always better at sports. I think his divorce, hard as it was for him, would've been even harder if I'd been married at the time, and my marriage stayed intact. He was always ahead of me. And you know what? I'd never really minded because he was my brother, and I was proud of him, and I loved him. But in that moment, standing there in his office as the reality of what he'd said sank in, all I felt was hurt.

"You'd better check your fucking ego." I turned on my heel and left before I said something I'd regret. Because there were a lot of things I wanted to say that I would likely regret later. Nothing he didn't deserve, but I wasn't a mean person, and I didn't say mean things just to be mean.

I got to my desk and hastily shoved my things in my bag and turned off lights. The fact that Perry didn't follow me, didn't fall all over himself trying to apologize, just made it all that much worse. I left loudly, slamming the door behind me.

My blood was boiling. I'd never really understood the meaning of the phrase until that day. As I sat in my car and started the engine, everything within me was tense. My jaw was clenched, my teeth firmly together. My grip on the steering wheel turned my knuckles white. My breathing was slightly more rapid than normal, and I could feel the heat of anger running through my body as if my blood had grown hot.

I didn't want to be there when Perry came out to get in his own car, so I shifted into Drive, went two office buildings down, and parked in that lot.

I picked up my phone, typed, *Where are you?*

A response came quickly. *Working from home this afternoon. Why? Miss me?* Followed be a winking emoji.

"God, you have no idea," I said into my empty car. Then I typed, *Absolutely. Wondered if you had some time for me.* That was a good generic way to put it, right?

I haven't eaten much today and was just about to forage in my kitchen. Wanna come here? I'll make us something. I have wine.

That answer could not have been more perfect if I'd scripted it for Zoe myself, and my heart soared. *Yes, please.*

Zoe texted me her address and then followed it with, *You okay?*

She could read me already, and while that thought would normally settle me, ease my mind, it only fueled the heat within me. *I just need to see you.*

I put my car in gear and drove, barely remembering how I got there. I pulled into her driveway, parked behind her car, and hurried up her front walk. I didn't even stop to admire her house. Or even look at it. I lifted my hand to knock, but she opened the door before I could. She'd been waiting for me, and she looked positively edible. Black leggings, a flowing tank top in red and white stripes, hair piled up in a mess on top of her head. She showed me those cheekbones, said hi, and that was it.

I pushed through the door, kicked it closed behind me as I grabbed her face with both hands, backed her against the opposite wall, and kissed her with everything I had.

CHAPTER SIXTEEN

Zoe didn't miss a beat, which told me she wanted this contact as much as I did. Maybe not as much as I *needed* it in that moment, but she was right there with me. I felt her hands on my hips, pulling me into her, and a small moan rumbled up from her throat.

How to describe kissing Zoe...

It was everything. All at once. It was equal. A partnership of mouths. I might have made the move, but she caught right up, and it wasn't until lips parted and tongues came into play that I *really* understood how very much I wanted this. It was as if the lid I'd tried so hard to keep sealed on my desire for her just flew off like a manhole cover being blown up into the air by the steam from below the street.

We were moving. I didn't even realize it until my legs reached the couch, and I fell back onto it. Zoe followed, her weight on me, and it was the most delicious feeling.

"Am I hurting you?" she whispered and attempted to shift.

"No." I held her fast with both hands. "Stay."

The blue of her eyes was hot, if that was even possible. People describe blue eyes as icy, as cool, but in that moment, Zoe's were filled with heat, like the hottest blue flame in a burning fire. Her pupils were large, her lids lowered slightly, an exact picture of desire, and I wasted no time pulling her head down, crushing her mouth to mine.

Arousal ran through my body. All of it. My limbs tingled. My stomach tightened. My underwear grew wet. I cupped Zoe's ass in both of my hands, squeezed, and pulled her against my center, and both of us whimpered. Then we looked at each other and laughed.

Zoe held my gaze for a moment before she reached a decision of some sort—I could see it on her face. She reached up and brushed my hair off my forehead.

"So, as much as I am absolutely loving this—and you should know that a big part of me is screaming right now because I paused the sexy times—I need to know that you're okay. Don't get me wrong. You can show up midafternoon and launch a kiss attack on me like this any time you want. But it seems like something's different, and I'm worried about you." She furrowed her brow. "Should we talk?"

I scrunched up my nose. "If we talk, can we resume sexy times after?"

Her smile was tender and she nodded. "How about I make us something to eat, and you can tell me what's going on?"

Just like that, I felt safe. It was a surprising realization, and then I was surprised by my surprise. Which makes little sense, I know, but it was true. I'd never felt so protected with somebody before, and I wasn't really sure how that was possible, given the relatively short time I'd known Zoe.

My body nearly cried out when she got up, taking her heat away. I wanted the weight of her back on me, but I managed not to whine and stomp my feet like a toddler about it. Instead, I took a moment to take in my surroundings. I'd completely ignored her living space in favor of having my tongue in her mouth, and come on, who could blame me?

I stood up, straightened my clothes, and looked around. "This is adorable," I said. The location downtown told me it was an older house like mine. But the inside had clearly been renovated, and the entire first floor was open concept. A couple pillars stood where I imagined they'd taken down a load-bearing wall, but rather than be in the way, they added some character to the space. Zoe's kitchen was all white cabinets and dark countertops, and the whole of the first floor was painted in a gray that was both cool and warmly inviting.

"Thanks," Zoe said as she held up a bottle of wine, and I nodded. "From what I understand, it was a flip. I was worried about corner-cutting because I know that sometimes, flippers use cheaper materials and fixtures to make a bigger profit, but my inspector said it was nice, solid work. No issues so far." She approached me and handed me a glass of what looked to be a crisp white. "I put a pizza in the oven. I hope that's okay."

"It's perfect." I gestured to the gas fireplace with my chin. "I've got one of those."

"That was in the top three things I wanted in a house."

"Mine, too. I love sitting near it at night and reading."

"One of my favorite things to do."

Kindred spirits, we were. I held up my glass, and she touched hers to it, and when we sipped, our eye contact held solidly. I wanted nothing more than to sweep her off her feet and back to the couch for make-out session number two.

As if reading my mind, she blushed, her cheeks tinting a pale pink. Instead of the couch, she led me to her bistro table, and we sat.

"What's going on?" she asked. A sip of her wine and she set the glass down, folded her hands, and watched me, and honestly? I have never felt so…paid attention to. She made me feel like the most important person in the world just by looking at me and waiting for me to talk. I liked that feeling. I liked it a lot.

"I like you," I said. Seemed like as good a place as any to start.

"I like you, too." The way she tilted her head just then spoke volumes. She wanted me to be real with her. I could tell somehow.

"All right. Listen. I don't date often. I'm not great at…" I searched for the right words. "Expressing my interest, and it's not terribly common for me to be approached."

"I find that hard to believe."

Right then? I loved Zoe more than life itself.

"Well, trust me, I don't click with women often. For whatever reason. It's been a long time since that happened." I snorted a laugh. "A *long* time." She grinned, and that gave me a shot of confidence. "But you and me? We click."

"Damn right, we do." She covered her grin with the rim of her glass. Took a sip. "What about your brother? I don't want to cause any problems between you two." A shadow crossed her face. "Or between him and me, if I'm being truthful. You know?"

I nodded. I liked that she wasn't afraid to say that, to say, I really want to keep his business. It might have been a little icky, but it was reality, and I liked that she faced it head-on. "I get that. Totally." The timer for the pizza went off then, and I was grateful as I watched Zoe stick her hands in oven mitts. I was going to just come out with all the details, but it wasn't really my place to talk about my brother's private life, and—also?—it felt really weird to tell Zoe that Perry was already dating somebody else. I'm not sure why, but it did, and I decided to… not lie, but gloss over the truth a bit.

"Two?" Zoe asked, yanking my attention back to where she was pointing a pizza cutter at the pizza.

"Yes, please." I made myself useful and got up to refill our wineglasses. "We're day drinking on a workday," I pointed out.

"That's because we are rebels." Zoe slid plates onto the table, tipped my chin up toward her, and kissed me softly on the mouth. "Super sexy rebels."

"Extra super sexy ones."

"You were saying about your brother?" We sat down to eat, and once she'd blown on her pizza and taken a small test bite, she focused those eyes on me.

"We talked through things and worked it out. It's fine."

"It's fine? Just like that?"

"I mean, yeah. It's good." I took too big a bite and burned the roof of my mouth. I felt my eyes water as I did that thing where you try to pretend you're not in excruciating pain. A sip of my cool wine helped, but only a teeny bit.

Zoe gave one nod and took another bite of her pizza, and that was it. No more questions. She trusted me, clearly, and that made me feel all squishy inside.

The subject shifted to our jobs and we chatted about them and fun people we'd dealt with—names excluded, of course, as we had no intention of tromping all over patient privacy—as we finished our pizza. I stood up to clear the plates from the table.

"No, no. You're my guest. Sit."

"Listen, clearing the table has been my job since I was old enough to carry a plate. You would take that from me? My entire identity and sense of worth?" I feigned hurt and shock, which didn't stop Zoe from taking the plates from my hands.

"All I care about is that you're sexy and that you're going to kiss me some more. Identity and sense of worth mean nothing to me."

"You intend to use me for your physical pleasure, I see." I held my palms toward her, sighed loudly, and turned my head. "Fine."

Zoe grabbed my hand and led me back toward the couch where this loveliest and sexiest of visits had begun. We sat down, and she toyed with the collar of my shirt before whispering, "Oh, I intend to use you for *your* pleasure, too, don't you worry."

And then we were kissing again. I couldn't pinpoint a beginning or a middle or an end. It was kissing, plain and simple. Or actually, no, not so plain and simple. It was kissing, hot and wet and erotic, and my body was on fire. We stayed sitting for a long time, and we switched off taking the lead. But I was lost, in the best of ways. Nothing existed but Zoe's mouth. Her hands on my body. The little whimpers and ragged breaths. I hadn't come over to take her to bed. Or to have her take me to bed. But that's exactly where we were headed, and I think we both knew it.

I tried to file away everything I felt. Every sound. Every touch. Every softly whispered word, and there were a lot of them. Turned out Zoe was a bit of a talker when it came to make-out sessions, and she said things like, "You're so beautiful," and "I can't get enough of this mouth," and they filled me with a throbbing, sensual anticipation.

We finally came up for air, our foreheads pressed together as we tried to catch our breath. When Zoe sat up and brushed hair off my face, she asked, "Do you have any idea how beautiful you are? How sexy?"

I was already hot and flushed, but I felt things deepen then. I swallowed, licked my lips. "As long as you think so, that's all that matters."

"Seriously. Your eyes are the most amazing shade of green, and there's so much more depth of color when I'm close to you like this. Your smile is infectious, and your skin is silky, and your mouth feels exactly the way I imagined it would—soft and hot and wet and so damn sexy."

"You thought about my mouth?" I didn't mean to sound quite as shocked as I did, but I was.

Zoe sat back and focused on my face, and her eyes widened just a bit. "Oh my God, yes." Then she laughed and blushed as she admitted, "I've been having fantasies about you since the first day we met."

I blinked at her. Blinked again. "Seriously?"

"Yes, you weirdo." She pushed at me playfully, but something shot across her face, and I wondered if I'd hurt her feelings. It was time to fess up, at least to this part.

"Zoe. My God. I've done the same thing." What I thought might've been hurt vanished instantly, and she grinned. Goddamn those cheekbones. They were going to rule me, I just knew it, and I told her as much. "By the way, if you ever want anything at all from me, just smile, because those cheekbones of yours are the highlight of my day."

"Yeah?"

"Yeah, and they have been since that first day. So there. Feeling's mutual."

Something dark and sensual floated in and settled behind Zoe's eyes. She stood up and held out her hand. "I think it's time the highlight of your day featured more than cheekbones, don't you?"

Three p.m. on a Friday and I was being offered sex by the most attractive woman I'd ever known in my life. I was a lot of things. I could be petty and insecure. Impatient at times. Frustrated by things beyond my control. What I wasn't, though, was stupid. No, no, I was not a stupid woman.

I put my hand in Zoe's and let her lead me upstairs.

Just like with the living room and the rest of the downstairs, I noticed exactly zero about Zoe's bedroom. Normally, I'd look around, see what I could learn about her from the most intimate room in her house. I'd stroll slowly, pick up things and look at them, take in the colors and textures, get to know her a little better through her decorating.

Not then. Nope.

All I could focus on was Zoe. The warmth of her hand in mine, the way her yoga pants hugged her ass the way I wanted my hands to. The scent of strawberries that drifted off her as I followed. I remembered the stairs were hardwood, as was the upstairs hallway, and her bedroom was large, roomy, and bright with sunshine—which was odd given where we were headed. Not only had I been day drinking, I was about to be day sexing. I couldn't remember the last time I'd been with someone *not* in the dark. My nerves kicked up a notch or seven.

Zoe turned to me, took my face in both her hands, and kissed me, and every last worry I had melted away. What was it about her touch? Her mouth on mine? There was a tenderness that was firm, a giving that was demanding. She was a sexual dichotomy, and I was completely, utterly there for it.

I forced my focus from insecurity about myself to simply reveling in Zoe. I wanted so much to see her, to bare her body and feast on her with my eyes, my hands, my mouth. I shoved everything but her out of my head.

I pulled back from her long enough to whisper, "Take your hair down? Please?"

"Only because you asked so nicely." She lifted her arms above her head, and that view alone—her standing there, arms up, unfastening her hair for me—cranked my arousal up so high I thought the top of my head might burst into flames. And then it happened. Her hair came tumbling down in a dark wave of gorgeousness, and I practically dove at her, dug my fingers into it.

"God, do you know how long I've wanted my hands in your hair?"

"As long as I have?" was her perfect response.

We stood there next to her bed, kissing, for what felt like hours, and I could've done it endlessly, but my body wanted more of her. I wanted to touch more than her hair, kiss more than her mouth. I grasped the hem of her shirt and slowly pulled it up and over her head. Her bra was white, simple and elegant, perfect for her. I ran my hands down her sides, held her waist, just took her in. I could feel her eyes on me, watching me watch her. She gave me a moment longer and then reached for my shirt.

A very brief flash of panic shot through me. I hadn't dressed that morning with the intention or idea or prediction that I'd be having sex with the most beautiful woman I'd ever seen that day, and I hoped I'd worn a decent bra and underwear. I couldn't remember—my mind was empty of everything but her.

"God, you're beautiful." When she said it, her eyes hooded, darkened with a hunger that I instantly recognized, and it sent a surge of desire through me that was so strong, I felt my knees go weak. Zoe didn't wait for a response. She cupped my breasts with both hands and kneaded them, watching my face as she did.

I felt myself flush. So Zoe was going to be that kind of lover, the kind that watched her partner's face. The last person I had been with preferred the lights off and seemed to focus on *the act* rather than on the individuals involved, and while I can admit that I did feel less self-conscious in the dark, there was something so sexy and erotic and *important* about feeling like Zoe was right there with me. Not only that she saw me, but that she *liked* what she saw. As a person with insecurities about my looks, that was huge for me, and I embraced it, embraced her, and I was *there*. I was *in*. All in.

I kissed her. Hard.

She made a sound that was a combination moan-whimper that sent a surge of arousal due south, and my underwear paid the price. I made quick work of the clasp to her bra, and then she was topless and oh my God. Her tousled hair cascading over her bare shoulders, her creamy skin, her bare breasts that were larger than I expected and indescribably sexy...I couldn't stop myself. I bent forward and peeled her leggings off. She stepped out of them and stood before me, and I swore to God I was looking at not just a piece of art, but a masterpiece.

"You are stunning," I said, a soft, reverent whisper as my eyes roamed her body. She never squirmed or shifted, never seemed at all uncomfortable. Rather, she was confident and patient and let me simply take her all in, every inch, every dip and curve.

"Thank you," she said. "I love that you think so."

"Well, I have eyes."

Her smile grew, and that was enough looking for me. I stepped toward her, but she held up a finger. "Oh no. Not until it's a level playing field." Then she swept her finger up and down in front of me.

Something about her assertiveness sent even more arousal pumping through me, and I held her gaze as I removed the rest of my clothes, and that was another amazing thing about being with Zoe: the eye contact. Not my strong suit by a long shot, but with her? It was easy. Comfortable. I could look into those eyes all day long, and even though it felt like she could see right into my soul, I had no desire to look away. Again, I felt safe. The second time I'd thought about that with her.

"So," she said as I stepped out of my underwear and stood up, our two naked forms face to face. "This taking our time has been lovely, but I've had enough of the waiting." With that, she spun me so I fell backward onto her bed—which smelled like her, God help me—and followed me there. My legs opened automatically to make room for her, and I was amused by that, by my body taking things over from my brain. Too much thinking, not enough acting, clearly.

Zoe settled her center on my thigh, and I gasped at the hot wet of her. "That's what you do to me," she said, then kissed me with a passion that I felt from the top of my scalp to the tips of my toes and everywhere in between.

Much as I wanted to savor every individual moment, every single second of being with her, things began to blur into one big event of erotic sensation. Her hands were everywhere. Her mouth was everywhere. My body was on fire, and I know I grasped at her. My fingers dug into her hair, her shoulders, her back. My mouth couldn't get enough of her skin, her nipples, her lips. We rolled more than once, battling for control, for the top, sometimes laughing, sometimes gasping. But Zoe was taller than me and stronger than me, and she won more often than not. At one point, when I was trying to reach between her legs, she grabbed both my wrists and pulled them above my head, pressed them into the pillow, and gave them an extra push. Her eyes had gone so black, her pupils dilated with arousal, and she looked down at me and said, very quietly, "You're distracting me from my mission. Don't make me tie you to the bed." And then she kissed down my body as I lay there, my insides completely liquified.

She owned me.

On her knees between my thighs, she pushed my legs wide apart, gave me another one of those smoldering looks that were going to be the death of me, and bent to my center. My very hot, *very* wet, majorly throbbing center.

The rest is a blur.

I don't know what she did or for how long. I only remember that when my orgasm rocketed through me like a freight train, I was pretty sure I'd died. In the best of ways. Didn't the French call the orgasm the little death? They were right. That was exactly it. I'd died for a minute. Checked out. Moved on to the next plane, which involved lots of bursting colors and pleasure sizzling through my body like electricity. I never wanted to come back. Ever.

Time passed. I think. All I know is that when I opened my eyes, Zoe was on her side next to me, propped up on her elbow and looking down at me with such a gleam of satisfaction in her eyes that you'd have thought she was the one who just came super hard.

"You're vocal," she said, one dark brow arched in what I could only describe as amusement.

Super hard and very loudly, apparently.

I winced and covered my eyes with a hand. "I'm really not, though."

"Oh, I beg to differ."

"I'm sorry."

"What? Sorry for what? Why? Do *not* be sorry. That was incredible and I love that you let me know how I was doing." She bent toward my face, kissed me lightly. "I loved every single sound." Another kiss. "I bet my neighbors did, too."

I gasped in horror. "Stop that!" Smacked at her playfully.

"I'm kidding. You weren't that loud at all. Let me put it this way—you gave good directions."

"And you took them well."

A beat passed. "You're so sexy."

That was something I knew I'd never tire of hearing, but I didn't say that out loud. Not yet. "Just let me lie here for a minute until my body decides to work again. And then you'd better gear up."

"Is that a threat?" she asked, her eyes sparkling, her cheekbones sharpening as she grinned.

"Oh, it's a promise."

CHAPTER SEVENTEEN

My phone said it was after two in the morning. I had never had so much sex in my entire life, and still, I wanted more. I lay there in Zoe's bed, listening to her deep and even breathing, and all I wanted to do was wake her up.

I wasn't the least bit tired. In fact, I was wired. We'd had sex until dark, ordered a pizza from Vinnie G's, and brought it up to the bedroom with us. Its leftovers were on Zoe's dresser across the room because we were too busy having more sex to actually walk it down the stairs and into the kitchen. We'd finished the bottle of wine, and I had also guzzled a couple glasses of water, as dehydration was an issue, what with all the fluids I was losing.

I'd thought about going home. Ross and Rachel had plenty of dry food in their dishes. They would survive an evening without their usual wet, though they'd make their irritation known when I did finally return home. But I just couldn't make myself leave Zoe. It's like I thought if I left and went home, the next time I saw her, the whole afternoon and evening and night would turn out to have been one big sexy dream, and we'd be back to simply pharmaceutical rep and doctor's office admin, smiling at each other and sharing doughnuts.

I never wanted us to go back to that again.

I didn't care what Perry thought. And I didn't even feel bad about it. Not then. All I wanted was Zoe.

I turned to look at her in the moonlight, and she couldn't have been sexier if a movie director had positioned her. She was on her stomach, arms up under the pillow, all her dark hair fanned out around her head. She was still naked—frankly, I never wanted her to put clothes on again, but I was pretty sure I'd lose that argument—the sheet covering just her ass. Her back was bare, that large expanse of skin turning me on all over again. One leg was bent, so her legs made a number four, and as I stared at her, my heart rate picked up, my mouth filled in anticipation, and I knew I was wet again. See what I mean about the dehydration? There was no way I wasn't going to touch her. I reached out, ran my fingers across her back, and when she didn't move, I scratched lightly. That got her attention—I could tell by the shift in her breathing. I scooched closer to her, ran my hand down her back and under the sheet, over her shapely ass, stopped briefly to squeeze it, then slipped my fingers between her legs. Just like me, she was wet, and when I glanced at her face, her eyes were open and fixed on me.

"I'm sorry," I said, not really sorry at all. "I just couldn't help myself. You're so fucking gorgeous." And before she could say anything at all, I slid my fingers inside. She was hot and wet and slick, and her small gasp sent a shot of arousal right to my center. She shifted her legs to give me better access, lifted her ass slightly, and I took the invitation, pressed in more deeply, stroked her slowly, but with a firmness borne of a newfound confidence. I knew her body already. Hell, I'd spent the last nearly twelve hours studying it. Mapping it with my fingers, my tongue. I knew how to make her squirm, how to make her shiver, how to make her softly beg me to give her release. I was aware of how corny it sounded, how unrealistic it would seem to anybody looking in from the outside, but I *knew* her body already.

Zoe picked up my rhythm, rocking her body with each stroke of my fingers. And when she pushed herself up on all fours, I raised myself up to my knees and took the opportunity to palm her breasts, first one, then the other, zeroing in on a nipple, rolling it between my finger and thumb the way I'd learned sent little shocks of pleasure to her center. No gasping this time. A small whimper, then a moan that came from deep in her throat. Another thing I'd learned in my hours of study: that moan signaled her orgasm was imminent, and I increased my efforts, listening to every sound she made, feeling every shift of her body. I watched her hands clutch the pillow in her fists as she dropped her head and then leaned back into my hand.

While Zoe was much quieter than I was, she was physically more expressive when she came. Her back arched. She threw her head back. She clamped her legs together, imprisoning my hand until she decided to set it free. And she let go of a long, deep moan. It wasn't loud at all, but it was so fucking sexy it sent a surge of wetness to my center every single time. I'd counted. This was the fifth time, and as with one, two, three, and four, I was soaked. *My reward for a job well done*, I thought, which made me grin.

Zoe collapsed back down to her stomach, and when I lay back down next to her, she scooted over so she was lying half on me. "What are you smiling at?" she asked me, her voice husky.

"You. I could do that to you every minute of the day."

"Not sure I'd survive."

"I'd give you plenty of food and water between orgasms."

"You have it all planned out, I see."

"I am nothing if not pragmatic."

Zoe tucked her head under my chin. A beat passed, and I felt her body slowly relaxing, muscles easing, a twitch here and there that told me she was well on her way back to sleep. Her whisper surprised me. "You're amazing in bed, you know. You're gonna be the death of me."

I kissed her forehead and tried not to be too obviously giddy. I wanted to get up and do a little football dance around the room, be silly, give myself a trophy, and make an acceptance speech. Instead, I pulled her close, gave her another forehead kiss, and whispered to her, "No way. I want you around for a long, long time."

She snuggled in as I pulled the sheets up over us and let sleep finally take me.

"You know what I appreciate about you?" Zoe asked as she popped a K-Cup of hazelnut coffee into her Keurig for me.

"My sexual prowess?" I shoveled a forkful of scrambled eggs into my mouth and shot her a goofy grin.

"Well, duh. Goes without saying. I'm sore in places I didn't know could be sore."

I wrinkled my nose. "Sorry about that."

"*No.*" She said it firmly and held up a hand to punctuate that. "Do *not* apologize. I love it." She made sure I was looking right at her before she repeated herself with emphasis. "*I love it.* That kind of soreness just reminds me of how incredible the night before was. Does that make sense?"

It absolutely did because I felt it, too, so I nodded. My inner thighs felt like I'd done a million and three leg lifts. My nipples were sensitive to the touch that morning from all the attention—even my borrowed T-shirt against them sent sizzles through my body. My lips were slightly chapped, and I had been sucking down water since we got up. All signs of a night of fabulous sex.

"What I love about you is your realness."

"My realness?" I took the coffee she slid toward me.

"You're so genuine." She popped another K-Cup in, this one tea, and set it to brew. "You're just you. No pretense. No lies. That I know of," she added with a grin and a wink. "I know there's so much more for me to learn about you, but I really appreciate starting off on even ground. I haven't had that in a long time." A shadow crossed her features then, but she shook it away and focused on doctoring her tea.

That shadow was infinitely safer than discussing even ground because we weren't exactly on it, and I knew that. But the way her eyes had darkened made me slide into protection mode—someplace I realized I was going to visit often when it came to Zoe—and I decided my stuff could wait while I got to know more about her.

"Tell me about your last relationship," I said as she sat across from me at her kitchen table. I finished my eggs and chewed while she seemed to look for the right starting point.

A sip of tea as she gazed off into the distance. I could almost see her memories floating in the room like little clouds of vapor, waiting to be chosen. "I was seeing a woman, Annie, for a little more than two years. I met her online, and I realize now that I overlooked a lot of things that I shouldn't have. But she was pretty and successful and sane—three things you don't often find together when you're online dating." She raised her eyebrows and I laughed softly. "We got along great, had a lot in common, were both very driven by our jobs. She was in time management and traveled a lot to different companies in different states to give presentations on how they could improve productivity. We never lived together, which was probably a good thing, because my mom got sick just after our first year together. It wasn't long after that when I started to feel Annie kind of...drift."

"While your mom was sick?"

Zoe nodded sadly, sipped her tea, and she looked so incredibly beautiful right then that I felt my breath hitch in my throat. A ray of sunlight caressed her dark, tousled hair, and her eyes held such vulnerability I wanted to wrap her in a hug and never let anything harm her ever again, be her own personal Bubble Wrap. Not something she needed, I knew, but it surged through me with such force I'll never forget it. "About eight months in, we knew she wasn't going to make it and had to figure things out. Get her affairs in order, as they say. I think Annie visited her three or four times, but she just slowly kind of faded away. When I did call her on it, she said I hadn't been very emotionally available, and maybe we should just move on."

"*Your mom was sick*," I said, this time with more emphasis, my voice laced with disbelief. "Of course you were emotionally unavailable for her. Your emotions were elsewhere. *With your sick mom*. Who was *dying*." I shook my head, disgusted. "Jesus. Sounds like you were definitely better off without her."

"I definitely was. I see that now. But at the time, it was just so hard to realize that this person I thought I knew wasn't at all the person I thought she was. It was like I'd been catfished or something. Hi, I'm Annie, I'm solid, I get you. Oh, wait, you need me to be there for you so you can fall apart? Yeah, no. Sorry. Bye. A slight exaggeration, but that was how it felt at the time. She wasn't at all who I thought she was."

"I'm so sorry you had to go through that, Zoe. Both the Annie thing and your mom's illness. I can't imagine how alone you must have felt." And my eyes welled up right then because I really could not imagine how lonely she must've been, nursing her dying mother—the only family she had—while her girlfriend decided sticking around and being supportive was too much effort.

"There you go again, tearing up for me." She smiled at me so tenderly that my eyes welled further, and a few tears escaped.

I shrugged, wiped them away, a little bit embarrassed. "I'm a sap."

"You're not. You feel things. Deeply. I'm learning it's one of your best qualities." She sipped her tea, her eyes on me the whole time.

"Sometimes, I wish I didn't feel things as deeply as I do. It would save me some embarrassment."

"There are not enough people in the world who feel empathy for others. Be grateful you do. It's very much needed."

And just like that, any shame over my habit of crying at the drop of a hat vanished. Zoe had some powers. I was beginning to see that.

"What about you?" she asked then, as she stood and collected our dishes, silently waving me back to my seat when I made a move to get up and help. "Last girlfriend? No, wait. Last relationship. I shouldn't assume."

"Girlfriend," I said. "I was with Kendra right out of college. That had its challenges, and when she got offered a job in Atlanta, she took it, and that was that. Then I met Mandy about a year later, and we were together for almost three years until her ex came back and swept her off her feet. Again."

"Ouch."

I shrugged. "I took it as a sign. It sucked, but it made me accept that there had always been something about our relationship I couldn't pinpoint, but it never felt exactly right. You know what I mean? It sounds kind of silly now, but maybe I'm just not explaining it well."

"No, I get it." Zoe closed the dishwasher, then leaned back against the counter. "When it doesn't click, you can feel it."

"Exactly."

And then there was a moment when our gazes held, and it was just that: the two of us looking at each other. Softly, if that makes sense. Tenderly. Because us? *We* clicked. We definitely clicked.

Zoe inhaled and turned her gaze toward the window. "It's such a gorgeous morning. How do you feel about going for a walk?"

In that moment, I would do anything I could to have another minute—hell, another second—with her. "A walk sounds great. Can I borrow some clothes?"

❖

I was honestly not sure I'd ever just walked with a—what should I call Zoe? date? girlfriend? love interest?—before, but there was something crazy peaceful about doing it with Zoe. We simply strolled the neighborhood. No hurry. No specific destination. We didn't hold hands, but we walked close. Bumped shoulders every now and then.

"Do you know flowers?" she asked me as we passed a house with a lovely display of color in front.

"I do," I told her, then pointed to each as I said, "Those are yellow flowers, those are red flowers, and these over here are what's known as the elusive white flowers."

Zoe laughed. "So that's a no."

"Afraid so. My mom knows them, but I'm ashamed to say I zone out when she starts giving me specifics."

"Rude."

"What about you?" I asked, curious. I mean, I wanted to know every single thing about her, and if flowers were the next subject, I was in. At the next house, it was her turn to point.

"Geraniums." She indicated some full, red potted flowers on the steps, then turned her attention across the street. "Hydrangea bush. Needs pruning." We continued to walk, and for the next several houses, she listed flowers. "Tulips. Pansies. Petunias. Impatiens. More geraniums."

"You know, you could just be making things up. I'd never know."

"That's true. I could be. I'm not, but I could be."

We walked out of the residential neighborhood area and toward Jefferson Square where it seemed like lots of other folks had the same idea about a Saturday morning walk. People strolled Jefferson Avenue, sat at outdoor dining tables, walked their dogs. Zoe and I stopped to pet as many as we could, and it was another thing I realized I loved about her—she loved animals as much as I did.

"Would you ever get a dog?" I asked her as we reluctantly said good-bye to the cutest corgi puppy I'd ever seen.

"Oh my God, yes. Absolutely."

"Yeah? What kind?"

"Gah, that's a hard one." She dropped her head back and seemed to examine the sky as we strolled. "I mean, who doesn't love a big, dopey Lab or golden retriever? A dog you can lie on the floor with and play Frisbee with and let your kids crawl all over without worrying?" My heart did a little hop-skip at the mention of kids, but I wisely kept my mouth shut. Discussing future dogs was one thing, but kids was a whole different door to open. I left it shut for the time being and let her continue. "But I would also love something I could swoop up in my arms. Something fun size. Like a terrier or a poodle." She jerked a thumb over her shoulder. "Or that corgi that I wanted to stuff under my shirt and run away with."

A laugh bubbled up from my chest. "I wanted to, too!"

"That settles it. We'll get a corgi."

We both felt the weight of the words, I think, because we both got quiet for a bit. The weirdest part was that it wasn't fear. It wasn't that she said what she said and freaked me out. In fact, for me, it was the opposite. It felt like, of course, we'll get a corgi. Like, foregone conclusion kind of stuff. Normal. Regular. The next logical step because the idea that we'd be together in the future was already planted firmly in my brain. I wondered if Zoe felt the same way but, again, thought maybe I should just let it lie for the moment. When I did brave a glance at her, she had her head up, seemed to be taking in the hustle and bustle around us, and had a big, beautiful smile on her face. The last thing in the world she looked was freaked out or frightened in any way. She turned then, and those sparkling eyes met mine, and she bumped me gently.

"You have plans for the rest of the day?" she asked.

I wanted more than anything to say no, to tell her I wanted nothing else but to stay right next to her all day, take her back to her house, undress her, have my way with her body for an entire Saturday. Instead, I sighed in defeat. "I promised my mother I'd have lunch with her and then take her shopping."

"That sounds like fun. I've got some work I need to deal with since I knocked off early yesterday."

"For what it's worth, I'd much rather spend the day with you." After the things we'd talked about and the thoughts that had parked themselves in my brain during our walk, I didn't feel at all like I shouldn't have said it. It felt right. Besides, it was true.

"It's worth a lot." She ran her hand down my arm to my hand, linked our fingers, and pressed a kiss to my temple as we turned a corner and headed back toward her house. "What about tonight?" she asked.

"I should be done with my mom by late afternoon. I'll tell her I have dinner plans because I'd really like to take you out. On a date." I grinned at her. "We did this kinda backward, you know."

"We really did, didn't we?" She wrinkled her nose. "Dinner usually comes first."

"And we come second."

"I see what you did there. Clever."

"I can be." I lifted her hand to my lips and kissed her knuckles. "How about I pick you up around seven? We will have a proper date."

Zoe nodded, and I felt as much as saw her eyes roam over me. "And then I'll rip your clothes off, and we'll do things in the right order."

I swallowed. Nodded. Took a moment to collect myself. When I felt like I could speak rather than croak, I asked, "Can I use your shower when we get back?"

"Of course." We were back on her street already. "I mean, I should probably help you, you know? Taking off your clothes. Washing your back. Stuff like that."

"I could definitely use some help." I mean, seriously, who was I to argue?

Laughter burst out of us both as we realized we'd picked up our pace.

CHAPTER EIGHTEEN

I love spending time with my mom. When it's just us? I love it. Growing up, I did have her to myself a lot, it's true. Perry being ten years older than me meant he had his own life and friends and sports and such, and while he always looked out for me, his schedule made it difficult for us to do things as a family. More often than not, it was my dad taking teenage Perry and Carter to their games or to practice while Mom took me to things like ballet, which I had no business even attempting, or gymnastics—I cannot be trusted with a pit of foam pieces because I never want to get out—or just shopping with her. It became our thing. Lunch and shopping. We did it together at least once a month, if not more often, and it was time alone with my mother that I treasured.

We had eaten our lunch and were wandering the mall that day. Some days, we'd wander around Jefferson Square, visit Stefan at his shop and say hi, pop in and out of little stores. Other days, it was the mall, and that day was a mall day. We were in Bath & Body Works when my mom finally brought up what I suspected she'd been dying to talk about all day.

"I talked to your brother last night," she said, not looking at me as she picked up tester bottles, smelled them, then set them back down.

"Oh? And how is Carter? I feel like I haven't seen him in ages." Yes, I was being purposely obtuse. I didn't care.

"I mean Perry." She arched an eyebrow at me.

"What, you didn't want to launch right in at the restaurant, so you saved this for later?" I shot her a grin so she'd know I was teasing her. Kind of.

"He says you're seeing that Zoe."

I bristled because hearing her referred to as *that Zoe* just rubbed me the wrong way. "And he's seeing somebody new."

"He said that was just a date. Nothing serious."

"And that means…what?" I was trying hard not to take offense, not to let that simmering of my blood bubble into a boil. I rubbed something that smelled not unlike fabric softener into my hands just to give myself a few seconds. "That as long as he's not dating somebody seriously, he still gets to hold on to Zoe? They didn't even date, Mom. Nothing was ever going to happen between them because Zoe is *gay*." I purposely didn't lower my voice because, while my parents were perfectly accepting of my sexuality, my mother still lowered her voice whenever she used the word gay. I'd decided she wasn't even aware she did it most of the time. This time, she did take a quick look around as if to see if anybody'd heard. But when she met my eyes, there was some shame there. As there should have been.

"Isn't there a rule, though? Like, no dating your siblings' exes or something?"

I blinked in disbelief. "You can't be serious right now." And then the boiling *did* start to happen.

"I'm just saying." She shrugged. Actually shrugged, like it was no big deal, like she didn't see the ridiculousness of the situation.

And that did it. I blew.

"Why are Perry's hurt feelings so much more important than me finding somebody I really like? I'm not a horrible sister, and if he'd actually *dated her*, I would never in a million years think of seeing her. But he did not date her. They had one date, which was lunch, so barely even a real date. They played in a golf tournament together because *he needed another female on his team*." I kept my voice steady and at a normal volume, and I was proud of myself because it took massive effort to achieve that—I was so mad. "They never touched. They never kissed. They were not an item. I don't understand how that qualifies her as anything even remotely close to being an ex of his. And also? When's the last time you saw me happy with another person?"

My question surprised my mom, I think, because she stopped pretending to shop and actually looked at me then. Truly looked. In the eye. She glanced down. Glanced back up. Cleared her throat. "It's been a while," she said quietly.

"That's right. It's been a *long* while. And Zoe?" I shrugged. "I mean, we're not anything other than just kind of seeing each other." No way was I going to tell her that we'd already slept together. It wouldn't help my argument at all. No, I'd keep that little tidbit to myself for now. "But I'm happy when I'm with her. She's smart and kind and beautiful, and she makes me laugh. I don't know about you, but I think it's about time for me."

She nodded, and I knew she agreed, but I could also see her worrying about her middle son. As usual.

"Perry will be just fine, Ma."

Her nod became a little more determined. "He will. I know." Testers were sniffed once again. We were headed back toward normal. Slowly, but on our way. "Maybe if…" Her hesitation seemed like she was looking for the right phrasing. "If things continue to move forward with her, you can bring her over for dinner. So we can get to know her."

I could feel the grin spreading across my face, but I caught it before it became too wide. I didn't want her to think she was automatically off the hook for dismissing my happiness in favor of my brother's bruised ego. "I'd like that," I said simply and left it at that.

If things continue to move forward with her…

Things were already way farther along than I'd ever expected or predicted or dreamed about. I was trying hard to guard my heart, to slow down my pacing, though I probably should have been trying harder. Especially after we'd talked that morning about doing things backward. Taking a breath seemed to be a smart move. The question was, could I actually do it? Could I actually slow down? Take that breath? Get my bearings? Because all that sounded a lot less awesome than simply being with Zoe.

Slow things down?

My brain pushed on the gas pedal instead.

❖

I had never been to dinner at Blu, but I'd heard nothing but raves about it from friends, patients, and relatives alike. It was upscale—or as upscale as things got in a casual, laidback city like Northwood—and because of all those recommendations, added to the overwhelmingly rave reviews on Yelp, I decided that's where I was taking Zoe for dinner. It would cost a pretty penny, I knew, but I didn't care. My date would be worth it.

The second she opened the door when I picked her up, I knew I was right.

Her dress was simple. Black. Knee-length. Capped sleeves. And a V that dipped not far enough to be scandalous, but far enough to tease me, and I knew my eyes would be roaming to that spot directly between her breasts all night. I was totally okay with that, and I hoped she was, too. Strappy black heels, a silver bracelet. All that gorgeous dark hair was pulled gently back and gathered at the nape of her neck. My eyes fell on the necklace I'd noticed before, the one with the two ruby stones.

"Okay, first of all?" I let my eyes comically bug out as wide as possible. "Oh my God, you look scorchingly hot. Like, people are going to be so jealous of me. Somebody will probably try to take me out as we walk through the restaurant. Steal my date. Be prepared." Zoe's gentle blush did nothing but make her even prettier. "Second, this is so pretty," I said, touching the tip of my finger to the necklace. "I've noticed it a couple times."

"Thanks. My mom and I were both born in January, so that's our birthstone. Garnet. We each had a necklace. When she died, I took the stone charm from hers and put it on mine, so she's always with me."

"I love that." I held my arm out like a guy in a forties movie, and Zoe tucked her arm in my elbow. "Shall we?"

"You know," she said, as we walked to my car, "you're one to talk. Did you manage to look in the mirror before you left your place?"

I shook my head as I opened her door for her. "Nope. No mirrors at my place. Don't believe in 'em."

"I would say that's a lie, but since I've never been to your house…" The way she let the sentence dangle said a lot more than the actual words did.

"Play your cards right, and that'll change," I said and shut the door. I could feel her eyes on me as I rounded the front of my car and climbed into the driver's seat.

As I reached for the ignition, Zoe placed her hand on mine. "Seriously, though. You look amazing. I think I'm the one who's going to get her date stolen."

She leaned toward me, pressed her lips to mine, and I completely forgot my name. Where I was. What day it was. I opened my mouth more, deepened the kiss, and felt her hand come up to the side of my face, fingers digging into the back of my neck. When tongues started dancing, I wrenched away. Breathless. Flushed. Sure she could see by my expression and my wide eyes that it shocked me how quickly she could ratchet me up, stoke that internal fire, until I felt like I was about to ignite into flames.

"God," I said and forced myself to lean back into my seat, away from those lips of hers. Our gazes held for a beat before I laughed and pointed at her. "No. We have to have dinner first. Like civilized people, not sex fiends."

"You know, I don't think you should be knocking sex fiends. They seem to have their priorities pretty straight. So to speak."

I held up my hand as she leaned toward me again. "Stay back, temptress," I said as I started the car.

Zoe laughed that musical, gorgeous laugh of hers and placed her hand on my thigh as I drove. Nope. Not distracting at all.

"Wow," Zoe said softly a few minutes later as we walked into the restaurant. "This is beautiful."

She wasn't wrong. Blu was hopping and just as gorgeous as its Instagram page would have you believe. Dimly lit, like all good fancy restaurants, the entire place was cast in an inviting ethereal blue, because of course it was. The entire dining area was open, with a long, elegant bar along the left wall. Lines of blue light ran under its edge and along all the shelves behind the two bartenders, shining through the clear glass and giving a really cool vibe to the whole place.

Surprisingly, the openness didn't equate to noisy. Maybe because everybody was dressed up, many having intimate two-person dinners, and conversation was at a lower volume? I wasn't sure, but it only made it feel even more inviting.

I gave my name to the hostess, and she showed us to a small round table for two, which could not have been more perfect if I'd chosen it myself. A staff member pulled our chairs out for us and slid them in as we sat. Then he folded our napkins into our laps, filled our water glasses, told us to enjoy our dinners, and was gone.

Zoe leaned an elbow on the table and propped her chin in her hand. All the blue lighting in the restaurant only made her eyes that much bluer. "Well. You do not mess around when it comes to taking a girl to dinner."

"I do not." I held her gaze and everything south of my stomach tightened up deliciously. Getting through dinner was not going to be easy.

Zoe was having the exact same thought—I could tell by the way her eyes darkened—and she wet her lips with just the tip of her tongue. I groaned. She laughed.

I'm pretty sure the wine was terrific and our dinners were fabulous, but I honestly only remember trying to get through it without lunging over the table and ripping her clothes off. It was not an easy feat. Holy sexual tension, Batman.

"I want to know more about you," Zoe said after we'd placed our orders and had wine. She held her glass cradled in the palm of her hand as she sat back, and the view from my side of the table was beyond sexy. How? How did she just sit there with a glass of wine and say something simple and turn me into a puddle of goo right there in my chair? I couldn't figure it out, but I loved every second of it.

"Yeah? Like what?" I propped my elbows on the table and leaned toward her. You know how they say a room just fell away? Or all the sound faded? I always thought that was complete romance novel bullshit until that night because that's exactly what happened. The rest of the restaurant just…muted. Dimmed. Muffled. The hum of conversation lowered, the lights seemed to shift so they were only trained on our table, and there was no one else but us.

So weird.

And also, so amazingly *good*.

"I'm actually trying to figure out why your last girlfriend let you go."

My initial thought after that was one of warmth because it was a nice thing to say, let's be honest. Until you replayed it in your head a second time and it sounded more like, *I'm trying to figure out what's wrong with you.* I grabbed my glass, took a big sip.

"She was obviously an idiot." Zoe smiled, her eyes crinkled and darkened, and I felt better. So much better that I blurted before I thought.

"I'm a little insecure."

Zoe's brows rose, but the smile stayed as she lifted one shoulder and asked, "Who isn't?"

"You're not."

A snort of a laugh. "Please. Of course I am."

"Seriously? What do you have to be insecure about?"

"What do *you* have to be insecure about?" There was a fire of challenge in her blue eyes as she leaned forward to match my stance, and then we were both tipped toward the center of our little table, staring in each other's eyes like an ad for two prizefighters who were facing off on pay-per-view on Friday night.

A beat passed. Another. And then we both burst out laughing and sat back in our chairs.

"I think you get me," I said and was surprised when the words left my lips.

Zoe must've noticed my expression. "That's a good thing, though, right?"

I nodded as the waiter arrived with our meals, and I waited until he'd left before I added, "It's a very good thing. I'm not sure somebody has before."

"Oh, the pressure..." Zoe made a face where she clenched her teeth and grimaced. Then she grinned widely and said, "I'm kidding. There's nothing I like more than that."

"Than getting me?"

"In every way possible." And her eyes went dark again. And my underwear got wet again.

We ate, but like I said, I don't remember much. What I can remember with startling accuracy is how gorgeously sexy Zoe was sitting across the table from me doing something as simple as raising a fork to her lips or sipping from her wineglass, and how incredibly lucky I felt to be there with her.

"What were you like in school?" I asked, as I tried to picture six-year-old Zoe on the playground.

"Me? Hmm." She tipped her head in an adorable display of thinking and seemed to search the restaurant for her answer. "I was outgoing. I had a lot of friends. I was probably a little on the bossy side." I laughed at that. "Perils of being an only child. You expect things to always be your way, and sharing is an entirely new concept."

"I wouldn't have a clue what that's like."

"No? Isn't Perry quite a bit older than you?"

"Ten years. But he liked having a little sister, so he often let me hang with him. He showed me off." I took a sip of my wine. "I do think if I'd been two years younger than him instead of ten, I'd be telling you a different story, though." I cut into whatever my dinner was—chicken?—and stabbed a piece. "Did you play any sports?"

"I was a cheerleader." She said it with no shame or embarrassment, and I loved that. But decided to tease her anyway.

"I mean, they can take your lesbian card away for that, can't they?"

"When they"—she made air quotes—"can toss a hundred-pound girl in the air and catch her on the way down without dropping her, they can, sure."

"I am so turned on right now." I arched an eyebrow at her. I wasn't lying.

"Good." She took a bite of her pasta something or other and never broke eye contact. "What about you? Tell me about teeny, tiny elementary school Morgan."

"I was not outgoing, and I did not have a lot of friends. Super shy. Very self-conscious. Probably part of the reason Perry was so protective."

"Aww, that makes me sad. Were you picked on?"

"No, not really. I was more…invisible." I gave a shrug and did my best to be nonchalant, even though it squeezed my heart to think about that version of me. "I took a longer time to find myself than most kids, I think. I did better by high school. Not popular by any means, but not as unseen as before. I got decent grades, played volleyball."

"Ooh, now I'm the one who's turned on." A wink.

"Good." This time I held the eye contact. I took one last bite of my dinner, set my fork down, and sat back with my wine. "You know, it's kind of fitting that I'd end up with a cheerleader. Lord knows I fantasized about them enough."

"I don't know. Do you think a volleyball player can keep up with a cheerleader? We're deceptively athletic."

"Maybe, but I have kneepads for a reason."

"Oh, my."

Yes, we shamelessly flirted to the point of being ridiculous, but it was fun and amazing and downright sexy, and I couldn't get her out of there fast enough. I paid our bill, and we headed out to the parking lot. Once inside the car, doors shut, we turned to each other and spoke at the same time.

"Come home with me," I said.

"Take me home with you," she said.

I stared at her for a beat with what I'm sure was a goofy grin on my face. "Buckle up."

CHAPTER NINETEEN

We barely made it through the door before we were pawing at each other, and I briefly wondered how long it would be like this. I knew sexual excitement wanes after a while, and I'd only been with Zoe a couple times, but in that moment right there in my entryway? Unable to wait and pulling her dress up and over her head just inside my door? It felt like I would always be this desperate to touch her, to bare her skin for my eyes and my hands. I had never felt such intense desire in my entire life, and I never wanted it to end.

That night, the sex was different. Once we were in bed and that frenzied tearing at each other's clothing was behind us, we slowed down. Everything. Our kissing. Our touching. Even our eye contact lingered, softened. We took our time. I listened to every sound Zoe made, every flinch or twitch or sigh went into the record of Zoe in my head, as if my brain was keeping a file on her. What she liked, what she didn't, what kind of pressure was good where. I went slow, cataloged all of it, even as I glowed with such arousal and joy. I would've been perfectly happy to stay right there, in my bed with Zoe's naked body pressed into mine, and never leave.

I wondered if she felt the same way at the time, because after she'd come—harder than the last time, I was sure—and turned the tables, she too seemed to take her time, to pay more attention, to touch me in different places in different ways to see what worked for me. Frankly, it all did, but the intensity of her eyes as she watched and studied was the sexiest part of all of it.

"I've never felt like this before, Morgan." She whispered it while I had my eyes closed, and I opened them to study her face. That intensity was still in her eyes, but the rest of her face had softened, relaxed, and then her eyes welled up.

My heart felt like she'd taken it in her fist and given it a gentle squeeze. In that exact moment, I knew I never wanted to be the cause of her tears. And if I saw them, I wanted to wrap her in my arms and hold her until they passed. In that exact moment, it was all I wanted in life, and I spoke honestly to her. "It's the same for me, Zoe. The exact same."

She grimaced. "Are you freaked?"

"Not even a little." I lifted my hand and brushed her hair behind her ear. "I feel safe. With you."

"Same."

And that seemed to be all we needed because she leaned down and kissed me, and we were right back on track. My orgasm tore through me a short time later, and I was pretty sure I left some scratches on her back. Sexy, throes-of-passion scratches. She didn't seem to mind.

Neither Kendra nor Mandy had been big cuddlers. I, on the other hand, am. I'm a huge cuddler. But I learned to get along without. I learned to sleep on my side of the bed, maybe reach out a foot or a hand for the warmth of contact, but it was always a little bit of a bummer. Zoe was a completely different animal. She slept all over me. I think she'd been cautious the first time we were together, reined it in a bit. Because this time, she was like ivy, entwined with and wound around me until I couldn't tell which legs were hers and which were mine. Where her arms ended and mine began.

And it was glorious.

I had honestly never been that happy sharing a bed with another person.

"Is this okay?" she asked as she got close. I could hear the hesitation in her voice and wanted to chop that away forever. I wrapped my arm around her and pulled her in tightly.

"It's better than okay. It's perfect."

She snuggled in.

I don't remember falling asleep, but I do know that I slept insanely hard.

❖

Apparently, Zoe was a morning person.

When I woke up and opened my eyes, I had zero time to recall anything about the night before because she was right there, propped on her elbow, smiling down at me.

"Were you watching me sleep?" I covered my eyes with my hand.

"I was."

"Such a rom-com thing to do." I uncovered my eyes, squinted at her. "Or a creepy serial killer thing to do. Are you plotting how to murder me?"

"Oh no. I've already done that. Just trying to decide how to dispose of your body." She peeled the sheet away to reveal my still naked self. "Though...yeah." She ran her fingertip from my throat down between my breasts and circled each one. "Forget it. It's too sexy for me to give it up. You're off the hook."

"Thank God."

She palmed my breast, then bent to take a nipple into her warm mouth.

We didn't get out of bed for a while.

I drifted off once we'd finished, and when I woke up the second time, Zoe's side of the bed was empty. I had a split second of wondering whether I had completely dreamed her before I heard the soft sound of dishes and knew she was in the kitchen. With no reason to stay in bed, I hauled myself up.

"Why is it so damn sexy to see a girl wearing your clothes?" Zoe turned and smiled at my question. She was dressed in a pair of red shorts and a white T-shirt, both of which I recognized as my own.

"I hope you don't mind," she said as she approached me. "I couldn't bring myself to get back into a dress and heels." She kissed me softly. "I made you some coffee."

"You did?" I didn't hide my surprise. "You don't like coffee."

"You do." She shrugged as if that was the most natural of answers. "I found some tea in your cupboard."

I went to the counter, poured myself some coffee, and brought the mug up under my nose so I could inhale deeply. That aroma alone conjured up mornings and comfort and anticipation of the day. I could just smell it and be ready for whatever lay ahead. Okay, no. Lies. I needed to drink it, too.

"Do you have a charger? My phone's almost dead."

I leaned the small of my back against the counter and gestured in the direction of the living room. "On the table by my chair there should be one." My eyes locked on her ass as she walked out of the kitchen. All on their own. Not my fault. I take zero responsibility for them objectifying her.

I inhaled, took in a huge breath, and let it out slowly. How had this happened? How was it that I woke up this morning and felt so completely content in the direction my life was suddenly going? How did it not feel even the slightest bit uncomfortable to have this gorgeous woman—a woman I had only known for a short time, if I was being realistic about things—making herself at home in my kitchen while wearing my clothes and making me coffee? How did I get here, and why wasn't I freaking the hell out? Well, I still was a little, but why wasn't I more?

Ross and Rachel had been surprisingly calm all morning. Shocking, considering how little attention they got the night before. Rachel looked up at me from her spot at my feet and blinked her big yellow eyes in something that translated as unimpressed, so I gathered their bowls, gave them breakfast, and sat on the floor with them while they ate their wet food. I stroked the soft silky back of each one, which always brought me peace, then headed back to my coffee.

"Hey, where'd you go?" I asked as I made my way toward the living room. "Did you get lost along the...?" I saw Zoe sitting in my chair, her tea in one hand, my notebook of poems on her lap and being held by the other. My heart began to hammer in my chest.

"Morgan, these are amazing." Her voice was quiet. Reverent. "Your words. They paint such a picture. It's breathtaking. Why didn't you tell me you wrote poetry? I had no idea." She turned the page, and her expression changed. Her brow furrowed and a shadow arrived, settling over her face like a veil, and I knew exactly what had happened. She'd started at the beginning, at the poems I'd written a while back. Poems for me. Now she'd reached the more recent ones.

She glanced up at me, her blue eyes slightly wide, the question clear on her face. Then back down to the notebook, turned a page, went even darker.

"Did...were you...did your brother not even write the stuff he sent me?"

I swallowed hard, but the lump of shame that had lodged in my throat wouldn't go down.

Another page. A shake of her head.

"You wrote all his poetry?" Her eyes weren't hard, but they were definitely not as soft and inviting as they had been just a few minutes ago.

I nodded. It was all I could do.

"Wow." She stood up. I got the impression she wanted to read more but snapped the notebook closed instead. "I should probably apologize for helping myself to your work, but it was lying open on the table and it caught my eye and..." She pinched the bridge of her nose. "He didn't write any of it?"

I shook my head. Apparently, my voice no longer worked.

"God, I felt *so* bad having to tell him the truth. It was *awful*. Here was this swell guy who was so obviously into me, sending me love poems and—" Her head snapped up. "Did you write the short little cute ones, too?"

Another nod. My stomach churned.

"Of course. And here I thought he'd poured his heart out to me, sent such intimate words, so it made it a hundred times worse when I had to turn him down."

I almost chimed in with how he *was* super into her in a way I'd never seen before. But then I remembered his date and his ego and his demand that I not see Zoe, and my desire to protect him in the midst of my own crisis evaporated before my eyes.

"Why wouldn't you tell me, Morgan? I don't understand. After all my talk about how real and genuine you are?" She snorted a sarcastic laugh then, and I felt it as though she'd slapped me. It hurt more than anything else she was saying. "And now I find out you're neither of those things."

Ouch.

I needed to answer her, to say something. I knew it. I just didn't know what. There really was no excuse for my not telling her right away. "I didn't know how to tell you." My voice was barely above a whisper.

"So you thought, what? I just won't tell her ever and maybe she'll never find out? Was that your plan? That you played Cyrano de Bergerac for your brother and I'd just never be told?"

Yeah, it kinda was. I looked down at my feet.

"Did you two compare notes?"

Ouch again. I shook my head.

"Jesus, Morgan. How do you expect to build any kind of relationship on a shaky foundation? On a lie from the beginning?" She crossed the floor, pushed the notebook at me, then went into the kitchen and left her tea on the counter. "I realize it's not a life-altering omission, but it still feels really icky to me. Especially after I told you about Annie and that the exact issue with her was that she ended up not being the person she let me believe she was. You've done exactly the same thing." She seemed to roll her words around in her head before letting them exit her mouth. "I mean, if you're willing to lie about something like this, what bigger things would you keep from me in the future?"

Direct hit, that one.

"I'm so sorry, Zoe. I should've told you." I was miserable. My eyes welled. I could feel the heat in my cheeks as she studied me. I could feel her eyes on me, but this was by no means the same feeling I got when she was mentally undressing me. This was like she could see right into my head. I wanted to slink away and hide in a corner somewhere. Like a child. Which I felt like at the moment because why, oh why didn't I just tell her from the beginning? "I'm so sorry."

"I believe that. I do. I believe that you're sorry. But…what I'm not sure of is whether you're sorry for doing it in the first place or sorry I found out." Silence reigned for what felt like a hundred years but was probably more like ten seconds. She pushed herself away from the counter. "I think I need some time. Maybe you do, too." She unplugged her phone from the charger and headed for the stairs.

"Time? Wait, what?" I wanted to run after her. I wanted to shout at her. *No! No, I don't need any time. Not ten minutes ago, I was thinking about how perfect we are, how amazing it is to be with you. I don't need any time.* But maybe I did. Hell, I didn't even know. I felt blindsided. I was embarrassed. I was ashamed. I was angry—not at Zoe, but at Perry for going after her first. I was angry at myself for not standing up and beating him to it. And most of all, I was mad that I hadn't just fucking told her to begin with.

Of course, all of those feelings did nothing but keep my feet cemented to the floor as I watched Zoe come down the stairs only a minute or two later, back in her dress and heels. She stopped at the base and looked at me across the living room. So many things were clear on her face then. Hurt. Anger. Sadness. Betrayal. And something else that I couldn't even let myself think about.

"Please don't go," I managed to whisper, but I wasn't sure she heard me.

It seemed like she tried to give me a sad smile then. Or maybe it was just a sad grimace. Whichever, it didn't matter because she still left.

I stood there in my shorts and T-shirt, coffee in one hand, notebook in the other, feeling too many things to even sift through. She must've ordered herself an Uber because I heard a car slow, then a door slammed shut, and the car drove off. I didn't realize I was crying until I felt the first hot tear track down my cheek and my nose began to stuff up. If I hadn't been so sad, I might've found it amusing how quickly my world went from perfect to a mess in the space of about seventeen minutes. The Universe could be a cruel, cruel thing.

And then I groaned and shook my head because this had nothing to do with the Universe. This was me, plain and simple. I'd caused this mess. Not the Universe. Not Zoe. Not even Perry. Just me. I was solely responsible for Zoe walking right out my front door.

I didn't think I'd ever betrayed anybody before, but that's the thing on her face that had seemed the clearest. She felt betrayed by me.

How the hell do you come back from that?

Could you?

CHAPTER TWENTY

The days dragged by so slowly I wanted to scream. It was like a small child had been told to go to bed, and they walked as slowly as possible, dragging their teddy bear, their blanket, their feet. Except this Wednesday was also dragging August behind it. Everything that came with August also exemplified slowness. The heat. The humidity. I didn't do well with either one. Give me a crisp fall day or a lovely fifty degrees in late March, and I was a happy girl. August with its sweating and its bugs? Hard pass, thanks.

It didn't help that my mood was in the toilet. Had been since Sunday morning when Zoe unceremoniously left my house, and I hadn't been able to talk to her since. Well, aside from the one text she sent on Monday night, probably sick to death of my endless calls and texts and just wanting me to stop bothering her.

I'm still taking time...not sure it makes sense for us to continue if I feel like this.

Those words were like a punch in my gut. A hard one. The kind of punch that doubles you over and makes it feel like you'll never be able to get a full breath again.

Also? It made me angry. That was it? We were done? Yes, I'd kept something from her I shouldn't have. I knew that. I'd knowingly deceived her. I knew that, too. I'd admitted it and apologized a million times over for it. What else did she want? I felt terrible. I was not a person who lied—traditionally or by omission—on a regular basis. I desperately wanted a second chance, and it was not only hurtful, it was maddening that she seemed unwilling to give me one.

I sighed as I gazed out the front windows from my seat at my desk. It occurred to me that if Zoe and I had been together longer—a few months, a few years—maybe it would be easier for her to forgive and forget and let us move forward. But we'd literally been dating for a few weeks. We were still in the very early stages, so maybe she just thought it was easier to end things now.

A move I absolutely did *not* agree with, but there it was.

I mean, maybe I deserve better.

It was a thought that had crossed my mind more than once after I'd sent about a dozen and a half unanswered texts. Zoe had kind of bailed on me. Yes, I'd made a mistake, but it wasn't evil or underhanded.

I'd reminded her of her ex, that was all.

"Ugh." I dropped my head into my hands because I'd been going around and around like that for three days and my brain was fried.

"Headache?" Joanne asked from behind me. I didn't answer, and in the next minute, four small, orange ibuprofen pills were dropped on my desk in my line of sight.

I looked up at her gratefully. Joanne was the quintessential mother—she took care of everybody in the office, even the nurses and doctor. I swallowed the pills because what could it hurt? If I didn't have a headache, one was surely coming.

I managed to make it through my third workday of the week, which honestly felt like the twenty-third, and started wrapping up for the day.

"Morgan?" Perry's voice over the intercom made me jump in my seat. "You still here?"

I seriously considered ignoring him, letting him think I'd gone for the day, but I sighed and gave in. "Yeah."

"Can you come here for a second?"

"Yeah." More sighing. I was doing a lot of that lately, like every single thing in the world was just too big a burden for me. I gathered my bag and slung it over my shoulder, hoping to convey to Perry that I was on my way out. He was at his desk, his eyes on his monitor, but looked at me as I entered and immediately turned all his focus on me.

"Have a seat," he said, indicating a chair.

"I'm good." I stayed on my feet. "What's up?"

He squinted at me, and I tried not to squirm under his studious look. "You okay?" he asked, and there was real concern in his voice.

"Peachy."

He squinted again. Then he picked up a pen, set it down, picked it up again, cleared his throat. "Listen." He took a deep, audible breath and let it out slowly. "I was a dick."

I blinked in surprise. "I'm sorry?"

"Me. To you. I was a dick. I had no right to tell you who you can and cannot see. I was jealous and self-centered, and you deserve better from your big bro. I'm really sorry." As I continued to stare at him, he added, "And you seemed really happy, so that's a good thing. Except…not the past couple days." His sandy brows made a V above his nose, and I could feel his eyes on me even as I looked down at my shoes.

"Turns out, you don't have to worry about your dickishness because Zoe and I aren't seeing each other anymore." I looked up at him. "But I do appreciate the apology."

"What do you mean, you're not seeing each other anymore?"

I tipped my head slightly. "It's a pretty straightforward statement."

"I thought things were…" He shrugged. "It seemed like they were going well."

"Yeah, they were until she found out I wrote all the poems you sent her."

Perry clenched his teeth and winced. "Damn."

"Yeah."

"Did you tell her you had?"

A little finger of shame tickled the back of my neck. "After she found my notebook and asked me, I did." My turn to wince.

"Oh, Morgs."

"I know. But, I mean, what was I supposed to do? There wasn't really ever a time that seemed perfect to go, By the way, remember all those really great emotional poems my brother sent you? Yeah, I wrote 'em. Surprise!"

"I see your point. Still, seems like she could give you the benefit of the doubt."

It did seem like that, didn't it? If you didn't know about her past, and I wasn't going to share that with Perry. I dropped into the chair after all. Defeated. "I think I just have to let it go. I've texted. I've called. She's only responded once, and that was to tell me maybe it's better to just call it quits now. Maybe she's right."

Perry looked at me with sympathy.

I sat back in the chair and threw my hands up. "But it was so good. I don't understand why she can't focus on that part, you know? It was *so good*. We were fantastic together. In every way. I just…" I felt my eyes tear up, and I tried to blink them away. "I could see a future. For the first time. I could see a future with her."

Perry said nothing. Instead, he reached into his bottom desk drawer and pulled out two rocks glasses and a bottle of whiskey, then proceeded to pour us each a drink.

"Okay," I said, looking around the room for cameras and a set crew. "Am I on *Law & Order* or something? 'Cause I've only ever seen people do this on TV."

Perry grinned. "I have hard days sometimes." He handed me a glass and held his up. "To the Thompson siblings finding their matches. One of these fucking days."

"What happened to the Zimmerman chick?"

He shrugged, said something like, "Meh," and kept his glass up.

I touched it with mine, and we both drank, the whiskey burning its way down my throat. I wanted to agree with him. To laugh sarcastically at our terrible dating luck. To commiserate with him about the pros and cons of the single life. But I didn't do any of those things because I still truly believed I'd found my person. And lost her. In the space of about three months.

"Just say the word, and I'll never prescribe another drug from her company." His grin was wide, and I knew he was trying to cheer me up, to pull me out of my funk, and I appreciated it, but I didn't want that.

"No, don't do that. We are professionals, all three of us. It's fine. Business as usual, okay?"

"You got it."

The idea of Zoe walking into the office all cool and businesslike terrified me, but I decided I shouldn't worry about that until I had to. I put on a somewhat happy face for my brother because he was a guy and he was over the emotion and had moved on to a few work things he needed done that week, and just like that, it was exactly as I'd said.

Business as usual.

❖

My tendency to go all solitary, curl up in a ball, and lick my wounds was strong that weekend. I hadn't heard a thing from Zoe since her maybe we should just stop now text, and frankly, I had given up. I did have a shred of dignity, and the way Zoe had practically ghosted me stung. Badly. She should've treated me better than that, no matter what I'd done. So I did my best to chalk things up as dodged a bullet and got on with my life.

Of course, I didn't really believe I'd dodged a bullet. I believed I'd fucked up something that had been on its way to wonderful.

It was Saturday morning, and it was already hot. I sat on my back deck with my notebook and an iced coffee and tried to soak up some fresh air before it became too humid, and I had to retreat to my central air. How people survived without it, I would never know.

Something I'd learned about myself—and I suspected this was true of all writers, especially those who wrote poetry—was that I wrote much better if my emotions were extreme. If I was incredibly happy or bone-crushingly sad, that's when I'd write my best stuff. Pen in hand and listening to a couple of birds having what was apparently a serious disagreement near the bird feeder, I did my best to jot down what I was feeling. Instead, I only ended up writing about what I missed.

I glanced at the words I'd written in the last thirty minutes as I sat there.

Empty, cold
Not before you got here
Definitely now that you're gone
Alone, lonely
Fine on my own, always
Everything's different now
I gave you my power
All of it
And now you're gone and
I am powerless

God, it was pathetic. Sad and wallowing and one giant pity party, but it's how I felt. How could one woman cause so much emotion to whirlwind through me in such a short time? It hardly made sense to me.

I shut the notebook, no longer interested in writing in it and annoyed that I now felt an unfamiliar guilt around my poetry. Writing had always helped me organize my thoughts and clear my head, and now? I just felt passionless about it, as if Zoe had taken the joy I found in it with her when she stomped out my door in her sexy black dress and heels. Stolen it. And that pissed me off.

I went about my Saturday doing busywork. Cleaning and playing with my cats and staying occupied always helped to keep my mind from wandering off to undesirable corners, so when Stefan invited me to his house for early drinks and then dinner, I jumped at the offer. Plus, Stefan had a pool, and it was about three degrees cooler than the surface of the sun that day, so I packed up my suit, filled up the cat dishes with dry food, kissed Ross and Rachel on their heads with the promise I'd be back for nighttime snuggles, and got the hell out of Dodge. At least for a few hours.

Keeping in line with Stefan being a proud living, breathing gay man stereotype, his house looked like it belonged on the cover of one of those design magazines like *House Beautiful* or *Architectural Digest*. There was very little Stefan couldn't do, and I was often so envious of his talents. I knocked, then walked through the front door without waiting for a response because I figured he was in the backyard. His downstairs smelled like lavender and vanilla, relaxing and warm, and I inhaled deeply, feeling much of my stress melt away just from being in his house.

"Well, hello, gorgeous," Stefan announced, coming in from the backyard in a pair of blue and white striped trunks, his hair spiky and wet, an empty margarita glass in one hand. He kissed my cheek, kept his other hand on my face, and studied me. "You haven't been sleeping."

He wasn't wrong. I shrugged gently out of his grasp and pointed at his glass as I busied myself unpacking my suit. "Make me one of those, and I might."

"They're strawberry."

"Sold."

"Go put on your suit and meet me poolside."

I did as instructed and entered Stefan's backyard oasis, which never failed to completely relax me. It was like being at a resort. Kidney-shaped pool, surrounded by flowers and various flowering bushes. A tiki bar in the corner had been the center of many a party when he'd first moved in.

He was stretched out on a lounge chair under a huge tropical blue umbrella. A matching chair sat parallel, and the small round table between them held two big glasses filled to the brim with the lovely pink concoction.

If I hadn't been so miserable, I'd have thought I'd stepped into heaven.

"I don't often see you under an umbrella," I commented as I spread out my towel and situated myself on my designated lounge chair.

"It's too goddamn hot to be in the sun today."

"True." I settled in and reached for my drink. "How was business today?"

"Crazed. Maniacal. A zoo. We were booked solid and ended up with thirteen walk-ins. Thirteen! I was busier than a one-legged man in an ass-kicking competition, as my dad used to say."

"So...a good day, then."

"A very good day."

We touched glasses, sipped. I felt the cold of the drink itself, then the warmth of the tequila it was made with, and it was like my whole body relaxed into my towel. "God, I needed this. Thanks, Stef."

This was the way Stefan was. He didn't ask me to elaborate. He didn't push to know why I needed a good dose of alcohol and to lounge by his pool. Our friendship was long and close and had a shorthand. He knew I'd broach the subject when I was ready.

It took forty-five minutes, a dip in the pool, and a second margarita before that time came, but when I did decide to talk about it, I *talked*. I talked about all of it. Every single detail about Zoe came spilling out.

Stefan didn't interrupt. That was the other great thing about talking to him. Oh, he was very opinionated, and he didn't sugarcoat anything, but he made sure to get all the information before he let you in on what he was thinking.

He was quiet for what felt like a long while once I stopped talking. I could almost hear the gears in his head, cranking and turning as he processed the information I'd given him. I sipped my drink, squeezed some water out of my hair, waited.

"Tell me about her last relationship," Stefan said. "I don't think I know much about her."

"When Zoe's mom got sick and Zoe was taking care of her, her girlfriend told her she was emotionally unavailable."

"I hate that phrase," he muttered, and I wasn't sure if he was talking to me or himself. "Did they break up?"

"Eventually, yeah."

"I assume the girlfriend did the leaving."

I nodded.

Another beat went by. Might've been two. Stefan turned to look at me. Really look at me. "This girl of yours isn't all that complicated. You know that, right?"

I stared at him, felt my eyes narrow. "What do you mean?" But I kind of knew.

"I mean, she's got trust issues because people keep leaving her. Duh." When I didn't respond, he sighed and turned his entire body so he was facing me. "You broke her trust. No, you didn't mean to. No, it wasn't malicious, and you weren't hiding some horrible thing. You fucked up. That's all. And if she didn't have trust issues, this might not have been as big a deal. But she does, so it is. She ended it before you could. Essentially, she left you before you could leave her and be added to her list of people that left."

I had told Stefan more than once that he'd missed his calling as a therapist. I waited for him to go on, not wanting to impede his momentum, but he sat quietly for a long while. "She hasn't contacted you?" he finally asked.

I shook my head and felt that familiar sadness fall over me, once again confused by how such a short time with somebody affected me so intensely.

"I think you need to go after her." Stefan gave one nod after he spoke, as if punctuating it.

"But she said—"

He held up his hand. "I know what she said. But she's hurt and she's scared." He inhaled slowly and when his eyes met mine, there was an intensity I didn't often see. "If you guys connect the way you say—"

"We do." My turn to interrupt. "We absolutely do. She knows it, and I know it."

"Then you can't let that slip through your fingers. You have to *fight*."

I took his words in. Rolled them around. Examined them. Tasted them. The truth was, I was a good girl. I always had been. I followed the rules. I did what I was told. Zoe said we were done. It never occurred to me to say screw that and chase her anyway. I was not a fighter, and I hated the realization.

"You think?" I turned to Stefan then, feeling all kinds of uncertain. On top of that, emotions were at war inside me. Hope, doubt, fear, possibility. It was a lot.

"Do you love her?"

Oh, that was a big one. That was the question, wasn't it? *The* question. I hadn't asked it of myself because I was afraid of the answer. Because I knew the answer. And saying it out loud would make this all so much more real and so much riskier. But I had never lied to Stefan. I felt my eyes well up as I nodded and said very, very softly, "Yeah. I do."

"I thought so."

"You did?" That was a surprise.

Stefan tipped his head and gave me a look that said, *Really?* "I have known you for years and years, and not once have I ever heard you talk about somebody the way you talk about this one. Not once."

This one. That made me smile for some reason as I gazed out over the pool. *This one.* Dangerously close to *the* one, I was aware. There was a question that lingered, though. One I was afraid to ask, but couldn't not. "What if she doesn't feel the same way?"

I think Stefan knew it was coming because he answered way too quickly not to have thought about it. "Then at least you tried. And you can go on with your life without wondering what might've been. You know? I think that's got to be one of the saddest things to think about when you're old. What if I'd only tried? What might've been then?"

I turned to him, went for a little levity because the moment felt impossibly heavy. "I had no idea you were so cerebral."

"I have *layers*. I am a goddamn *onion*."

We were quiet again for a long time because it felt right. Just sitting, thinking. We finished our drinks. I went back into the pool to cool off. It was closing in on dinnertime and still close to ninety degrees and sticky. Welcome to August in the Northeast. I did a lazy breast stroke around the pool before climbing onto a floating raft and closing my eyes.

My head felt full. But my heart felt full as well, and they seemed to battle each other.

I don't know about you, but for me, the victory in that particular debate always goes to the same loving, beating side, and it knew what I needed to do.

CHAPTER TWENTY-ONE

I don't know if I've mentioned this yet, but I'm kind of a coward and a huge procrastinator. When it comes to basic, normal decisions, I can make them, but when it comes to actually doing something that makes me nervous or having a conversation that scares me? Yeah, I like to put those off.

And put them off.

And put them off.

Adriana gave me a T-shirt for my twenty-first birthday that said, *Why do it today when you can put it off until tomorrow?* and nothing has made me feel more seen. While I have gotten better as an adult at not being such a procrastinator, that skill never dies, and I could bring it out at any time, for whenever it suited the situation.

A situation like talking to Zoe.

The woman who put a stop to our very young relationship. The woman who I'd recently admitted to having fallen for. If I had gone right over to Zoe's from Stefan's, I'd have gotten this all out of the way because my heart had already won the battle over what to do. But no. I procrastinated, and while I was doing that, my brain decided on a rematch, and it tromped my poor heart into the ground with logic. Stupid, stupid logic.

That's why it was Monday, and I was sitting at my desk, not having talked to Zoe, still thinking about talking to Zoe, but even more nervous about talking to Zoe than I had been. Like, *way* more nervous. I was annoyed with my own indecision, and so I sat there and stared out the front window at the storm clouds rolling in. The sky was the color of a dull nickel, and the rumbling of thunder could be heard in the distance. Very apropos to my mood.

I answered the phones and dealt with incoming patients, but my filing, my billing, my follow-ups? They all lay untouched because staring off into space seemed like a better use of my time.

Things brightened a bit midafternoon when Brittany walked through the front door. She was smiling and had that happy bounce in her walk that she'd had since she was a kid, and I was wildly glad to see her.

"There's my favorite niece," I said and felt my world lift a bit.

"That one never gets old," said Brittany, my only niece. She was dressed in a subdued yet classy black pantsuit, her hair pulled back in a complicated twist, and she looked sophisticated and older than her twenty-two years.

"You look amazing. I'd buy stuff from you. How's work?" I checked the clock. "You're not playing hooky, are you?"

"No, I'm not playing hooky." She used a smarmy voice to mimic me, her favorite aunt, and the sophistication slipped just a bit, which brought a small grin to my lips. "I had a client meeting, and it ended early, and my boss told me I could have the rest of the day off."

"Nice of him."

"Her."

"Nice of her."

"She's pretty cool." Brittany leaned her elbows on the counter and made a show of looking through my little window at my desk, my computer, my stacks of untouched work.

"It's been over a month now. You like it?"

"My job? I do. Zoe's been a huge help."

At the mention of her name, my body did weird things. Went warm and cold at the same time, though, how that was possible, I had no idea. And everything stood at attention, pricked up, like a dog who'd heard a high frequency not audible to anybody else. "Oh yeah?"

"Seriously. She's given me some terrific tips, walked me through a cold call. She's a pro."

I nodded. I'd had no idea Zoe was still helping Brittany. I was glad she hadn't blown my niece off because of the rest of the crazy

Thompson family—I probably wouldn't have blamed her. At the same time, I felt a ridiculous twinge of jealousy that Brittany was seeing her, and I wasn't. Before that sank in too far, Brittany said something that pulled me up short.

"Have you seen her recently? She seems kind of…" She nibbled on the inside of her cheek as she appeared to think about it. "Off. I want to say sad, but it's not that. Or not just that. I don't know." She shook her head. "She doesn't seem herself."

Well, hell.

While I wasn't quite sure what to do with that information, part of me got a tiny thrill of hope. And then I scolded myself because how self-centered was I to assume that Zoe's happiness revolved around me and if she was sad—or *off*, as Brittany put it—that it must have to do with me? God, I sucked.

"Did you ask her about it?" I grabbed myself a Twizzler from the bag on my desk, held it out to her. *No big deal. Not at all concerned. Just sitting here asking totally innocent questions while chewing my Twizzler.*

Brittany shook her head as she took a piece of licorice. "I don't feel like I know her that well yet, on a personal level, you know? I mean, we talk, and we've spent a little time together, but it's been mostly focused on work stuff."

"I see."

"But I thought maybe you could see if she's okay."

I blinked at my niece. Chewed my Twizzler. Sat there without saying anything.

"Would you do that?"

"Do what?" *Yes. Play dumb, Morgan. That always works.*

Brittany tipped her head to the side and arched a brow at me. "See if she's okay? She's your friend, right?"

"Yeah." I nodded. She was, wasn't she? My friend still? Maybe she didn't think so, but despite my all-over-the-damn-place emotions, I cared about Zoe very much. Loved her. And if something was bothering her enough that it was noticeable to acquaintances, maybe I should check on her.

I promised Brittany I'd touch base with Zoe and waved as she headed off to meet some friends for an early happy hour. Then I spent the remaining two hours of my workday freaking out just a bit about the idea of seeing Zoe.

Maybe I could just text her. Or call.

Coward.

I sighed at that inner voice accusing me of being less than brave.

When Diane was getting ready to head out, she dropped a couple of files on my desk. "When do we get more drug samples?" she asked. "'Cause I've gone over a week with no surprise doughnuts or sandwiches, and frankly, I'm a little sick of it." She grinned to make sure I understood she was teasing. "Can't you call your pharma rep friend and tell her I need pastries, or I'll become unbearable?"

"Become?" I asked and Diane barked a laugh and pointed at me.

"See you tomorrow."

Perry was taking care of his emails in his office, Joanne was gone, and with Diane taking her leave, there was only me left. I hadn't gotten much done, but I reveled in the quiet of closing time. Brittany's assessment of Zoe had stuck with me, made a little nest inside my heart and settled in, and the idea of her being not herself was more than I could bear.

I took in a big lungful of air and held it for the count of seven, then let it out very, very slowly. I always felt better after I did that, like it centered me somehow.

"Okay," I said aloud in the empty office. "Decision made."

I would go see her. I wouldn't stay. Just knock on her door, assess her myself, since I thought I knew her a little better than Brittany did, and see if I also thought she seemed off.

What I would do after that, I had no idea. Zero.

Nerves starting to uncurl and jangle against my bones, I locked up the office and headed out to my car where it sat in the parking lot next to Perry's BMW. The sky had gotten darker and the thunder closer. I reached for my door handle, and when my car beeped the signal that it had unlocked, I glanced up.

There was one other car sitting in the lot, way over in the corner, about ten spots from mine, the driver inside and looking my way. My heart began to pound.

Zoe.

It was like an invisible tether connected us, and neither of us looked away for what felt like a really long time. Probably only a few seconds, but it was intense. I felt like she was looking right into my soul. When her car door opened, I jolted into action. I threw my stuff into my own car, slammed the door, and took steps in her direction. Neither of us hurried. In fact, we each walked almost comically slowly, strolling, until we met in the middle, several spots away from each of our cars. Two women, standing in the middle of an almost empty parking lot, thunder rumbling. I felt a tiny splatter of wet on my face. The rain was coming.

"Hi," she said, and I was relieved she spoke first.

"Hey." There was a lump in my throat all of a sudden—nerves? concern? fear?—and I tried to swallow it down. "It's good to see you," I said softly, and it was. Good God, it so was. I knew I'd missed her. I knew I'd felt lost without her. But those things were amplified a hundred times by actually seeing her in the flesh. I wanted so badly to reach out and touch her, but I balled my hands into fists and kept them by my sides.

"How are you?" she asked, those blue eyes dark, boring into me like she was trying to find the answer herself inside my head.

Miserable. Awful. Crushed. Ate an entire bag of Cheetos for dinner last night and chased it with half a bottle of merlot. They all ran through my brain.

"Hanging in there, I guess," is what came out instead, and I added a shrug to make my point. But as I looked at Zoe, I realized that Brittany was right. She was *not* herself. There were dark circles under her beautiful eyes, and those cheekbones were nowhere to be found. Her shoulders slumped slightly, as if she was carrying some invisible heavy thing, and she just looked really tired overall. I was instantly worried about her. "How are *you*?"

That's when her eyes welled up, and she looked away, and all I wanted to do was take her in my arms. Her throat moved as she swallowed, and I lifted my arms a bit, as if my body wanted to wrap her up regardless of my brain telling me to stand down and assess the situation. When she looked back at me, there was such anguish on her face that I felt my eyes widen in surprise. "I miss you so much," she whispered, and I was done.

Fuck this.

I stepped forward and pulled her into a hug as my eyes filled with tears. "I miss you, too," I said in her ear as a gentle rain started to fall. I felt her arms around me, her hands on my back, grasping my shirt, and one tiny hiccup of a sob escaped.

"I'm sorry," she said a minute or two later when she'd lifted her head from my shoulder to look in my eyes.

I held her face, wiped her tears with my thumbs. "For what? I'm the one who's sorry. I should've told you right away about the poems. I was an idiot." The rain fell a little harder, but it was warm, and I had no intention of letting Zoe out of my personal space just yet.

"I'm sorry I was so hard on you." Again, she looked away as if trying to find her words in the falling rain. "I talked to Perry a couple days ago."

Okay, that was a surprise. "You did?"

"He called me."

"He did." After I'd specifically asked him to leave it alone.

"Don't be mad at him," Zoe said, as if reading my mind. "He was worried about you, and he felt bad. He explained that he was terrible with words—which is very true, I can attest to that—and he'd always bugged you until you gave in and helped him. He said he realized pretty early on that you…I think he said had a thing for me." She made air quotes and I rolled my eyes.

"Eloquent as ever." But I felt the smallest bit lighter and motioned for her to go on.

"He said he should've stepped aside, but he didn't, and then after his ego took a beating, his pride got in the way."

"He told you all of this? I mean, my brother's a decent guy, but this is shockingly self-aware for him."

"He did. He felt terrible, said you were miserable, and he felt responsible."

"Wow."

"So, we talked a lot, and I came to some realizations with his help. After my mom and my ex and what I went through with each of them, I have…" She took a deep breath, toyed with my collar, and I wondered if this was hard for her to say out loud. "I have some problems with trust."

I thought for a moment about just how accurate Stefan had been before I said, "That makes total sense. I would, too."

"When I realized that morning what had happened with the poetry and that I'd been left in the dark about it, I acted instinctually. Walls flew up before I even realized they were about to. Putting an end to us seemed to be the best course of action for the safety of my heart, but I was already…" She looked down at her sandaled feet, the wet of the asphalt.

I wondered if she could hear my heart hammering in my chest, because to me, it seemed louder than the rain. "You were already what?"

Zoe avoided meeting my eyes for several beats, both of us pretty wet by then, and I wondered how it was possible that she could be even more beautiful while standing in the pouring rain in soggy clothes and flattened hair. When she finally looked up at me, the open, naked vulnerability on her face took my breath away. Literally stopped my lungs from functioning for a moment.

"I was already so in love with you." She whispered it, and I read her lips more than I heard her voice, the pattering of the rain on the pavement almost drowning her out. But those words. Her words. They shot straight into me, directly into my heart, evicting even the tiniest element of doubt, and they grew. Her words grew until they filled me completely. I felt myself stand up a little straighter, lift my chin, as if I was actually growing with the knowledge of how Zoe felt about me.

The pavement, the rain, the fact that we were standing in a parking lot. None of it mattered. "Oh, Zoe." I smoothed her wet hair off her face. "I love you, too. So much."

Kissing in the rain is the most sensual of experiences, let me just tell you. We were drenched, our hair and faces soaked, our clothes wet through. But I kissed Zoe Blake with everything I had in me, and if I could've stood in that parking lot in the pouring rain with her mouth on mine for the rest of time, I would've done it without question. I poured every emotion I had into that kiss. My hope, my fear, my worry, and my love. So much love. More than I'd even realized before my lips met hers. It was like our entire future together was solidified in that one rain-soaked kiss. Zoe deepened it, pressed her tongue into my mouth as she grabbed at my body in what felt like desperation, trying to pull me closer even though our bodies were nearly fused together from knees to mouths.

I couldn't get enough.

"I love you, Morgan," she mumbled between kisses, and I couldn't get enough of that either.

I pulled back from her just enough to look into those blue eyes. "I don't know where you came from, but I'm never letting you go. Just know that."

"Right back atcha," she said, and I pulled her into a hug, wrapped my arms around her neck, and could have sworn I felt our hearts meld right there as we stood on the pavement pressed against each other.

The rain fell.

The thunder rumbled.

We held on.

"Do you think the rain knows?" she asked softly after a moment.

I pulled back to see her face and squinted my confusion.

"Like your poem. Do you think the rain knows how we feel?"

My body filled with warmth at the realization that she remembered my poem. I nodded as I looked up, let the raindrops pelt my face. "I do. I think it knows everything."

"I reread the poems that you wrote for Perry. You really saw me like that? That early on?"

"It was killing me to think of you and him," I said honestly. Her face brightened, even in the gloom of the rain, and I stood up a little straighter, feeling that fleeting confidence come back to me like a power surge.

She pulled me into her arms again. Over her shoulder, I caught a glimpse of the office building, of my brother standing in the window, watching, a huge smile on his face.

He gave me a small wave, then spun the long stick that closed the miniblinds.

EPILOGUE

Snow didn't really start that year until December. We got an inch or two here and there a couple times in late November, but it wasn't until mid-December that we felt it. A storm hit and dropped nearly ten inches on us, and suddenly, just like that, it was winter.

I hate winter. I'll be completely upfront with that. I have always preferred to spend my winters inside. Give me a good book or movie, a warm fire and a blanket, a cappuccino or a glass of wine depending on the time of day, and I'm good until spring.

But I was with Zoe now.

And Zoe didn't do winter inside. Oh no. She was a let's-hit-the-slopes, let's-get-snowshoes, let's-go-sledding kind of girl, and I somehow did not see that coming.

So the last Saturday before Christmas, I found myself at the top of an enormous hill, surrounded by Zoe, Brittany, Brittany's new boyfriend Marcus, Perry, and Jennifer Zimmerman, who'd ended up being the perfect match for my brother after all. I was glad she'd stuck around. The six of us stood there watching people of various ages shrieking as they shot down the hill, which, after so much sled traffic, looked way more icy than snowy.

"We're gonna fly," Perry said with barely contained glee.

"Exactly what I'm afraid of," I muttered. Only Zoe heard me, and she leaned close. Her knit hat was the color of oatmeal with a jolly red pom-pom on the top. Rosy cheeks and a red nose made her adorable. And then she smiled, and her eyes sparkled, and her cheekbones popped, and in an instant, she went from adorable to downright sexy. I still had no idea how she made that switch so fast, but she did it all the time, and I loved it.

"I won't let you die," she said with a wink that made my toes tingle. I must have looked dubious because she bumped me with her shoulder and added, "Trust me."

Brittany and Marcus had zero fear. "Let's do it. We can fit." Brittany set a toboggan down. It was sleek and wooden and was just long enough for four people. She got on first, fit her legs up under the front part of the toboggan that curled up and back, and held the rope that was meant for steering, but I had my doubts about it helping with any accuracy if they careened toward a tree. Marcus got behind her, then Jennifer, then Perry until they made a human train. Zoe and I watched—her smiling, me wide-eyed—as Brittany shouted back to Perry, "Push, Uncle Perry!"

Perry used his gloved hands and shoved the sled forward. It only took three pushes before they were off, shooting down the hill like a rocket, past people that had already gone and were climbing up for another trip. Before they reached the bottom, Zoe dropped our toboggan flat onto the snow.

"Ready?"

"As I'll ever be."

Zoe directed me to sit up front. I did, situated my booted feet up under the front curve, held the useless rope, and wished for it to be over quickly. I mean, it wasn't like I'd never been sledding—I grew up in upstate New York, for Christ's sake—but I'd never really enjoyed it. However, when Zoe sat behind me, moved her legs around me, and I felt her body push up against my back, I started to think maybe this wasn't so bad after all. Even with all the layers we wore, I swore I could feel her body heat, and my own trying to match hers. Sitting there with Zoe all tight against me already made sledding infinitely better than I remembered.

"I've got you," she whispered in my ear, and then without warning, she shoved us off. I might have yelped like a surprised little girl.

Within the first three seconds, I realized I was exactly right about the hill being icy, and I thought about people on the luge in the

Olympics, flying down those twisty, turny runs, and I was certain we were going *at least* that fast. I was also right about the rope, which did nothing but give me something to clench with my gloved hands in a death grip.

Colors flew by. I think they were people. People in coats and hats. But all I saw were colors. Pops here. Pops there. And then we were past them before I could register what or who they were. I didn't realize how tightly I was holding on for dear life until my hand started to cramp around the stupid rope. But we were going to make it. We were almost there...

And then the lump happened.

I didn't know where it came from or how it got where it was, but it was a good-sized lump of snow, and our toboggan hit it dead-on.

Now, I'm sure we didn't fly far. But we flew. Sideways. There was a little-girl scream that I'm embarrassed to say was probably mine. We landed, and snow flew, and then we stopped in a pile of arms and legs and white. Snow everywhere. In my boots, down the back of my coat, in my face. I lay on my back, breathing heavily, watching the vapor my breath created float away above me. My arms were splayed out to either side. Zoe was laying across me. She lifted her head, and the joy in her eyes was so apparent, I couldn't help but smile, even though I tried to look annoyed as I recited an on-the-spot poem.

"Roses are red. Winter is snowy. When she tells you she's got you, don't listen to Zoe."

She snorted a laugh as she pushed herself up on her hands and looked down at me. "You okay?"

"You said you wouldn't let me die. I trusted you."

"And I didn't let you die."

"Are you sure?"

Zoe dutifully began poking and prodding me, and when she pushed on my stomach, I groaned. "Yes, I'm a hundred percent sure you're still alive."

"I hate winter," I said, and yes, I admit I was a little bit whiny.

And then Zoe's face took up my entire view as she leaned over, looked down at me, and said, "But you love me."

There was no denying that, not even a little. "I do."

She pecked me on the lips before I could say any more, then stood up and held a gloved hand down to me. "Come on, we've got time for a couple more runs before we have to be at your mom's. I bet she's making something amazing for dinner."

I took her hand, let her pull me to my feet, and we trudged up the hill together. Did I want to do a couple more runs? No. No, I did not. Would I follow Zoe anytime, anywhere without question? Abso-fucking-lutely.

At the top, we waited for a few sledders who'd set up ahead of us to go, my family included. Then Zoe flopped down our toboggan, held it in place with one boot, and looked at me with those gorgeous blue eyes. I could feel myself fall into the depths of them just like I did every single time she looked at me like that, like I was the only person in her world.

"Ready?" she asked.

To spend the rest of my life with her? I couldn't wait. "Ready." I sat down again, scrunched up my legs again, felt her body tight against me again. "You got me?" I asked.

"Always," came her reply, and she gave my hips a squeeze with her knees. "I love you."

And right then? With Zoe behind me, looking out for me? I felt like—no, I *knew*—I could do anything.

"I love you, too. Let's go."

Zoe pushed us off, and we headed downhill and into the rest of our lives.

Together.

Always together.

About the Author

Georgia Beers is an award-winning author of nearly thirty lesbian romance novels. She resides in upstate New York with her dog and cat, a wide array of plants, and at least the *desire* to learn how to cook. When not writing, she watches too much TV, explores the world of wine, and dutifully participates in spin class. She is currently hard at work on her next book. You can visit her and find out more at georgiabeers.com

Books Available from Bold Strokes Books

A Fae Tale by Genevieve McCluer. Dovana comes to terms with her changing feelings for her lifelong best friend and fae, Roze. (978-1-63555-918-7)

Accidental Desperados by Lee Lynch. Life is clobbering Berry, Jaudon, and their long romance. The arrival of directionless baby dyke MJ doesn't help. Can they find their passion again—and keep it? (978-1-63555-482-3)

Always Believe by Aimée. Greyson Waldsen is pursuing ordination as an Anglican priest. Angela Arlingham doesn't believe in God. Do they follow their vocation or their hearts? (978-1-63555-912-5)

Best of the Wrong Reasons by Sander Santiago. For Fin Ness and Orion Starr, it takes a funeral to remind them that love is worth living for. (978-1-63555-867-8)

Courage by Jesse J. Thoma. No matter how often Natasha Parsons and Tommy Finch clash on the job, an undeniable attraction simmers just beneath the surface. Can they find the courage to change so love has room to grow? (978-1-63555-802-9)

I Am Chris by R Kent. There's one saving grace to losing everything and moving away. Nobody knows her as Chrissy Taylor. Now Chris can live who he truly is. (978-1-63555-904-0)

The Princess and the Odium by Sam Ledel. Jastyn and Princess Aurelia return to Venostes and join their families in a battle against the dark force to take back their homeland for a chance at a better tomorrow. (978-1-63555-894-4)

The Queen Has a Cold by Jane Kolven. What happens when the heir to the throne isn't a prince or a princess? (978-1-63555-878-4)

The Secret Poet by Georgia Beers. Agreeing to help her brother woo Zoe Blake seemed like a good idea to Morgan Thompson at first...until she realizes she's actually wooing Zoe for herself... (978-1-63555-858-6)

You Again by Aurora Rey. For high school sweethearts Kate Cormier and Sutton Guidry, the second chance might be the only one that matters. (978-1-63555-791-6)

Coming to Life on South High by Lee Patton. Twenty-one-year-old gay virgin Gabe Rafferty's first adult decade unfolds as an unpredictable journey into sex, love, and livelihood. (978-1-63555-906-4)

Fleur d'Lies by MJ Williamz. For rookie cop DJ Sander, being true to what you believe is the only way to live...and one way to die. (978-1-63555-854-8)

Love's Falling Star by B.D. Grayson. For country music megastar Lochlan Paige, can love conquer her fear of losing the one thing she's worked so hard to protect? (978-1-63555-873-9)

Love's Truth by C.A. Popovich. Can Lynette and Barb make love work when unhealed wounds of betrayed trust and a secret could change everything? (978-1-63555-755-8)

Next Exit Home by Dena Blake. Home may be where the heart is, but for Harper Sims and Addison Foster, is the journey back worth the pain? (978-1-63555-727-5)

Not Broken by Lyn Hemphill. Falling in love is hard enough—even more so for Rose who's carrying her ex's baby. (978-1-63555-869-2)

The Noble and the Nightingale by Barbara Ann Wright. Two women on opposite sides of empires at war risk all for a chance at love. (978-1-63555-812-8)

What a Tangled Web by Melissa Brayden. Clementine Monroe has the chance to buy the café she's managed for years, but Madison LeGrange swoops in and buys it first. Now Clementine is forced to work for the enemy and ignore her former crush. (978-1-63555-749-7)

A Far Better Thing by JD Wilburn. When needs of her family and wants of her heart clash, Cass Halliburton is faced with the ultimate sacrifice. (978-1-63555-834-0)

Body Language by Renee Roman. When Mika offers to provide Jen erotic tutoring, will sex drive them into a deeper relationship or tear them apart? (978-1-63555-800-5)

Carrie and Hope by Joy Argento. For Carrie and Hope loss brings them together but secrets and fear may tear them apart. (978-1-63555-827-2)

Death's Prelude by David S. Pederson. In this prequel to the Detective Heath Barrington Mystery series, Heath discovers that first love changes you forever and drives you to become the person you're destined to be. (978-1-63555-786-2)

Ice Queen by Gun Brooke. School counselor Aislin Kennedy wants to help standoffish CEO Susanna Durr and her troubled teenage daughter become closer—even if it means risking her own heart in the process. (978-1-63555-721-3)

Masquerade by Anne Shade. In 1925 Harlem, New York, a notorious gangster sets her sights on seducing Celine, and new lovers Dinah and Celine are forced to risk their hearts, and lives, for love. (978-1-63555-831-9)

Royal Family by Jenny Frame. Loss has defined both Clay's and Katya's lives, but guarding their hearts may prove to be the biggest heartbreak of all. (978-1-63555-745-9)

Share the Moon by Toni Logan. Three best friends, an inherited vineyard and a resident ghost come together for fun, romance and a touch of magic. (978-1-63555-844-9)

Spirit of the Law by Carsen Taite. Attorney Owen Lassiter will do almost anything to put a murderer behind bars, but can she get past her reluctance to rely on unconventional help from the alluring Summer Byrne and keep from falling in love in the process? (978-1-63555-766-4)

The Devil Incarnate by Ali Vali. Cain Casey has so much to live for, but enemies who lurk in the shadows threaten to unravel it all. (978-1-63555-534-9)

His Brother's Viscount by Stephanie Lake. Hector Somerville wants to rekindle his illicit love affair with Viscount Wentworth, but he must overcome one problem: Wentworth still loves Hector's brother. (978-1-63555-805-0)

Journey to Cash by Ashley Bartlett. Cash Braddock thought everything was great, but it looks like her history is about to become her right now. Which is a real bummer. (978-1-63555-464-9)

Liberty Bay by Karis Walsh. Wren Lindley's life is mired in tradition and untouched by trends until social media star Gina Strickland introduces an irresistible electricity into her off-the-grid world. (978-1-63555-816-6)

Scent by Kris Bryant. Nico Marshall has been burned by women in the past wanting her for her money. This time, she's determined to win Sophia Sweet over with her charm. (978-1-63555-780-0)

Shadows of Steel by Suzie Clarke. As their worlds collide and their choices come back to haunt them, Rachel and Claire must figure out how to stay together and most of all, stay alive. (978-1-63555-810-4)

The Clinch by Nicole Disney. Eden Bauer overcame a difficult past to become a world champion mixed martial artist, but now rising star and dreamy bad girl Brooklyn Shaw is a threat both to Eden's title and her heart. (978-1-63555-820-3)

The Last First Kiss by Julie Cannon. Kelly Newsome is so ready for a tropical island vacation, but she never expects to meet the woman who could give her her last first kiss. (978-1-63555-768-8)

The Mandolin Lunch by Missouri Vaun. Despite their immediate attraction, everything about Garet Allen says short-term, and Tess Hill refuses to consider anything less than forever. (978-1-63555-566-0)

Thor: Daughter of Asgard by Genevieve McCluer. When Hannah Olsen finds out she's the reincarnation of Thor, she's thrown into a world of magic and intrigue, unexpected attraction, and a mystery she's got to unravel. (978-1-63555-814-2)

Veterinary Technician by Nancy Wheelton. When a stable of horses is threatened Val and Ronnie must work together against the odds to save them, and maybe even themselves along the way. (978-1-63555-839-5)

16 Steps to Forever by Georgia Beers. Can Brooke Sullivan and Macy Carr find themselves by finding each other? (978-1-63555-762-6)

All I Want for Christmas by Georgia Beers, Maggie Cummings, Fiona Riley. The Christmas season sparks passion and love in these stories by award winning authors Georgia Beers, Maggie Cummings, and Fiona Riley. (978-1-63555-764-0)

From the Woods by Charlotte Greene. When Fiona goes backpacking in a protected wilderness, the last thing she expects is to be fighting for her life. (978-1-63555-793-0)

Heart of the Storm by Nicole Stiling. For Juliet Mitchell and Sienna Bennett a forbidden attraction definitely isn't worth upending the life they've worked so hard for. Is it? (978-1-63555-789-3)

If You Dare by Sandy Lowe. For Lauren West and Emma Prescott, following their passions is easy. Following their hearts, though? That's almost impossible. (978-1-63555-654-4)

Love Changes Everything by Jaime Maddox. For Samantha Brooks and Kirby Fielding, no matter how careful their plans, love will change everything. (978-1-63555-835-7)

Not This Time by MA Binfield. Flung back into each other's lives, can former bandmates Sophia and Madison have a second chance at romance? (978-1-63555-798-5)

The Dubious Gift of Dragon Blood by J. Marshall Freeman. One day Crispin is a lonely high school student—the next he is fighting a war in a land ruled by dragons, his otherworldly boyfriend at his side. (978-1-63555-725-1)

The Found Jar by Jaycie Morrison. Fear keeps Emily Harris trapped in her emotionally vacant life; can she find the courage to let Beck Reynolds guide her toward love? (978-1-63555-825-8)